I0675449

THE
RED
CONCERTO

THE

RED

CONCERTO

S.F. HAYES

Boyle
&
Dalton

Book Design & Production:
Boyle & Dalton
www.BoyleandDalton.com

Copyright © 2025 by S.F. Hayes

All rights reserved.
This book, or parts thereof, may not be
reproduced in any form without permission.

This is a work of fiction. Unless otherwise indicated, all the names,
characters, businesses, places, events and incidents in this
book are either the product of the author's imagination or
used in a fictitious manner. Any resemblance to actual persons,
living or dead, or actual events is purely coincidental.

Paperback ISBN: 978-1-63337-928-2
Hardback ISBN: 978-1-63337-929-9
E-book ISBN: 978-1-63337-894-0
LCCN: 2025906633

For Adam, Jackson, and Lucas, who continually support, inspire, and challenge me.

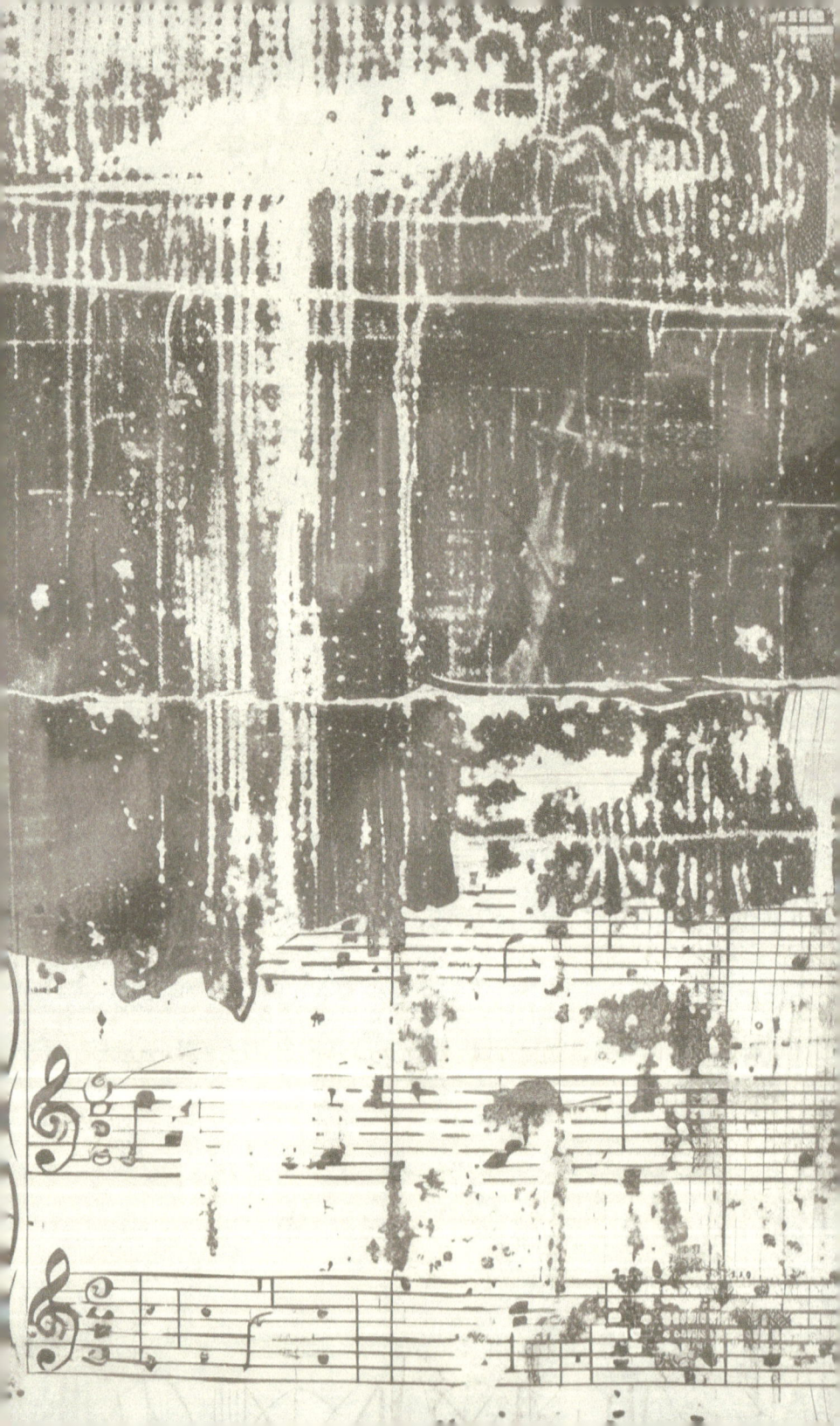

PART ONE
Prelude

CHAPTER 1

C harlie Emerson wasn't exactly suicidal. But whenever he got on his motorcycle, he longed, just a little bit, to die. He hadn't yet succumbed to the weakness—or was it that he hadn't gained enough courage?—to really try for it, but maybe tonight was the night. Because as he rode out of New York City, fists clenched tightly around the handlebars, something like hope nudged at him.

A few hours beyond the city limits, he rolled his wrist to accelerate toward the mountains, and on the road the darkness fell in increments as the distance between the streetlights grew. The traffic thinned to nothing. A road sign whizzed by, warning of dangerous curves ahead, and another commanded a speed of 15 mph. Charlie accelerated to 70.

Then the ascent began. The road narrowed and lifted, snaking up the side of a steep mountain. A sheer wall on one side; a sharp drop on the other. Charlie leaned into each curve, loosening his grip on the handlebars and relaxing into the seat, shifting his awareness from the tension of his muscles to the gradient of the road. His world contracted to a single focus on each new turn. Then there was only the few feet of gray concrete in his headlights, the taste of burning fuel in his breath, and the blare of the engine vibrating in his chest and ears.

Charlie had spent many nights like this in the fifteen years it had taken him to grow EmerSound Music into a successful recording label. At seventeen, he'd ridden occasionally and for the exhilaration, the pure enjoyment. But now, at thirty-two, he needed the rides as a relief from his long, regimented days—and *joy* was no longer the word he would use to describe them. They had merely become an indispensable outlet from his almost military lifestyle as CEO—a strict discipline of meetings and reports interspersed with media appearances as the celebrity CEO, always out for a good time, wooing audiences, controlling narratives, and destroying lives.

Once, music had been his respite—not the tripe EmerSound produced, but older pieces, Vivaldi and Beethoven, their speed and control echoing the way he rode through turns on the mountain. But he didn't listen to much music these days. Now he only rode and waited, as he always did, for the one moment when he'd welcome the crash offering him the end.

And then the moment came: His front wheel slid on something—even a small rock could do it at this speed—and he was headed for the drop down the chasm. He pulled back, skidding along the edge of the mountain, and for one long moment the choice was in stark relief: let go and fall into the abyss or hold on.

His heart pounded in a thrill of terror, the sound of his breaths, harsh and quick, drowning out the roaring engine. This, he knew, was his body's automatic reaction to the prospect of falling, an evolutionary tool, and yet it was enough; enough because he felt the release of an emotion at last—even if it was a preprogrammed fear—enough because the feeling ran pure, untainted by any sense of greeting toward death.

And so he would not die tonight.

He took control and pulled onto the road again, to continue on, empty of hope, but empty also of the need to feel. Ready to squeeze back into the uniform again and face another battle.

♪ ♫

His ride ended in time for him to turn the corner onto his street at 8 a.m., where the first event of the day was already underway as planned. Paparazzi jammed the sidewalk outside his building, blocking the way down to the underground garage—there to get a scoop on the "leak" of the most surprising engagement of the decade: his.

He'd expected them—had essentially invited them by planting the leak—but still, he slowed the bike more than necessary as he approached, allowing himself one more moment before transforming into Charlie-the-celebrity-CEO, reminding himself of the necessity to be in control of the story, else risk being the one controlled by it.

When he spotted his two bodyguards—dressed as cameramen and blending into the front row alongside EmerSound's own publicity crew—Charlie drew up to the group and stopped, pulling off his helmet but staying on the motorcycle. The mass erupted into questions and camera flashes. He affected his practiced public expression—a hint of a smile radiating exciting but untouchable celebrity—and ran a hand through his dark hair to tousle it. An image consultant had shown him specifically how to do it to make the most of what she called his "stunning good looks." She'd never been happy with his too-dark eyes, though, which along with his six-foot frame made him intimidating, but then he'd been painted as a character between villain and hero—the "bad boy"—which he'd parlayed into considerable media coverage.

He waited now for the three specific questions he'd planned to answer this morning. The first was planted and came from EmerSound's own—disguised—assistant publicist: "Is it true you're engaged to be married?" he asked.

"Yes," Charlie said, expanding his smile and adding a bit of wistfulness, but also a bit of annoyance—as if he'd not expected people to know yet. He'd practiced the smile specifically for this.

The crowd hurled more questions at him. "Who is she?" someone from the back asked. That was the second question.

"My fiancée would like to stay anonymous for the time being," Charlie said, "and I ask that you please not try to find her." They would try, of course, but they wouldn't succeed—there would be no one to find until he'd proposed to someone. And he'd have to find someone he could stand first.

Another beat of cacophony passed, and then he turned to a young woman—whom he recognized as a popular trend influencer—when she asked the final question: "How long have you been together?"

"All I can say," Charlie answered, "is that it hasn't been that long—but I fell for her from the moment I saw her. I promise you'll all get to know her soon enough. Now if you'd excuse me, I need to get to work."

That was the cue for Charlie's guards to make a path for him through the throng to the garage, but as he made his way, someone called out: "Is it true that you're partnering with Rafterty Studios again to produce a reality show? Is it about your wife? Is this all just a publicity stunt?"

Charlie stopped. It was true. He'd planned a lifestyle reality show, *Mrs. Music*, to follow his new "bride" as she settled into his supposedly extravagant life—a show designed specifically to capitalize on people's incessant curiosity about him while giving them a rags-to-riches love story. But he had to foil any rumor of it being a publicity ploy—they had to believe the marriage was real—or the thing would collapse before it got started. He gave his onlookers a considering glance. "Well, a show about her wasn't the plan, but is that something you guys would want to see?"

The mass broke out into loud chatter, questions, and even a few cheers.

"Would you do that?" the young influencer asked, excitement naked in her expression.

Charlie gave her one of his radiant smiles—calculated to make her feel like a cherished fan. "You know how much I appreciate you all. I could be convinced to let you share in my happiness."

The voices pitched higher, still begging for more answers. Satisfied that he'd stoked the excitement to a new high, Charlie left to drop off his bike in the garage, hoping for a hot shower and that he wouldn't have to think about the show again this morning.

CHAPTER II

Charlie was depositing his helmet on a table in the foyer when his hopes for a respite from the show collapsed. His personal assistant, Murdoch, hurried over, his bald head gleaming with a sheen of sweat. He was a stout man in his early fifties, a few inches shorter than Charlie, and though he maintained his usual demeanor of a soldier's carriage combined with a butler's severity, the sheen meant he was not happy. "Richard is here—in the library—and in one of his moods," he said.

Charlie sighed. Richard Stanton, EmerSound's head of public relations, was prone to hysterics. "What's wrong now?"

"He heard you didn't hire Brandy for the role of your wife. And he's worried there isn't enough time to find the right person."

"I don't know why he thought I would hire that girl. She's a simpering imbecile," Charlie muttered, heading down the hall toward the library.

Murdoch followed. "Also, the studio called to finalize the details for the show. They want to do a screen test with your fiancée. We can't keep putting them off—they're threatening to break the deal."

Charlie paused in the hallway, thinking for a minute. All of this publicity and scheming for the reality show would be moot if they lost the production company. "Get me a meeting with David Stuart," he told Murdoch. "He's producing the show, but he's out of the country and not due back for a month or so. It'll mollify the executives to know they have a meeting set with me—and give us the time to find the right girl."

"Will you see Richard?"

"Yes."

When Charlie had decided to start EmerSound in his Lower East Side studio apartment, he'd studied the music industry with the same kind of zeal he'd once brought to solving problems in differential calculus at graduate school: the same tenacity, the same cool observant methodology, the same hours even. He'd collected vast amounts of information on the industry: the music, the technologies, the companies, the media, the people. He'd found that in a certain part of the music sector—the very lucrative part—the music itself was the least relevant aspect of the business, and its quality didn't matter. Instead, there was a mysterious secret to what would sell, and this required a good marketer and a good barometer of customer preferences. That was a role Charlie himself could never fill. Richard Stanton, however, filled the role beautifully. He had a knack for finding music acts—and later inventing shows—that would sell. Charlie had never liked him personally, which was by design—he preferred not to like his employees in general—but some days he regretted that fact. Today was one of those days.

He sighed and entered the library—a space he usually didn't mind. When he'd bought the penthouse, the huge room had already been outfitted with rows of floor-to-ceiling shelves, leaving the front third as a sitting room, complete with a fireplace. Charlie had liked the brightness the skylight imparted, so he'd added a desk and wet bar to the sitting area, making the room double as his office.

Richard now paced behind the couch, catty-corner to the desk, with his usual nervous energy—a stuttering start-stop movement almost like a tremor on his overly thin body that was only partially offset by the fashionability of his gray suit. Charlie walked to the bar cart against the wall to pour himself a glass of whiskey—the only way to get through an early-morning meeting with Richard and his grating desperation.

Richard halted. "I thought we agreed on Brandy."

"You thought wrong."

"But she's pretty and she really likes you," Richard said.

"But I don't like her."

"Why not?"

Charlie sat on the edge of his desk to sip his drink, then tempered his voice, if not his annoyance, and said, "Just make another list of girls—maybe ones who aren't so vapid."

"We don't have any more time. People are already saying it's a publicity stunt, and after *Diva* they all know we need money. If we go broke—"

"Stop," Charlie commanded. He didn't need Richard to rehash the harrowing state of EmerSound's finances and the sizeable debt they'd mounted after their original reality show, *Diva Next Door*, had been canceled last year. Charlie planned to take the company public to generate cash, but first they needed a publicity-driving sensation to drive up the initial share price. Richard, who, along with his anxious need for approval, had an unerring knack for public taste, had come up with the *Mrs. Music* reality show concept—adamant that a Cinderella story never failed and that Charlie would make a perfect prince. The show would generate revenue from sponsored ads and music—and possibly even merchandise.

Except Charlie wasn't even dating anyone, at least not publicly, and he'd rejected all the girls he'd interviewed for the part so far, unable to stand the thought of any of them taking up residence in his penthouse. They fawned and they flattered, and he knew every single one, once she'd moved in, would try to get into his bed. After all, "philandering player" was part of Charlie's brand. But the idea of bringing so much of that brand into his own home had become unthinkable.

Richard was naming off more girls. "How about Madeline or Liz—you remember, they were in the running for *Diva* a couple of years ago. They both have their own following. We'd have a built-in audience before we even started."

"They don't fit the premise," Charlie said. "They're not… pitiful enough to be rescued."

Richard sank into one of the chairs facing the desk. "I wish Zoe hadn't managed to off herself. She'd be perfect, especially with a suicide attempt and all those rumors about her. You'd be the good guy—marrying her even though she's a pariah or whatever. It would be a reputational rags-to-riches. And people really thought you guys were together during the show, and they loved it. We could've totally capitalized on it."

Charlie took a long gulp of his whiskey, trying and failing to remember Zoe's face. He did remember that she had a little talent—not any more or less than any of the other girls before her—and they'd refused her a contract at the end of her *Diva* season because it was time to refuse someone. People claimed it was rejection, either for the contract or of Charlie's affection, that had devastated her. Either way, he should remember what she looked like. He was responsible, after all, for putting her there. For putting the events into motion that eventually led to her suicide. He closed his eyes for a second, but it wouldn't come to him. "Let's not talk about Zoe."

"But Charlie, I'm just trying to tell you what we need. We need someone like Zoe, someone who's in love with you so we can—"

"Enough," Charlie said, standing up. Richard was like a bug bite, itchy and irritating, and something you had to endure until it went away. And Richard would only go away if appeased. Softening his voice, Charlie said, "Look, Richard, I'm sure you can find someone we can both agree on for me to marry. You've never failed me."

Richard perked up a little, drawing taller. "Well, there are a couple more girls I could bring. And Simone probably knows some people. You should find a wife like Simone—honestly, she really keeps me together."

"Then it's settled," Charlie said, pressing the button on his desk to alert Murdoch to come take Richard away. "I want to see a list on my desk tomorrow."

When Richard had gone, Charlie allowed himself a minute to wonder if he would ever be able to find someone right for the role of wife in the new show. Then again, were any of the girls ever *right* for his shows? At least in EmerSound's previous reality show,

Diva Next Door, there had been no pretense of a relationship—technically no pretense had been required at all on the old show. Just a makeover designed to create a star, with a possible payout and recording contract at the end, if the girl had the "right stuff" and it was the right time. It wasn't his fault if the girls wanted to pretend to be better than they were, or if some of them were publicly outed as frauds. Or if one of them had killed herself.

It all made him weary, and he felt a longing—an old longing he'd never been able to root out completely—for the cold, hard facts of scientific analysis, where you said what was true, what you meant, and that was that. But no, the scientific world was almost as full of massaged narratives as the entertainment media, and the consequences were even more serious. It was why he'd hatched the plan all those years ago—to quit school, make piles of money, and then retire to work on his science alone and in peace. Alone was easy. Getting enough money was looking more questionable by the day. Peace, he might have already sacrificed away. And the work—well, he'd think about that again when the time came. If it came.

CHAPTER III

E very Wednesday morning, Charlie walked twenty blocks from his place to the City Academy of Music—no matter the weather—to meet his friend Lawrence Berg, a professor of music theory, for coffee and a chat. He'd started walking because he'd needed the space and time it gave him to think about his scientific work. He no longer needed that space, but the walks had become a habit.

Today, it was too hot for such a long walk, but Charlie did it anyway, unwilling to let the June weather bully his ritual out of him. He stopped at the sidewalk stand near the front gates of the Academy to order his usual summer drink, iced coffee, from the usual pale, slight girl who always served him, absently checking the latest email from Richard—a rant complaining about Charlie's continued lack of fiancée even though the new list of girls had been delivered a week ago.

A heavily gloved hand extended Charlie's drink. He looked up at the girl without taking it and she immediately dropped her head, revealing the top of a tattered black fisherman's cap.

"Seems a bit hot for leather work gloves and a woolen hat," he said.

She shrugged and jerked his coffee up, mumbling, "One dollar for the coffee."

He'd dealt with this girl every week for years, but he'd never really seen her until today. She looked to be in her twenties and of average height, but seemed smaller because she was overly thin, her bare shoulders and arms too fragile against the heavy gloves and the white ribbed tank top. He couldn't tell if she was malnourished or if it was an effect created by her hunched posture and bowed head.

Then, noticing sheet music on the counter behind her, he asked, "Are you a student at the Academy?"

"No." She placed his coffee down on the counter in front of him with a thump of finality.

"Do you write music?" he asked.

She didn't answer that one at all, and just stood there, eerily still. Over many months of visiting this stand, Charlie had seen her racing to fill orders, maneuvering in the tiny space to pour coffee and cut bagels, agile and quick, and her stillness now was an intriguing kind of discipline in contrast. He was tempted to draw her out, to see what she was about, but the line of customers was growing behind him, so he paid for his coffee instead. Walking off, he laughed a little at himself. He must really be hard up if this was the kind of thing he now found interesting. But then again, after all the hours he'd spent interviewing bride candidates—a revolving door of interchangeable girls who talked a lot but never said anything new—this girl's silence was unique.

Usually, Charlie would go to Lawrence's office, but today the man waited for him near the gates of the Academy, slouching against the wall. At six feet, he stood almost as tall as Charlie, but his lanky build and narrow face stressed the delicacy of bones rather than the power of muscles, and Charlie had always thought of him as a quintessential British aristocrat—which he was, down to the rich accent he now greeted Charlie in. "Am I late or are you early?"

"Either way, I'm not at your office yet," Charlie said with a smile, "so it doesn't matter. We can walk together."

They'd only gone a few steps when Lawrence said, "It seems congratulations are in order."

"Congratulations?"

"I hear you're getting married."

Charlie laughed. "I hope you haven't been following the story."

"Oh, not really following, but one can't help running into headlines now and then."

"I'll tell you all about it later."

"Ah, of course," Lawrence said. "I forgot." They had an agreement not to discuss anything important in public where they might be heard, and they walked for a bit without talking at all, but inside the building, Lawrence broke the silence to laugh and say, "I hadn't noticed how recognizable you are. Two of every three people stop to stare at you. And the third one only pretends not to know you."

"I'm sullying your reputation," Charlie said with a smile, and Lawrence laughed harder. But then an idea occurred to Charlie: Was it possible the coffee girl didn't know who he was? Is that why she seemed strange? "Do you know anything about the girl at that food stand?" he asked Lawrence. "She's always there when I go for my coffee."

Lawrence raised his eyebrows in a momentary surprise but then nodded. "As a matter of fact, I do. She audited one of my classes a few years ago. Maybe the advanced theory seminar? I'm not positive. But why the interest in her?"

"She had some sheet music out and it made me curious, that's all," Charlie said, though he wasn't sure if that's why he was interested in her. Maybe her oblivion. Or her air of living on a different plane of existence.

Lawrence's office was a cluttered place, with stacks of papers and books covering most of the surfaces, including the desk where the two men sat across from each other.

"So it's a publicity stunt then, this marriage?" Lawrence asked. He generally knew the true motivations behind Charlie's actions and had since college, when he'd taken Charlie—a thirteen-year-old college freshman—in hand. Lawrence had been new to the United States and said Charlie reminded him of a little brother he'd left back in England. "He's not the child prodigy you are," he'd told Charlie, "but you have the same exuberance." They'd stayed de facto brothers since.

So Lawrence knew Charlie's original plan—to use Emer-Sound as a way to fund his science—and at Charlie's nod, he asked, a little too casually, "Does that mean you're not retiring?"

"I'm just putting it off for a bit," Charlie said.

"You've been saying that for two years."

"I want to make sure I get the maximum value out of EmerSound."

"Two years ago, your excuse was you were doing too well, and if you jumped ship, people might get suspicious and not buy. So which is it?"

Charlie sipped his coffee. It might have been better if he had retired two years ago. Zoe would still be alive and Simone would've never been on *Diva*. "These things have to be timed right," he said. "And this new show will do it. Once we get a higher revenue stream going, I'll take the company public and cash out."

"Alright," Lawrence said dubiously, then his eyes brightened. "Oh, I have that paper on the new German acoustic technology for you—my friend Sanderson finally translated it," he said as he rummaged through a lopsided pile of papers on his desk.

Once upon a time, Charlie would've been excited about the prospect of new research, but he'd lost the taste for it. He had a growing collection of such papers from his friend on his own desk, all unread.

Lawrence was going on: "Sanderson asked me about you actually. What did he call you? I think it was"—he put on a German accent—"the boy who worked famous unsolved math problems like they were crossword puzzles."

"I only did that once."

"Yes, but it was in front of a two-hundred-person lecture hall." Lawrence snorted. "Did you read the last paper I gave you? It was rather too technical for me and I thought you might give me the gist."

"Not yet." Not ever, probably. "With the new show and all, I haven't had time."

Lawrence stopped searching and pushed away from the desk and the pile of papers, a faint smile ghosting his lips. "You've concocted that distraction with great skill."

"What distraction?"

"Your new show."

"It's not a distraction; it's my life."

"And you could make so much more of that life."

"I think I'm making plenty of it already," Charlie said, trying to sound nonchalant.

"Do you really? You're the quintessential rich bachelor leading an empty life—with your cars and your girls and your pictures in the news all the time. You're living a cliché."

"You forgot the mindless mass-pandering music and TV shows I produce."

"I didn't want to offend you."

"No offense. I've worked hard to build my empty clichéd life. And you've missed the only important part—I can step out of it at any time I choose. There's nothing to hold me to it, except my own whim." He didn't add that this was the whole point of it.

"And then you'll finish Acoustitech, publish your theory?" Lawrence had gone back to rifling through his chaotic desk, as if this were a casual question, though they both knew it was not.

So Charlie gave his pat answer—"That's always been the plan"—even though the plan had started to feel hollow some time ago and his inspiration had dried up, his scientific work stalled. Retiring from EmerSound no longer seemed like the next step on an exciting path. It only felt like an end, leaving him with a sense of lost purpose, as if he'd finally arrived at a long-sought destination only to find it abandoned. He'd never told Lawrence and didn't know how to tell him now. So he sat and watched his friend search the desk for a paper Charlie would never read.

CHAPTER IV

S imone Hawl had been a beauty queen in her late teens, tall and willowy with almost waist-long hair she'd cut to shoulder length and dyed auburn for her starring role on *Diva Next Door*. It was Richard Stanton who'd cast her on the show, but it was Charlie who had met her—and started sleeping with her—first. No one had known about Charlie and Simone's affair then, and no one knew about it now. Their weekly trysts were an easily kept secret even after she'd married Richard, as long as she left Charlie's just after the sun—and just before Richard— had risen for the day.

This morning, Simone got out of bed but stood admiring her own reflection in Charlie's full-length bedroom mirror rather than dressing. "They've started calling you Lucifer online," she said.

Charlie had not dressed yet either, and he lay stretched out on the bed behind her. He propped himself on both elbows at her words.

"Don't you want to know why they call you Lucifer?" she asked when he didn't say anything.

"You want to tell me."

"You know, like the Fallen Angel of Music." She turned to gather her clothes off the floor and began to dress, her movements slow and deliberate. Well-rehearsed. "*Rock Clash Magazine* said it first, because you corrupt young girls. They called you beautiful and dangerous, and..."

Charlie dropped back down on the pillow and closed his eyes. He detested talk of EmerSound in his bedroom but said nothing. Celebrity had become one of Simone's favorite topics in recent years, and he never stopped one of her rants. It seemed to make her happy, and he felt he owed her—after all, she was one of the girls he'd corrupted with his record label and his show and their affair.

"...as if you're some sort of unattainable god, but if they knew about us—Charlie, do you love me?"

Charlie opened his eyes but didn't move. This was the one concession he'd never made, even though he suspected her pursuit of Richard had initially been a ploy to get Charlie to confess his love. But he'd never loved anyone or anything and was probably incapable of it. He merely obsessed—and that obsession didn't benefit anyone. Still, he had enough affection for Simone not to lie to her, certain a lie of that sort would be the thing to destroy her, finally and completely. "Simone..."

"You never say it. I want to hear you say it."

"What will it change? Will you divorce Richard?" he asked, knowing she would never leave her comfortable and predictable life with Richard. *But then why is she tormenting me about my feelings?*

Simone had been buttoning her shirt, and her hands stilled for an instant before she pushed the last one through its hole. "That's not really the point."

"What is?"

"You say you love my voice. You say you love the way I look. But you never say you love *me*. I need to know that you're mine, Charlie. I want all of you."

There's not much left. "What makes you think you don't have it?"

"You never tell me anything. I don't know what goes on in that secret lab room. I don't know what the hell you even do all day." She turned to him, hands akimbo. Glaring. Waiting.

"You want to know the details of my wave theory? Want to give me a hand in finding the error in my experiment for Acoustitech?" he asked, knowing he was being cruel, knowing she had neither the interest nor the ability to understand that work, but the topic agitated him and he needed to make her stop. He got up and poured himself a glass of whiskey from the wet bar by the closet, then more quietly added, "I don't go to the lab anymore. The only thing I do now is run EmerSound." He took two long sips of the whiskey. It was much too early to drink, but he needed it, and besides, one drink never affected his work at EmerSound. Sometimes it even made his hours there more bearable.

"What about the show?" Simone asked, her words measured, unrattled by his outburst. "Why are you taking so long to pick someone to be your wife? I know you interviewed Brandy last week and didn't hire her. Richard was livid. He couldn't stop talking about it."

Now Charlie understood. "Is that what's bothering you? That I'm getting married?"

"Of course not. I'm curious is all." She faced the mirror again and made a show of adjusting her hair.

Charlie sipped his drink some more. He was a little weary of Simone's games today. What would it be like not having to worry about her pretenses and doublespeak? Not to feel this weight of trying to read between the lines, trying not to hurt her more than he had?

He let a moment pass, then asked, "Have you ever been to that little food stand across from the Academy?"

Simone frowned, shifting her head slightly from side to side, watching her diamond earrings sparkle. He thought she wasn't going to let him change the subject, but she asked, "The one on Seventy-Fourth? The thing's been there forever. Why?"

"You ever notice the girl who works there?"

"Why, Charlie, are you actually noticing other people?" Simone laughed, but he knew she was only partly joking.

"I notice people," he said. "I just don't usually care."

"Well, no reason to care about Alex, darling. She's kind of part of the school. You know, one of those odd little things that give the place character... She was already there when I was a student. I think there's something wrong with her. They let her sit in on one of the classes I was taking, and she never said anything. I guess they felt sorry for her."

"So she's a musician?"

"I wouldn't call her that, but she probably thinks so. She's got some music project she harangues the students about every once in a while. But no one's interested."

"What project?"

"Who cares? Wait, you're not suggesting she be the one you marry, are you?" Simone, now fully dressed, stared at Charlie incredulously.

"Maybe." He shrugged. He'd been toying with the idea vaguely, but if it assuaged Simone, he might take it more seriously.

A distant expression came over Simone's face as if she were calculating something, perhaps trying to figure out the media implications of the marriage. Then she grinned and swung her arms around his neck. Charlie put his drink down and held her by the waist, enjoying the bright gleam in her eyes, even if it was more about machinations of fame than it was about music, the way it used to be.

"Charlie, I think you might be a genius."

He wrenched out a smile, recognizing her attempt at a joke about his past—but he didn't much like the term, or being reminded of that past.

"I mean I've never seen you be so savvy about things like this," she went on. "It's almost Richard-caliber. She's perfect, of course! Think how it would look, how you could help her. Poor little thing doesn't have a chance of ever marrying anyone, much less someone like you! Every girl should know what it's like to be taken care of by a real man. Maybe it could even help her come out of her shell."

Simone knew as well as he did that his reality shows ruined people more often than helped them. For Charlie, that's what made this girl—Alex—perfect; she didn't have much to ruin. He let go of Simone and grabbed his drink again. "I just thought she wouldn't be any trouble; I'm not trying to save anyone. Besides, she can't even look me in the face. You think marrying me will miraculously cure whatever's wrong with her?"

"You don't understand women at all! Maybe she doesn't look at you when you're watching, but I'm sure she's *looked* at you. I mean, she may be a little slow, but she'd have to be dead not to think you're attractive. You'll use Glen Clarence, of course, to have her checked out, background and everything, and you'll see. Offer her a little money and she'll do whatever you want. No trouble."

"No trouble," he agreed.

CHAPTER V

The girl might be no trouble, but Charlie expected certain people at EmerSound to be harder to manage on the issue. As soon as Glen Clarence, private investigator, produced a write-up about the coffee girl, Charlie called a meeting with his key staff members to review the details, then sat watching from the head of the long conference table as they read through the report, sipping his coffee and taking measure of their reactions, trying to assess who would pose the biggest difficulty.

Richard Stanton trembled at a frequency slightly above his habitual one, and Jennifer Barnes, chief financial officer at EmerSound, frowned, her high forehead creasing deeply. But the show's producer, David, heavyset and bearded, seemed gleeful, grinning and nodding as he scanned the document. Murdoch, sitting on Charlie's left, took notes without reaction, his expression stoic. Each of these people had been hired for one main skill, a particular expertise Charlie needed, and he always asked for their advice where that expertise was concerned—though whether he took the advice was a different matter.

"Jesus, it says she's got some sort of orchestra music—we don't do that kind of thing," Richard said. "I thought we agreed on a singer."

Jennifer shook her head. "I know I never weigh in on your artistic decisions, Charlie, but I have to agree with Richard. Classical music is not what EmerSound does. We'd have to spend extra to get people with the right knowledge—producers, sound engineers, marketers."

"I like it," David said, his gruff voice matching the unkempt air of his wrinkled T-shirt. "An orchestra gives me a lot of cast to work with. Think of all the intrigue we could get going. Love triangles and in-fighting and jealousy."

Charlie had a few reservations about the music genre too at first, but he'd bought coffee from the girl several more times in the intervening weeks and had again liked her lack of sophistication and ambition. If she didn't expect much, she'd have no hopes to dash and no dreams to crush. And the report on her proved it—she was penniless, on the verge of eviction, and wasn't doing much to change it. The more he thought about it, the more certain he became of his decision. "We don't have to put too much money into the music," he said. "The show's not about that. Besides, aligning the sales numbers to audience polls for *Diva*"— he motioned to Murdoch, who pulled out two sheets of paper to hand to Richard and Jennifer—"tells me that the viewers are sick of the same old songs, even if they're sung by a new person. We need a new type of material, and I like giving the impression that we're expanding, becoming more sophisticated."

Jennifer narrowed her eyes, then said, "Maybe. And maybe we can get someone from that industry to serve on the new board of directors for the company when it's gone public. I'll look into it."

"But Charlie, have you read all these details about her?" Richard asked. "It's no good."

"I always read the details." Charlie ticked them off on his fingers as he recited, "Heart condition, Swiss clinic, two heart transplants, GED, apartment in the Bronx, coffee stand. Seems fine to me."

"No, no, the stuff about her dead mother and being estranged from her father—"

"It's great—real juicy stuff." David's overly loud voice drowned out whatever else Richard was trying to say. "And we'll get the sympathy card with all this illness crap. I can make something out of the father thing. Like it says, some patient at his clinic murdered another doctor—scandal-worthy stuff, maybe made her life at home hard, you know? Even if not, we can certainly make it look that way—she's probably already unhinged. All the better to get a rise out of her on camera."

David didn't rub his hands together or cackle, but those things wouldn't be out of place after his speech. It made Charlie a little sick, but it had struck the right note of confidence and bullying to persuade Richard—who didn't raise another objection. David, however, was on a roll now.

"We'll start her off as like this kind of new kid trying real hard to fit in. A sort of newbie airhead. And Charlie can be a bit of a villain—they love you as the bad boy—you know, like not understanding she doesn't belong and how she's uncomfortable. I'll find her a friend to help her and then maybe stab her in the back—and then I'll get her really drunk at some point and she'll explode. Everybody will be waiting for it. The quiet ones always go crazy if you needle them enough and then take away their inhibitions."

Charlie winced a little, imagining the feeble girl in the midst of David's sordid plan, but he said nothing.

Jennifer pointed down to her copy of the report. "On page eleven…it says she isn't online anywhere. I find it strange that a twenty-eight-year-old woman doesn't have any sort of internet presence."

"Not everyone cares about that kind of thing," Charlie said, but he read that portion of the report again, because it was strange—the girl didn't even have an email address. But then again, she was an introvert and it could be a good thing; people could say whatever they wanted about her online and she wouldn't ever know, much less care.

David guffawed. "Either it's a blank slate, which will make it that much easier to create whatever I want, or she's got some dirty past—naked photos or a sex tape or something—which is even better. Think of the scandal!"

This is why they'd hired David, Charlie reminded himself. He was the best in the business and he'd made *Diva* a success. And this time, Charlie would pay more attention, make sure the girl survived it all. Besides, if the scandal were of her own making, they had to neither manufacture a story nor feel bad about it getting out. He pushed away the annoyance niggling at him and stood up. "It's settled then. We have our *Mrs. Music*."

CHAPTER VI

Alexandra Weiss loved the rhythms of the city: the beat of traffic echoing off buildings, the rumble of trains underneath the street, the chatter of pedestrians hurrying along the sidewalks—a symphony of activity and purpose. Every morning she added her own harmony to the melody: the creek of rickety wheels from the coffee cart latched to her ancient bicycle as she pedaled the seven miles south from her room on West 167th Street to her spot in front of the main gates of the City Academy of Music.

By the time she'd unlatched her stand and squeezed herself inside, espresso machine on her right, pastries on her left, a shiny aluminum counter between her and the outside world, the morning commute had started its crescendo. The busy chaotic tune had panicked her on her first days in the city, causing the aberrations in her vision—which she'd gained control of years before—to come flooding back, wild and unruly. There had been no music to the city then, and she'd resorted to drowning out the chaos and her own panic with a pair of headphones and a gentle cello suite, as she eked out her living one coffee and one bagel at a time.

She still worked without rest for hours, and though the mayhem had settled into a pleasing warble, those hours felt ripped out of her life and away from her own music. Her one luxury during these long days came when she snatched a stretch of time for herself, during her breaks or when the customers thinned, to work on her own composition.

But recently, she'd had to give up most of her breaks because she couldn't risk losing any sales, already behind on her rent and power bills. And then all of it got even harder because of *him*, the Wednesday morning regular with the deep blue baritone who'd ruined the semblance of comfort she'd built. She'd noticed him a long time ago, because he was beautiful in that severe way of defined cheekbones, hollow cheeks, and strong jaw, over an athletic build and broad shoulders. She'd remembered him because he was like the final movement of a Beethoven sonata, tempestuous and elegant, his approach swift and legato, his order a terse staccato—"Coffee, cream, no sugar"—and she'd watched him the way she listened to a piece of music and for the same reason: He was art in motion. Then a month ago, he'd stood at her cart, waiting for answers, noticing things other people never did—her gloves and the sheets of handwritten music strewn all over the prep counter—and had refused to feel uncomfortable, no matter how hunched her shoulders, how downcast her glance, or how terse her manner.

And even though he'd not uttered an extra word in her direction since then, he'd unsettled her, intuition telling her she did not want to be examined by him again, and she'd started keeping her music hidden, even on days that weren't his regular day. Now she wasted time rummaging through her bag for her manuscript every time she needed to look at it, and she'd started to nurture an ambivalence toward him for the lost minutes—which cost even more time. He'd become less anonymous and more than art, and she could no longer enjoy watching him in the same way.

Today was again his day. A typical sweltering day in July, the sun had risen early and vengefully, and through the endless succession of cups of iced coffee and bottles of water handed out to faceless hands, she kept looking for *his* hands. But his regular time came and went without him, and when the morning rush thinned at eleven and he still hadn't come, she thought she should be relieved. But she only felt caged by her stand, stifled by the heat, and desperate to take a break or at least take her gloves off. But she couldn't do either—couldn't give up the money or risk her hands getting cut with a bagel knife or burned on the hot coffee machine—and so she trudged on.

Finally, that afternoon, when there had been no customers for some time, Alex sat on her stool in the stand, notebook on her lap, trying to work out the fourth and final movement of her *Red Concerto*. She'd worked on the piece for years, piecing together the first three movements in her little increments of stolen time, and it had been difficult—Alex liked difficult—but the fourth movement was grueling in a different way, because her imagination had waned and she had no time to nurture it. What she needed was long, uninterrupted stretches to focus on her music, to try new things and to experiment, but time was the one thing she couldn't find more of.

She crossed out the first four bars—again—because the structure and tempo were too mechanical, all edifice and no emotion.

Should she change the key? Would that put her in the right mental state? But the question had to wait, because a shadow fell over her notebook—the sign of someone waiting to order—and she looked up. It was *him*. The Wednesday regular with the too-sharp focus, here hours past his usual time.

"Hello," he said.

She closed her notebook and stood up to make his iced coffee.

"Wait," he said, and she stilled with the empty cup in her hand, but she didn't turn toward him. "I'm Charlie Emerson and I'd like to speak to you for a moment."

"I'm listening," she said, putting the cup down and then busying herself by wiping down a clean counter. An ambulance sped down the street, siren wailing, and for a moment it was all she could hear.

Finally, when only echoes of the racket remained, Charlie said, "Not here. Somewhere a bit more...private."

She glanced at him. "Private?"

"How about over there?" He pointed to a bench just inside the Academy's gates, nestled beneath a row of trees. The leaves swayed in a faint breeze, their shadows quivering across the bench.

"What do you need to talk to me about?" she asked.

"Please, just a few minutes. I'd rather not speak here."

His deference calmed her down and piqued her curiosity—his notice would haunt her until she knew what he wanted. And then she was so hot inside the tiny stand. "Alright," she said, "but I can only take ten."

Once her cart was secured and they were sitting in the shade, side by side, Alex huddled with her knees pulled up, her feet on the bench, and her chin on her knees. She swiped her gloved hand across her forehead. She was finding it difficult not to look at him.

He sat with his legs extended and crossed at the ankles, holding the back of his head in his laced fingers and gazing up at the tree. "You're Alexandra Weiss," he said.

He knows my name? With an effort to keep her voice steady, she said, "I go by Alex."

"Okay, Alex, I have a proposition for you." He paused, as if this preamble would be enough for her to understand what he meant.

"A proposition?"

"I'd like you to marry me."

She snapped her eyes up, focusing on him, but there was no humor in his face. Just a stoic watchfulness. She tensed her body, making herself smaller, and shook her head, in denial or confusion. She couldn't begin to understand what sort of scam this might be. She dropped her focus to the bit of pavement in front of the bench, again.

"I'm making a show and it's going to be about my new wife—a *musician*—who's just getting her start. You fit the characteristics I'm looking for."

"What characteristics?" she asked, focusing on the easiest detail first.

"Not important. I—" Charlie stopped midsentence.

The low murmur of a conversation grew closer, then changed to female titters as two sets of feet appeared in Alex's field of view, the *slap-slap* of their sandals slowing—almost stopping—as they passed by.

When their voices had drawn away, Charlie said, "It wouldn't be a real marriage. You won't have to sleep with me."

Alex was finding the whole scenario ridiculous. "I don't know what this is," she stammered. "I don't even know anything about you."

He didn't answer right away and she spared a glance at him. He was staring at her, one eyebrow raised. Then he shrugged and said, "I'm thirty-two years old, I own EmerSound Music, which I started out of a studio apartment on the Lower East Side fifteen years ago, and most recently, I coproduced and appeared as a judge on *Diva Next Door*, which ran for seven years." He recited the list of his accomplishments with the same tone someone else might use to read a list of groceries.

She hadn't heard of any of the things he'd mentioned. "What's *Diva Next Door*?"

"You really don't know, do you?" he asked, smiling faintly. "It was a reality show—where we picked an average girl and made her into a superstar."

"And it was popular?"

"We had the highest-rated show in the country for several years."

He must be famous, she realized. "You assumed I'd know who you are."

"I figured the probability was high."

"I don't really follow pop culture," she said, but the word "probability" jarred her memory. "Are you related to Charlie Emerson, the mathematician?"

At this he laughed. It was a light, attractive laugh. The lightness was incongruous. "You've heard of that, but not *Diva Next Door*?" he asked.

She shouldn't have said that. People didn't expect normal girls to know about that kind of math. She shrugged, trying to be casual.

"I used to do math," he said, still smiling, "but I don't anymore."

"Why not?"

The remnants of his amusement faded. "My past in mathematics is hardly relevant here. What do you think of my proposal?"

"That's your whole argument, then, of why I should marry you?" she asked.

"No." Now he was all business. "I've had my lawyers prepare a contract that states all the particulars of the marriage and the show, how we'll produce your music, the amounts to be paid and when, our living arrangements, what you will and won't owe me. All of it. That'll be the whole argument. My lawyers can explain it to you—"

"You want to produce my music?"

"That's what I do."

How did he know about her music? Had he chosen her because of it? It seemed impossible. "But you don't know anything about me or my music."

"I've done my research."

Alex rubbed her eyes with the palms of her still-gloved hands, which were now shaking. Of course he'd checked up on her. He must be rich beyond imagination. It would be so easy for him to dig up her past. But here he was, anyway, offering her this contract. She felt like she was standing in the middle of the road and the light had just turned green to oncoming traffic, and Charlie Emerson was behind the wheel of a semi-truck headed straight for her. He wouldn't even notice what he'd done afterward. But still there was the offer to produce her concerto. The possibility to finish writing it and bring it to life.

"I'm sorry—this must feel intrusive," he said, more appeasing now. "But in my line of work, it's important to vet people."

"And what have you found out about me?"

"You're twenty-eight. You've had a hard life so far. You've written music and you've approached a lot of students at the Academy, but they weren't interested. You can't afford to hire musicians and record your own demo. You're behind on your rent and your power bills. You're about to get evicted."

He knew a lot. But perhaps not everything. "Don't you need to hear my music first, before you produce it?" she asked.

"The music isn't relevant. We can fix anything."

What kind of music producer didn't care about the music? What kind of person did any of this at all? She needed to end this conversation, needed time to think. "Let me have the contract," she said. "I can read it."

He leaned forward just the smallest bit, maybe to try to see her expression, but at the last minute stood up instead. "I'll have the contract delivered to you within the hour. You'll have to sign a nondisclosure when it arrives. We'll proceed from there."

And he was gone.

CHAPTER VII

Alex's first mistake was taking the contract. A messenger from Charlie's lawyer brought it to her and she put it straight into her bag, determined not to look at it. But her curiosity grew as the details of Charlie Emerson's life trickled out of her memory.

When she'd hit an age when she could understand such things, Alex had grown fascinated with young geniuses—and perhaps because her own life was small and limited, she'd spent time finding and following stories of kids who did great things. Charlie Emerson was among the first of these. Admitted to a prestigious college at age thirteen—the first and only student to accomplish it at the Asher Institute of Technology—he'd been a math prodigy and had already made progress on a difficult physics equation by that age. She'd followed him intermittently, whenever she could find mentions of him online, through his three years as an undergraduate and then into graduate studies, even trying to read a few of the papers he'd published, although the math had been beyond her at the time. Then, busy with the drama of her own teenage life, she'd lost track of him.

So she knew enough to reason that there was nothing to trust about him or his show, no matter who he'd been as a child. Maybe *specifically* because of who he'd been as a child. How and why did a person go from astounding math prodigy to pop record producer? And after the years she'd spent working, and the events of her own life, it wasn't possible that by simply marrying this man and being part of his show she could finally finish and record the *Red Concerto*.

But in the next few hours, as she brewed coffee and handed out pastries, her eyes kept returning to her bag. Maybe it wouldn't hurt to just read the thing? She couldn't reject it outright without even a glance.

So, in the evening, when her bike and cart were secure and she'd returned to her little room, she settled on her bed with the contract. She held the stack of papers in one hand and lightly ran her other hand over its surface. The first page only said, *For Alexandra Weiss.* She stared at the name and closed her eyes. Then she opened the document and read.

The proposal wasn't a bad one. It amounted to exactly what he'd said: She'd marry him and be the star of his show, a forty-three-minute spot plus ads, to run once a week for a single season, where Alex's journey as the so-called Mrs. Music would be shared with the audience, culminating in the performance of her music in a live finale episode.

The final episode will be the premiere of "Red Concerto," after which time the marriage will be terminated via a no-fault divorce, following an appropriate interlude to be determined by EmerSound Music Inc.

She reread the sentence several times, not only because they already knew the name of her concerto, but because it represented the fulfillment of her dream of almost a decade.

There were other details: a prenuptial agreement, a "modest" monthly allowance—though the amount listed was almost ten times what she made at the coffee stand—a generous lump sum at the end of the marriage, her royalties on the sale of her music, and the pretense that the marriage was real. None of it meant anything to her in the face of that phrase, *the premiere of the "Red Concerto,"* and the lure of spending more time on her music. No more coffee stand, no more constant interruptions, only music. Being on the show couldn't be much worse than the coffee stand, could it?

She spent half the night on her computer researching EmerSound and Charlie Emerson, streaming the music and shows they had produced, knowing there must be a hitch—which, of course, there was. EmerSound's music and shows were clichéd, pandering knockoffs of better ones. The music was unremark-able, the sets exaggerated, the stories overly dramatic—all clearly done to appeal to sensationalism and cash in on the trend of the moment without thought or artistry. The company produced everything she detested and avoided in art. How could she and her music ever fit at such a place, even if she wanted it?

Charlie Emerson himself was even harder to understand, and she learned no more of him than what he'd told her. There were many details to be learned from the online gossip sites and posts, but even if they could be trusted, they told nothing of the man, not really. They told only of Charlie the music executive who'd risen from a small recording label owner into media-per-sonality fame through *Diva Next Door*. She learned of his extrav-agant lifestyle, his millions, and saw pictures of him with beau-tiful women: actresses, pop musicians, models. But these last details could just as well be for the media—as Alex herself could be—merely a show; no one ever talked of him having long-term relationships. In any case, what she'd seen of him in person wasn't consistent with the wild bachelor they presented, though she couldn't exactly say why.

Charlie's life before fame as CEO and president of Emer-Sound was harder to decipher. She found only one recent mention in an obscure online magazine from an article about famous people with surprising pasts. It referenced Charlie's old life as a mathematician and scientist:

A well-known and celebrated mathematical child prodigy, Mr. Emerson quit his mathematical and scientific work shortly before receiving his PhD at the prestigious Asher Institute of Technology. His early work was promising, and he had been widely expected to present a revolutionary set of equations on his so-called unified wave theory, but these never came to fruition.

Some have claimed that Emerson tried to pass off fake data to validate his theory and was asked by Asher to leave both the institute and the mathematics and physics fields. After leaving, Emerson withdrew into self-imposed exile as far as mathematics and physics were concerned.

By the time he was back in the spotlight, he had already owned the EmerSound record label for several years, his mathematical past mostly forgotten. He has never talked publicly about the time surrounding his departure from Asher or his mathematical work.

Alex couldn't believe that Charlie had needed to fabricate his work. Why, with that kind of mind and ability, would he have tried to cheat? She found free access to two of Charlie's old papers from his graduate days—the one she'd tried to read as a teenager and a later one introducing his wave theory—and now having the necessary knowledge to understand the material, she spent several hours working through them. She was astounded. Even with her amateur ability in physics and math, Alex could see the scope of his vision, how he'd brought together disparate fields to solve problems in a feat of creative genius. This was not a man who needed to fake his work. But then how could he quit that work and turn to producing pop music and reality shows—and not very good ones at that? What was he doing with all his extra mental energy?

She couldn't figure him out. For Alex, who would've done anything for the *Red Concerto*, who would have accepted anything to keep composing music, he was incomprehensible.

But even though she had no idea what made her appropriate for his show, or what exactly she'd be in for, she knew she couldn't say no to his proposal. It was like a fairytale—only she wasn't sure if it was the happy story of the rescued princess or the cautionary tale of a pact with the devil.

CHAPTER VIII

Once Alex had made the only decision she thought possible, she had to tell the only person in her life who would care enough to disapprove. She dialed the number, which she hadn't done in a long time. He picked up on the third ring.

"Hi…Dad," she said. "It's me." There was a pause. A very long pause.

"Hello," Dennis Weiss said, his voice barely audible, and then he cleared his throat and said in a sterner voice, "Hello…Alex."

"How are you?" she asked, trying to ease the way into the conversation.

"Same as ever. Things are calm. Is something wrong? I wasn't expecting a call for another month."

"No, not exactly wrong. But I've received…a sort of offer. Which you should know about."

"What offer?"

"A marriage proposal."

This second pause stretched even longer. "I didn't realize you were seeing anyone," he said finally.

"It's not like that. It's for a…show. The wedding would be legal—contractually speaking—but the rest would be acting."

"Why would you want to do something like that?" Weiss said, the anxiety present in the low, controlled tenor of his voice. "Who made the offer? What show?"

"Charlie Emerson."

"*The* Charlie Emerson? From that *Diva* show?"

"You've heard of it?"

He sighed loud enough that she could hear it through the phone. "Yes, of course. Has he offered you a part on one of his reality shows?"

"Yes, but it's going to be a different kind of show than the *Diva* one. It's not a competition," she said, adding quickly, "He's that math prodigy who went to Asher when he was thirteen. Remember him? We talked a lot about him when I was little."

"The one who quit? *That* Charlie Emerson?"

"Yes."

He didn't answer and she knew he was trying to figure out what line of questioning to pursue. She got off her bed and paced the narrow strip of floor beside it, ten steps from one side of the room to the other and back.

Finally he said, "How did he find you?"

"He's been a regular at my stand for a couple of years."

"And suddenly he decides he wants to produce a show with you in it as his wife? Why?"

"I'm an up-and-coming musician," she said, quoting Charlie because she still didn't really know. "It's a good offer. There's a contract."

"And have you ever seen *Diva Next Door*?"

"I watched some of it online recently."

"Do you understand the point of his shows then? His strategy? To find a random—a *normal*—girl and make her famous. *Really famous,* Alex—and not just in the tiny world of classical music. He's all about publicity."

"He's offered to produce the *Red Concerto*."

"Just how much does he know about you?"

"Everything he's supposed to know. And I don't think—"

"He seems to know enough to make you the one offer you wouldn't be able to refuse. But you must refuse. You can't be one of those famous stars from his show."

"I have a plan—with the right sort of look I don't think anyone will realize—I think it'll be fine. I can't say no. You have to understand that—"

"How can you even consider this?" All his efforts at being calm were gone and he was yelling now. She had expected it and listened, but her steps became faster, more agitated as she continued to stalk back and forth in her little room. She'd never liked disappointing him, though she often had.

"It's not worth it," he continued. "You'll be exposed to all that media. This is the most outrageous thing I've ever heard. After all we've done to keep you safe!"

"What good is it to be safe if I can't do the one thing—the only thing—I've ever wanted?"

"Listen to me carefully. I know what you feel about the concerto—haven't I done what I could to help you, to promote your musical ability? But this man—that he's intellectually gifted is not a good thing. He'll see through you. It'll be harder to hide what you are from someone like him."

"He won't pay any real attention to me. I'm a nobody in his eyes." *And maybe if he really sees me, he'll understand.* She stopped her pacing at the wall and leaned back against it for support—she hadn't admitted this to herself before.

"But if he does pay attention, it'll be a disaster. It's too risky."

"I'm going to accept," she said. "There is nothing that I won't risk for the concerto."

He cursed.

"I won't let it hurt you, I promise," she said.

"It's not about that!"

She closed her eyes. "It may be my only chance," she said, not wanting to say it but knowing it had to be said.

"I'll give you the money to produce the *Red Concerto*. I'll mortgage the house. Or you can sell the music to someone else to produce. Anything is better than this plan."

"I won't let anyone else produce the concerto—they won't do it right. And you've already mortgaged the house for the medical bills—you think I didn't know? Besides, Charlie Emerson's fame is what will make the musicians even consider playing for me. If I can offer enough money, I might even be able to get decent ones. I've tried for three years to get the students from the Academy interested and no one will really even talk to me about it. I've got no credentials." This was more than she'd intended to tell him but he needed to know. She could imagine his furrowed brow and deep frown.

But when he answered, his voice was calm. "And where are you going to live?"

"He has a place in the city and I'm going to have a room there." She pushed away from the wall and resumed her pacing.

"It won't be easy, living with someone like that. He'll have staff and they'll be around all the time. They'll have access to all of your things."

"I'll be careful."

"It won't be enough. You have no idea what you're getting into."

CHAPTER IX

The diner where Alex had asked to meet Charlie was busy when he arrived. Evening was falling and the building shadows had grown long enough to shield the avenue from the sun's harsh glare, but the heat continued, merely changing direction, as the sidewalks exhaled the day's accumulated hot air.

Charlie hesitated inside the entrance, letting the cool air wash over him and surveying the restaurant—one large room, situated on the corner of bustling streets, with two full walls of windows, the kind of place you could sit in leisure with a cup of coffee and watch the city's activity and think. He smiled at that thought, remembering a similar place near his lab in graduate school where he'd spent so many hours thinking and working through problems.

Alex had left a message asking him to come alone to discuss the contract—no lawyers, no producers, no assistants—and he'd accepted, not wanting to scare her off, though he was wary of being recognized and mobbed in a place like this. But today, no one noticed him.

He spotted Alex's black fisherman-style cap and her thin arms in a booth against the far window, a giant backpack next to her on the bench. She wrote intently in a notebook, more graceful and less anemic than he'd remembered, and pretty in a delicate, waif-like way, a smattering of freckles highlighting fragile cheekbones. Charlie watched her for a moment, enjoying the prospect of someone so completely engrossed in their work, then made his way over to the booth. He sat down across from her, intending to get a look at her notebook, but she shut it with a loud thwack.

"Hello," he said.

She mumbled a low "Hi," huddling into the corner of the booth, head down, though her hands remained on the notebook, the worn black leather of her gloves camouflaged against the hard cover.

"Have you ordered?" he asked.

"Just having coffee." She tipped her head in a tiny nod toward the mugs on the table, hers half-full.

"I'd like to order some food. Let me get you something. You—" Charlie stopped short of saying *you look like you need it.* Partly out of good manners and partly because she *hadn't* looked like she needed it just a few minutes ago.

"Apple pie," she said, her voice still low.

He smiled. Easy to persuade, wasn't she? He motioned for a waiter and ordered two slices of pie and another coffee, then leaned back in the red vinyl seat. Alex leaned over to rummage through her bag.

"How have you been?" he asked her.

She didn't answer his question but instead pulled out a packet of papers to lay on the table. "I read over the contract and made a few changes," she said, pushing the stack toward him slowly, almost cautiously.

He had the absurd urge to pull her cap off and make her look at him, but instead he reached out and put one hand on the stack of papers. "Why don't you explain it to me first?" he said.

She lifted her head slightly—now he could see the rounded point of her chin—and her words came succinctly: "I want to hold auditions right away and choose the orchestra for the *Red Concerto* myself. We need to offer enough money to draw the right kind of musicians. And I want to be the conductor."

This surprised Charlie into silence, the moment stretching on when the waiter arrived, placing slices of pie in front of them and filling his mug with coffee. When the waiter had gone, Charlie asked, "Have you ever done any of that before? Hiring musicians, conducting?"

"No," Alex said, "but I can figure it out."

He'd already worked out the budget with Jennifer to hire someone to "help" Alex with her concerto. He figured they'd have to rewrite a lot of it, because even though he wasn't concerned with putting out good music, it did have to pass as music, at least, and he wasn't convinced she was any sort of musician. There was no training mentioned in the background report, and she didn't seem to have the right sort of emotions for it. Not enough passion, he decided. He knew what kind of emotional capacity music needed   especially in the classical genre—the sorts of highs and lows one needed to experience for it. "You have no formal training in music, am I right?" he asked.

"I had music teachers growing up."

A few piano lessons didn't count, but he couldn't say that. And anyway, he wasn't in the business of setting people straight on their delusions of grandeur. The exact opposite, in fact. He stirred cream into his coffee and took a sip. "Any other changes?"

She stared into her pie. "I don't want to be followed around by cameras all the time. Two hours a day at most after the makeover."

"And before the makeover?"

"I don't want to be on camera…like this. I don't want a 'before' stage."

Of course she didn't want to be on camera before she'd been made glamorous. Charlie put his mug down on the table with a sharp clank, disappointed to find her conventional after all, then annoyed with himself for expecting differently. "The show's premise depends on the before-and-after. It is not negotiable," he said.

"One before episode only, then, and I get to approve it before it airs."

"Miss Weiss, I don't think you understand how reality shows work. You don't get to set the terms; the producer does. We'll certainly need a lot more footage than just two hours a day. And"— *be delicate*—"classical music is difficult. All of it, including conducting, requires training. I will let you do it, but you'll have to let my experts help you."

"Your *experts?*" She finally raised her face to him, but it seemed like an involuntary reaction born of incredulity.

"Yes. It is my company and my show, after all."

"No experts. That's not negotiable." She shook her head, her almond-shaped eyes cold, clear, and brilliantly blue.

Charlie let his lips suggest a smile, allowing her to see his curiosity, and a fleeting confusion passed through her eyes. Then, as if suddenly noticing that she'd looked up, she dropped her head, grabbed a fork, and stabbed it into the pie in front of her. Was she panicking? About the experts or him? He should give her a bit of time to recover. "Let me have a minute with the contract," he said.

He perused it quickly, flipping pages with one hand and drinking his coffee with the other. Her proposed changes included additions to clarify the precise number of on-camera hours required of her, approval of her appearance in every episode, and detailed specifications for her orchestra—including the number of musicians, the types of instruments, and the length of daily rehearsals. "Did a lawyer do this?" he asked absently as he turned a page.

"No," she said, and quickly added, "You don't have to worry, Mr. Emerson. I understood the contract perfectly."

"I was only thinking the additions are very professional." A strange incongruity. Charlie's mind kept working, noting as he read that she hadn't stipulated anything about what EmerSound could or couldn't do with her music in post-production, leaving him plenty of options to fix things later, and so he could give her the "no experts" stipulation—she'd never see the experts. He could increase the budget for the musicians as she'd asked. Jennifer wouldn't like it, but he needed to give Alex some of what she'd asked for, so she'd accept all the things he wouldn't give, especially the minimal camera time. He understood not wanting to be on camera before the big makeover—that was just vanity—but why so demure about camera time after? All the girls he'd ever dealt with for his shows were desperate for more attention.

"How is your heart?" he asked, looking up from the contract. Maybe her attitude had something to do with her heart condition or the transplants, somehow.

She poked her fork at the half-eaten pie in front of her. "It gives me no problems."

"And do you have any other medical issues we should know about? Physical or mental? There are insurance considerations and the like."

"No," she answered without hesitation, but she put her fork down, and her hands disappeared under the table.

She seemed rational enough, he decided. "Alright. Here's the proposal: Two hours of camera time a day is impossible, but we will put in a maximum hours-per-day that's reasonable for all involved. We'll also make sure that you don't look terrible for the pre-makeover episodes, so you don't have to worry about that. Most likely, it'll be just one episode from what the producer's told me. I cannot give you final say over any of it—that part of the show is left up to the studio. As to your music, I'll give you what you want with your musicians and conducting, but if there are problems, someone else will need to get involved—the producer or an expert. Can you agree to all that?"

"No experts," she said firmly.

"The producer, then."

She hesitated for a moment, but then answered, "Agreed."

"Good. I'll have the contract drafted to show those changes, and my assistant, Murdoch, will be in touch with you about the next steps. We need to proceed quickly—the show will premiere in early September, and that only gives us a little over a month to produce the first episode. Please don't delay." Charlie took a pen from his pocket and jotted down some notes for the lawyers on the contract. Then he took one bite of his pie, put some cash on the table, and stood up, contract in hand. "Please feel free to stay and finish your food."

Alex lifted her hand, gesturing a goodbye, and as he left, she took up her fork again. He thought of the clarity in her eyes and wondered again at her incongruities. In another life, he might try to unravel them, might find her interesting. But not in this one. In this one, Alex would be a border in his house, where his staff would take care of her needs, and where there was enough space so that he'd never have to see her unless they were shooting for the show. She'd remain an androgynous waif ghosting the corners of his life.

Before leaving the diner, he found the waiter and ordered a sandwich and a whole apple pie for Alex. He'd left enough money to cover it.

CHAPTER X

C harlie shifted uncomfortably, though the back seat of the car was objectively very comfortable, even for his height. But he'd crashed his bike last night, bruising his hip, and the constant low-level throb was beginning to aggravate him.

Murdoch, though, looked plenty comfortable—he'd taken his jacket off and loosened his tie while giving his report, oblivious to Charlie's plight. "According to Richard, the publicity for the show is going well, especially because people believe you're doing it in response to fan requests. Alexandra Weiss is hitting the right note of girl-needing-to-be-rescued, but Jennifer says the PR has yet to turn into revenue, though there might be added interest in the IPO…"

Charlie repositioned himself again. He shouldn't have gone out on the bike, knowing the first shoot for the first episode of *Mrs. Music*—the proposal scene—was scheduled for today. But somehow he'd forgotten the endless hours of inanities required for taping these shows, only remembering because of the steady unease that had plagued him as he'd read through the synopsis for the episode last night—and that feeling had turned into the sharp restlessness that could only be eased by the blistering speed of his motorcycle. So he'd gone out despite the rain-slick streets, but no amount of acceleration had gotten him the rush he needed to relieve the vise closing in on his chest. Then he was slipping, swerving to avoid a rocky wall, and slamming down on the pavement.

"…We should be at the club in about ten minutes," Murdoch was saying as he checked his watch. "They'll tape the proposal first, upstairs in the VIP lounge, then the party scenes on the main dance floor. I've told David you won't stay for the second part if it goes past one o'clock, since you have meetings in the afternoon and—"

The car went over a pothole and Charlie grunted as pain shot through his hip.

Murdoch paused and glanced at him, expression uncharacteristically laced with concern. "Are you hurt?"

"Just a little fall off the bike last night."

"The way you ride, it's as if you don't care whether you live or die. You have to stop," Murdoch said, then hmphed.

Charlie gave a bark of laughter at the truth of those words. But also because they were coming from Murdoch. "I don't think I've ever seen you angry."

"Well, I do get angry. And you haven't been taking care of yourself lately."

"Maybe I should wear suits more often," Charlie said, smiling a little at Murdoch's loosened tie and lack of jacket.

"Suits?"

"You're usually so impervious to everything," Charlie said. "As if when you're in a full suit, nothing affects you. Thought I should try it."

Murdoch shook his head. "I'm serious. After the accident last year, I thought you'd be more careful."

"It was just a few broken ribs." Though one of those ribs had punctured his lung and he'd spent five days in the hospital struggling to breathe.

"And a concussion," Murdoch added. "It's like you're trying to kill yourself."

"I'll be fine," Charlie said and leaned his head back again. Last year's accident hadn't been on purpose, just a coincidence of a bad decision and bad luck. That Murdoch might think it had been intentional was not a good thing—he'd have to be careful of showing too many injuries from now on. Also, there was more than one way to make yourself impervious. "Is there any whiskey back here?"

♪ ♫

It was ten in the morning and Charlie had just finished a double as the car pulled up to Polar, the club where they were shooting the first episode of *Mrs. Music*. The chaos started as soon as he stepped out of the car and onto the sidewalk.

"You have to do something with that girl!" a woman said, accosting him, her shrill voice oddly unmatched to her round face and plump cheeks.

Murdoch came hurrying around the car, still struggling to get into his suit jacket. "Charlie, this is Grace Morris," he said, a little out of breath. "Alex's personal stylist."

"I see," Charlie said. "And is there a problem with Alex, Grace?"

She nodded and sputtered on. "The pictures they sent me were clearly of a blonde. This person who's shown up today—the hair—I don't even know how to describe it. And the makeup, if you can call it that, is, like, the most awful—and she won't let me touch it. I can't work like this! You have to understand this is my reputation and—"

"You're talking about *Alex*—the girl I'm marrying?" Charlie asked, unable to reconcile Grace's description with the strange, vulnerable girl he'd negotiated with at the diner. He hadn't seen her in the intervening weeks, leaving Jennifer Barnes and the lawyers to settle her contract, but this didn't sound right. Probably Grace was exaggerating, the way image-conscious people usually did.

Grace's eyes went wide and she stammered. "Well…I mean… I know she's your fiancée…and I wasn't trying to be rude…or anything… Of course, you must like the way she looks or else…well…" She went silent, finally, and her fingers moved to the silver chain around her neck to fidget with it, while she looked everywhere but at Charlie.

Her teetering panic reminded Charlie of Richard Stanton, and his old annoyance bubbled up—annoyance over time spent dealing with people like this when he could be in his lab. He cut off the thought. "Where is Alex now?"

"She's upstairs on set," Grace said, hope sparking in her eyes.

"Murdoch, please find me a drink," Charlie said, walking past Grace and toward the club. "I'll deal with Alex."

The set was on the mezzanine, an oversized balcony, not very large, crammed with cameras, lights, and crew, and barely leaving space for the little table where the proposal would happen. Alex, standing away from the commotion, alone in the shadows next to the wall, was almost unrecognizable. Her hair had become an enormous mass of bright red frizz; her face was buried under a thick film of foundation at least two shades darker than her original color, and her lips were hot pink. Even Charlie, who was not in the habit of noticing such things, knew this pink was the exact wrong hue against the red hair. He burst out laughing, catching several people's attention, including Alex's. But she quickly dropped her head and withdrew into herself.

"What happened to your hair?" he asked when he'd reached her.

Alex touched her hair lightly with one hand. "Manic Monday."

"Excuse me?"

"The hair color—it's called Manic Monday Red."

"But why?" he asked, unable to mask his appalled incredulity.

She shrugged. "To stand out. For the show."

"I believe Grace had a different look in mind."

"The contract said I'd get to be me before the makeover."

Charlie closed his eyes briefly. "But this isn't you."

"This is what David wants, though, isn't it?" She swept her right—gloved—hand down in front of her, gesturing at her shapeless, flower-printed dress—an overly colorful monstrosity, at least a size too big, sleeveless, and hanging past her knees. Her gloves were a white cotton today.

"I'm not sure he wanted you to look like a clown," Charlie said more harshly than he'd meant to, but he wasn't cruel enough to let her go on camera like that.

She glanced up at him and smiled, almost bitterly. "What better character is there for a circus than a clown?"

He threw his head back and laughed, despite himself, because the answer was so unexpected and she was so right. And what argument could he make against the truth?

"Charlie, there you are." Simone appeared from behind one of the camera setups and paused, letting her gaze slide over Alex. The whisper of a smile formed on her lips. "This must be Alexandra." She offered her hand. "I'm Simone."

"Hi." Alex didn't accept the hand, merely raising hers in a vague wave. The contrast between the two women was laughable. Simone—auburn hair hanging in symmetrical waves around her shoulders and body outlined expertly by a form-fitting dress— looked as if she'd been polished to a high shine and shellacked. Next to her, Alex looked like a little girl who'd gotten into her mother's cosmetics to play dress-up.

"I just ran into Grace and she seemed so flustered I thought I'd come to see if I can help," Simone said. "Alex, darling, what's going on with your...face?"

"My face?" Alex asked, all innocence.

"Well, I know this is supposed to be some sort of before-and-after story," Simone said. "But even a 'before' has to be plausible, darling. You'll make Charlie a laughingstock with that...look. You have to let Grace fix it."

"What are you doing here?" Charlie asked, belatedly realizing Simone had no official involvement with this show.

Her lips turned up in a peculiar expression, both demure and cunning. "Oh, didn't Richard tell you? He's hired me as an advisor. I hope that's not a problem?"

He shrugged, knowing without asking that she'd convinced Richard to hire her, but what he didn't know was why. Simone liked, above all things, to be in the spotlight. Simone as behind-the-scenes advisor was laughable. He knew, too, that she wouldn't explain—after all, she hadn't mentioned it a few days ago, when they'd last met in private.

"Well, Alex, what do you say? Shall we go see Grace?" Simone asked.

Alex looked from Simone to Charlie and back again, her eyes sharp. "Alright," she said. "But just the makeup."

"I totally understand," Simone said, putting an arm around Alex, extra syrup in her voice. "Come on, I'll explain everything to Grace."

As the women walked off together, Simone turned back briefly to shrug at Charlie as if to underscore her skill in getting Alex to capitulate.

He watched them go, then frowned, thinking of Alex's sharp observation about the circus that was this show and her even sharper eyes. None of it fit. He'd always liked a good mystery—it was one of the things that attracted him to math and science. But today, the idea of untangling all this was distasteful.

Then he shook his head and looked away, the old leaden weight settling in his stomach. He was thinking of the large chasm between contemplating the petty motivations of these women and unraveling the secrets of the physical universe—that chasm between the life he'd thought he could live and the one he was actually living.

He needed another drink.

CHAPTER XI

Her makeup fixed, Alex stood again at the mezzanine wall, watching the staff, the crew, and the actors—taking in the various characters present, weaving together the tapestry of who belonged here and what was accepted.

As a child, Alex had often been told she was "too much" or "overly excitable," that she needed to be quiet, composed, still, and her mother had pointed to a neighbor's daughter, Carrie-Anne, the perfect model of an agreeable little girl. Alex watched her and tried to learn, not because she wanted to please the adults around her, but because she saw that by doing what was expected, Carrie-Anne was left alone and safe. In the years since, Alex had adopted Carrie-Anne's personality whenever she needed to be normal enough to disappear in plain sight.

She was, however, beginning to see that the old personality wouldn't work on the set of *Mrs. Music*. Shy and quiet stood out too much. EmerSound was like an orchestra made mostly of heavy percussion instruments—kettle drums or cymbals—the people aggressive and loud, either intentionally seeking attention or like that by nature. Simone was a little different—she flittered around the set, smiling warmly and chatting with everyone; she belonged without being a complete stereotype. But people watched her as she moved through the room, with admiration or envy or lust—she wasn't invisible enough.

"Oh, there you are," Grace said, materializing in front of Alex, plump cheeks flushed. "I've got the perfect idea for how to color your hair," she said. "I know, I know, not today—but for the wedding, we'll go blonde and then add highlights in the front here. What do you think?"

Knowing she'd have to submit to the full makeover eventually, Alex nodded.

Grace made a grinning motion and continued, "I think maybe a little darker than the color in the picture… What was that, a number nine? Maybe if…"

This woman melded well on the set of *Mrs. Music* and people actively avoided her—probably because of her incessant chatter. But Alex didn't think she could keep up that level of constant prattle. It had too many details and too much information, even if none of it was particularly interesting. Alex would be exhausted within ten minutes trying to come up with so much trivia.

"…I mean the eight range would work but nothing with any red—oh!" Grace had gone on, heedless of Simone's approach and startled when Simone linked arms with her.

"Don't look now," Simone said, "but here comes David and he's bringing Brandy."

"Who's Brandy?" Grace asked, eyes widening at the prospect of intrigue.

Simone's expression turned conspiratorial. "She's some sort of internet sensation—sings and dances. Charlie can't stand her, but David absolutely loves her so he booked her for the show. Not that I can blame Charlie. Her stuff is so annoying." The two women chuckled, enjoying their cruel gossip.

The girl, whose shoulders David had his arm slung over, was all bleached blond and blue eyes, and her beauty would've been remarkable if her lips weren't quite so unnaturally plump, and if she didn't teeter quite so much on her very high heels.

"Alex, this is Brandy," David said. "She's playing your soon-to-be best friend."

"Brandy," Simone gushed. "It's so great to see you, honey. Your latest video is adorable."

The two women made hugging motions—though barely touching each other—then Brandy turned to Alex. "Hi-yee, I'm, like, so excited to be on the show, and, you know, to be friends and everything."

David nodded and stomped off, calling, "Get to know each other! Later on the dance floor it has to look like you could actually be friends."

Brandy clapped her hands together once and started talking. "Okay, so I'm thinking we can pick a song and, you know, make up a dance that we do together—or no, I know, I'll teach you one of my dances and it'll be, like, so cool…"

Brandy kept up her monologue for many minutes, her hands flapping around at the same rate as her speech, and Alex listened carefully—to the lilt of the voice, the speech mannerism, the word choice—while also noting that no one else gave Brandy a second glance. Where Simone garnered attention, Brandy was completely invisible through utter conspicuousness. Plus, her conversation had very little substance. Like that constant drone of traffic outside your window that you eventually stopped hearing because it was so predictable and inconsequential. She was perfect.

Eventually, David called for everyone to take their places, and Alex took hers across the dinner table from Charlie. His glance skimmed over her face briefly and away, without the deep regard from earlier, but she noticed a severity in his eyes that hadn't been there earlier. He took a sip from his glass—half-full of whiskey, she thought from the scent—then called out, "I need another drink." Someone scurried over with a full glass, exchanging it for the empty one, and Charlie took a hearty gulp, leaning back in his chair and slouching with an air of boredom.

"Okay, Alex, we'll start with you," David called out from the vicinity of a blinding light. "Look at camera one, behind Charlie, on his left, and say something about how lucky you are to be with Charlie. Really lay it on like we talked about earlier. Everyone, quiet! And…action!"

"I'm, like, so lucky to have found you, Charlie," Alex said, pitching her voice higher, to a light orange, matching Brandy's. "And, like, I just can't believe it, you're, like, so famous and everything."

Charlie raised an eyebrow, surprise flashing through his expression at her speech. Then he snorted, emptied his glass again, and went back to looking bored, as Alex did her monologue to different cameras. But later, in the few seconds of gap between takes, he sat up and leaned over the table, eyes narrowed. "I'm impressed—you had me fooled before." There was an edge to his voice, not enough to call it disdain, but enough to be disconcerting.

Confused by the non sequitur, Alex said, "What?"

"The acting—" Charlie began, but David cut him off.

"Charlie, start the proposal to camera four, then come around the table slowly."

Charlie leaned away from Alex but reached across the table to take her hand. Then his demeanor shifted, the ennui and disdain disappearing, and he morphed into...a normal person—although Alex wasn't aware of having thought of him as abnormal before. But, after all, he'd been a child prodigy and a genius, and there was nothing normal about that. Still, she couldn't pinpoint the exact difference.

"Wait! Cut!" David stomped over to them. "What's with the gloves, Alex?"

She widened her eyes and blinked several times. "Oh my God—I'm so sorry, but, like, I didn't have a chance to get a manicure or anything, and my nails are, like, something awful. Seriously, you totally don't want those on camera."

David rolled his eyes, then shook his head, cursing. "Someone needs to get these details right, people. Let's take it again. Don't focus on the hands. Action!"

Charlie, still holding Alex's hand, now stared directly into her eyes, his own soft and affectionate. "I know it's only been a short time, but I feel like I've known you for years," he said, his voice changing tone enough to shift into a light blue. Then he stood up and came around the table—slowly to let the various cameras catch all the angles—and capped the cliché by getting on one knee in front of her. "Will you make me the happiest man on earth and marry me?"

And that's when Alex saw it. The difference in him was the emotion: the real Charlie—the one she thought of as the real

Charlie, anyway—betrayed very little emotion. He was almost stoic. Even when he'd laughed at her hair and called her a clown, there had been no joy, only sarcasm. But here he was, convincingly a man in love. The juxtaposition—and the heavy drinking—made her wonder if he enjoyed any of this, and if he didn't, why he'd orchestrated it.

But even though she sat across from him for the next hour, repeating takes and pretending to be ecstatically in love, she found no clues and reached no conclusions. Then he was gone and she was left to the exhausting task of pretending to be friends with Brandy on the dance floor.

CHAPTER XII

After a week of submitting to dress fittings, facials, hair appointments, body scrubs, and salt baths, Alex was exhausted. That's probably why her first reaction to the enormous and dimly lit lobby of Charlie's building was to think of black holes. If she'd had more rest, the black marble tiles wouldn't seem so foreboding, and she wouldn't feel like she was going to get swallowed up here, devoured by some silent void that she hadn't anticipated.

"This way," Murdoch said, walking past, carrying her duffle bag. "David and the crew are upstairs already."

Alex picked up her violin and backpack, trying to shake off her apprehension as she followed Murdoch into Charlie's private elevator to the fiftieth floor. But as they rode up, the secluded, darkly paneled interior only compounded the feeling of being erased: The ride was so suffocatingly quiet and so smooth that Alex felt the movement only as a pressure in her ears, without even the relief of ticking numbers on a panel to show their progress.

Then the elevator doors slid open to the foyer, revealing four people: two with cameras, one with a giant microphone on a telescoping pole, and David, who stood behind the other three and gestured to indicate the cameras were rolling and then silently mouthed "Say something" to Alex.

If the lobby had been a void, the foyer was a kind of blinding over-presence in its brightness—circular and with a domed skylight, done entirely in white marble shot through with dim gray veins. So bright, the crew hadn't even needed to set up extra lights. Alex opened her mouth as if awed—although the wonder wasn't all fake—and said, "Oh. My. God. Am I, like, really going to live here?"

David nodded enthusiastically and motioned for her to put her bags down, then pointed toward one of the three hallways off the foyer before heading there first himself. He was followed by the crew, who were followed by Murdoch and Alex, and they all took a tour of Charlie Emerson's penthouse mansion.

Despite the equipment, the cameras, the professionally decorated rooms, and the six people traipsing through the place, the penthouse reverberated with an air of emptiness. And though Murdoch spoke continuously—"There are three hallways...the central hallway leads to all the shared spaces... living room...dining room...ballroom...library...theater... kitchen..."—Alex felt a silence underneath, and her attention turned constantly to the echoing *tap-tap-tap* of their steps down the granite-tiled hallways. David kept having to remind her of the cameras, motioning wildly for her to talk, and each time she performed by throwing out platitudes—"Wow, it's, like, so huge!...We're on such a high floor!...When Brandy sees this, she's totally gonna die!"—expecting David to scold her, ask her to say something less inane, but he just grinned and gave her a thumbs-up, and on and on it went.

Alex had hoped to glean some insight about Charlie from his place, but almost everything felt scrubbed of color and personality—even the grand piano in the ballroom was white—and she began to think nothing could be learned about Charlie here, as if, like the man himself, the place wore a mask of sterile opulence to hide its soul.

Three hours later, taping was finally over for the day, and as the crew members were packing up, Murdoch brought Alex back to the east hallway and told her, "You may choose any of the rooms here as yours. And please remember that the west hallway"—which he hadn't shown her—"belongs to Mr. Emerson. You should have no reason to go there unaccompanied." He said it the way he said everything—in that monotone of fact-giving—but a threat whispered through anyway. She just shrugged again, because he was right, and she had no reason to seek out Charlie.

Alex waited for the crew to leave before retrieving her violin from its case in the foyer and returning to the east hallway to choose the room that would be hers. She took her time, walking from room to room, testing each space by shutting the door and standing in the center to play on her violin the Russian lullaby she'd learned from her mother.

She'd been four years old the first time she heard the piece. Her mother had just brought her home from preschool and had been standing at the kitchen counter cutting an apple when Alex told her about a song they'd learned in class. "It was purple and green, Mama."

Her mother, a tall, skeletal woman with a mass of frizzy brown hair and deeply arched eyebrows, looked down at her with a severe frown. "What do you mean, purple and green?" she asked in her thick Russian accent.

"Those are its colors."

"You mean this is song about colors?"

"No, Mama, it is those colors. That's how it looks."

Her mother put down the knife and took Alex by the hand to march her to the couch, where they sat down together. "Now, you listen to me," she said. "Other people, they don't see colors when they hear music. Do you understand?"

Alex shook her head.

"They only hear sound with ears. They don't see anything with eyes."

"Oh," Alex said, confused.

"This is important. You must not tell people that music is like this for you. They will not understand. They will take you away."

"Is it bad, Mama? Am I sick?"

"I don't know. But they will be scared and maybe some think it is bad. I had to escape from home, very young, alone, because I told them I was different. They wanted to lock me up and take my music away. You must not tell anyone at all."

"Do you see the music?"

Her mother smiled—an enchanting sight to Alex, because it transformed her mother's face, highlighting her almost unearthly, delicate beauty. She hugged Alex. "Yes, my little one, I see it too. And I will show you how to use it, how to control it."

Her mother went to the closet and, from the back, pulled out a black case, worn and old, unlatching it to reveal a violin nestled inside. "This will be yours one day. For now, it is too big, and we will have to get you a smaller one. The violin, it will be your tool. This is how we control the problem."

Alex hadn't had any problems and didn't understand, but then her mother played—that slow, haunting tune, Russian in origin, with a mesmerizing rainbow of blues—and Alex fell in love with the violin, and knew she had to learn to play, problems or not.

Her mother was her first teacher, drilling into Alex the need for secrecy about her "sound visions" with the same intensity she drilled her on technical perfection. It was a grueling regimen, but Alex heeded her mother's instruction and progressed quickly, and though she still didn't understand the problems her mother had spoken of, she began to fear them.

And then it happened. A year later, Alex accompanied her mother to a holiday party at a studio apartment in a neighborhood with tightly packed buildings, many on the verge of dilapidation. The room was crowded with people and decorated with red and green lights on the walls along with bright silver bows placed haphazardly on the few pieces of old furniture around the room. Alex's mother held on tightly to her hand as they navigated through the crowd of adults, and Alex was hot, lost in the forest of legs and constantly pushed and jabbed by elbows and knees.

Music played from a stereo system on a high shelf, obscured by the chatter of the guests until someone yelled, "Time to dance!" and turned it up—something loud and nonsensical that made Alex's vision swirl with a clamor of colors, an ugly, horrible mess she'd never seen before. *What if this ugliness was the problem her mother had told her about?* A stab of terror shot through Alex, making her heart pound too fiercely, and then she couldn't catch her breath, and the colors swirled until she was dizzy. She covered her ears, losing her mother's hand and wanting to scream—maybe she had screamed, she wasn't sure—and then everything went black.

She woke up in a hospital, her head and neck hurting—from having fallen, they told her—and there was a great deal of worry from the doctors who came to prod her and run tests, but she told no one about the visions and her mother nodded at her in approval, and when the doctors had left, her mother said, "This will get better. You must practice on your instrument many hours to calm the brain. To practice the control and make it stop."

And Alex did practice. She practiced for many hours every day, and by the time her mother died several years later, though Alex's sound visions hadn't stopped, she'd learned both how to control them using music and how to keep them a secret. She only needed time and a proper space for her practice.

For the past decade, her own little apartment uptown had been passable—though not ideal—acoustically, as a practice space, and she now found herself daring to hope for something better as she tested the rooms in the east hallway of Charlie's penthouse.

The luxurious guest room with open views of the river would have great light, but the parallel walls produced a merciless echo—a muddled undulating brown. The second master suite had a separate sitting room and an irregular shape but was outfitted with thick wall-to-wall carpeting—a recipe for the black blobs of flat, booming music.

The last room she came to was all the way down the hall, situated at the back of the penthouse in a shadowy corner, with its only window facing another building, older and shorter, with a soot-grimed roof. The room housed a few boxes of books, old clothes, and used furniture, but the walls were a bright white, utilitarian and incorruptible. The only softness in the room was the faded yellow curtain on the window—a gossamer remnant from some other time and, like the memory of happiness, vaguely disappointing for having grown dim.

The storage room was, however, acoustically perfect: bare wooden planks on the floor, walls slightly askew, not too small, not too large. An ideal place for a single violin. The music dripped from the walls and ceilings, and Alex felt like she was floating and weightless as she played.

Murdoch didn't object when she claimed the storage room. He merely raised his eyebrow in a gesture reminiscent of Charlie, and then had the room cleared for her within the hour despite the fact that it was ten o'clock at night. A bare minimum of furniture was brought in: a full-sized bed, a nightstand, a chair. At some point Murdoch brought a squat man with an abrupt manner and white overalls to deliver a rug in an attempt to cover the floor, but Alex made him remove it immediately.

Then, as Murdoch was walking away down the hall, just before he'd turned the corner, she called to him. He stopped and turned to her.

"Have you known Charlie very long?" she asked, dropping her act as a concession to getting some information.

If he noticed the difference in her, he didn't show it. He approached her again—he never spoke to anyone from more than three feet away—and said, "I've known Charlie for almost sixteen years."

"Since he was in graduate school then?"

"Yes."

"How did you meet him?"

He considered her a moment and she saw the first break in his stern manner as he smiled a bit, his voice coming out almost relaxed when he answered, "I was a night janitor at the Asher Institute of Technology. He used to work all night in the lab and we became friendly."

"You were a janitor?" It was shocking—she had always imagined him from some well-to-do background, with his exacting manner and extreme propriety. "But you don't sound—I mean you're not..." She stopped.

But he didn't seem offended, answering in the same relaxed tone, "No, Charlie didn't think so either."

"How did you end up here, as Charlie's...assistant?"

"It's a long story," Murdoch said slowly, as if he wasn't fully set against telling her. Alex replied more earnestly than she wanted to, "Please tell me the story. I'd like to know something real about Charlie."

Again, Murdoch considered her, then he nodded, and his expression softened. "Along with my janitorial position, I was boxing for money when I met Charlie," he said. "The boxing was something I'd done in the military, but he never liked it—thought a concussion would ruin my brain. He was so young, but he was the only person I'd ever known who thought my brain was worth anything—the only person I knew who could decide something based only on his own judgment—and there's a force in that kind of certainty. Eventually, I stopped boxing and started reading books he suggested. We kept this up, even after he left Asher, and once EmerSound had become profitable, he offered me a loan to go to college, where I studied business. He hired me even before I graduated. Now I'm sort of a manager of Charlie's life, both at home and at work."

"Does he do that very often then?"

"Do what?"

"See the potential in people."

Murdoch smiled at her, a hint of recognition in his eyes, though she didn't know what he'd seen. "Charlie sees everything."

When he left her alone, she frowned, thinking that his last statement had sounded like a threat, also. *Neither of them knows anything about me that's dangerous*, she told herself, but the thought, rather than calming her, made her sad. After all, here was Charlie, a man who saw everything, who had the potential to understand, and she had to hide from him.

She sighed and unpacked. Then she stood in the middle of the room and played her mother's lullaby, then the theme to the *Red Concerto*, and as the colors of the music aligned and came to life, she felt something inside her simultaneously relax and spark to life—as if she were being caressed by a lover—and she played, consumed by the music, heedless of the time and the hours that passed.

CHAPTER XIII

Charlie put his pen down and glanced at the clock. It was late, nearing midnight, and he'd been working in his library office for nearly four hours, reading reports and making notes for Murdoch. The task should've been done hours ago, but he'd been distracted, constantly remembering his old scientific work, thinking of how it had been left unfinished for years. He didn't further the work, even in thought—it was merely as if he were glancing into a room through a slightly ajar door, surveying the contents and refusing to enter—but it muddled his brain and he couldn't seem to make it stop.

He was hungry, he decided, remembering that he'd skipped dinner. That's why he couldn't focus. He got up and headed to the kitchen, but on the way, he heard sounds coming from the tiny room in the east hallway, and confused that anyone should be in that room at all, he changed direction to investigate. It couldn't be Murdoch—he'd waved good-night on his way to bed as he walked past the library an hour ago. And because Charlie had insisted on receiving detailed schedules of when the *Mrs. Music* crew was in the apartment and where they'd be setting up and taping, he knew the crew was supposed to be gone, as well. Could this be the room Alex had taken? Why hadn't she been offered a proper guest room?

As he neared, he thought the sound might be music, but it dropped off, softening too much for him to be sure. He opened the door just as the music swelled again and he froze, feeling absurdly like he'd stumbled onto the site of some accident, a simultaneous urge to turn away and keep watching. It wasn't a reaction to Alex herself, though she had changed, both in looks—the clown hair had been replaced by a cascade of golden hair hanging down her back, luxurious and delicate—and comportment. Her stance was confident, legs set wide apart and firmly rooted. It wasn't even her nearly ferocious expression, eyes closed, mouth set in determination, or that her hands were gloveless.

It was the music she was making with the violin she held to her chin that made him feel like he did when he was on the precipice of a mountain, his bike careening toward the edge, out of his control—a thrilling, intense, and dangerous thing that could only lead to his destruction.

And yet the music itself was joyous, like a frolic through a meadow where green flowing grasses waved in the wind and tiny white flowers bloomed in carpeting swaths of delicate life. Alex's fingers ran through scales that gained in speed and volume, lifting up, the way you'd ride a motorcycle up the side of a mountain. But where he was looking for death, she celebrated life. And it was devastating—like someone had crashed through one of the huge walls of windows in the living room, and he'd thought he had light before only to find that the glass had been opaque with muck and this was real light, but it was too much and his eyes couldn't adjust.

The sunlight of her music was an assault on his senses—a live, electrified wire pushing current into him, making his heart beat too hard and his chest hurt, and he wished it were a heart attack and he could die afterward, after hearing this, because he couldn't continue on the way he had before. But he knew it wasn't a heart attack because whatever was coursing through him was not death—it was the opposite—it was life. It was the vulnerability of finding something that can be torn from you, something that makes you weak. Something that makes you want.

Then, finally, the music came to an end and Charlie exhaled in a gasp. Alex turned toward him, her hair swinging with the motion, and though he tried, he could no longer see her as the androgynous waif he'd come to expect; instead, he felt something he could only sum up as an astonished kind of respect, laced with something sharper, something almost violent.

"What's wrong?" she asked.

What's wrong? he wanted to yell. *You are wrong—you should not be here—not in my show and not in my life. You were supposed to be a moldable canvas. A talentless nobody. I don't want the responsibility of you.* But he hardened his face into an expressionless cast and said, as casually as he could, "It's rather late. Your music was disturbing me."

"I'm sorry, I didn't realize. I'll stop."

He nodded—one sharp movement of his head—then spun around and marched away, with the conviction that no one, not even himself, must ever know the things he'd felt here tonight. He clamped everything down until the only thing left was anger—at her for not being what she'd seemed, at himself for misjudging her, at the world, which just wouldn't leave him alone. Then, he allowed himself one thought: He needed a drink.

PART TWO
Allegro

CHAPTER XIV

"Why so preoccupied, darling?" Simone asked, leaning over the side of Charlie's bed to retrieve something from inside her purse. Then came the click of her lighter and a momentary flash in the dimness, followed by the faint perfume of the joint she lit. Her spine curved gracefully, displaying the smooth skin of her back as she moved to lie back down beside Charlie, but he didn't touch her again. It hadn't worked to distract him the first time; he was still thinking of Alex's violin performance.

"There's no way she's some kind of goddamned virtuoso," he said, mostly to himself. Of course not—he'd merely been hungry and tired last night, so his reaction was over-exaggerated. Why would she have been working at a coffee stand if she were good?

"Charlie, what are you talking about?"

"Alex."

Simone giggled, probably too high to process what he'd said, though she'd heard the name—evidenced in her next comment: "Oh, did you read today's *City Chronicle* article about Alex? This guy, Chris Donner or Donnelly or something—apparently, he was friends with Alex when they were kids and he says she's a real bitch. He was at her house all the time because they were neighbors and his mom took care of her—you know, because of her heart thing—and then when Alex moved out, she never talked to them again. I mean not even a phone call."

"Never mind," Charlie said, annoyed at himself for mentioning Alex and in no mood to hear gossip. Why was he fixated on the violin playing anyway? Yes, he'd been shocked she could play, but he was over it now. Lots of people could play an instrument. This was nothing to obsess about.

He forced his focus back to Simone as she blew smoke out and sighed, her breasts falling and rising with the movement. She'd drunk a lot of wine and, he suspected, taken some other substance too tonight besides the pot. There was that tinge of youth to her, the way she'd been when he'd first met her, relaxed, affectionate, and open. "You've been doing a lot of drugs lately," he said.

"God, you're not going to get all uptight, are you?"

"You'll ruin your voice."

She rolled toward him and smiled, holding up her joint. "*You* don't have to sing. Want a hit?"

He shook his head, still watching Simone, but now seeing her as the girl he'd first encountered five years earlier in performance, while she was still a voice student at the City Academy of Music. She'd sung an aria from a Mozart opera—a difficult and haunting piece—her voice echoing strangely in the silent hall, the harsh German words offset by complex, delicate runs in the melody. It hadn't been a perfect performance but she'd stood with her fists clenched, the lines of her face taut, the angle of her head proud, and there had been a quality of abandon and purity to her performance that gave him a sense of wonder and cleanliness. He used to ask her to sing for him often in those first few years, but the special quality had seeped out of her performances and he'd stopped asking. He didn't like to think of it anymore.

There seemed to be so many things he didn't like to think of anymore, so many things he could no longer do, either because he couldn't do them or because he couldn't stomach doing them. His life had become a series of small intermittent events, each designed to give him the strength to make it to the next one. Four nights of Simone each month. One weekday morning with Lawrence. Motorcycle rides that left him bruised and broken. Originally, these things had been the respite—small breaks from his other work—but with EmerSound's increasing tedium and his scientific work stalled indefinitely, the respite had become the meat of his life.

But this was what he'd wanted. To be like everyone else, to stop obsessing about science, to be impassive to failures and betrayals, to carry on with the habits of yesterday without consideration or thought until his life was half over and his choices had dried up—Charlie shook himself mentally. Why was he thinking like this? One piddly piece of obscure music played in a minuscule storage room by a girl who was practically homeless and he was having an existential crisis? He jolted up to sitting, needing to do something, anything, to stop the thoughts. He succeeded only in startling Simone into a little scream.

"What is it with you these days?" she asked with a huff. But the question was rhetorical; she took another drag of the joint, dropped it into her almost-empty wine glass on the nightstand, and flopped onto her back again, her muscles loose, as if the scream had used up all of her energy.

Charlie braced his arms on bent knees and focused on her over his shoulder, on her body again, anything to rekindle his desire for her and not think of the thing he'd just glimpsed. But it was no use tonight. The desire was lost.

He groped for a distraction and finally processed what Simone had been saying about the article in the *City Chronicle*, and then thought of Glen Clarence—the balding little man who'd done the background check on Alex—of how his report had said nothing about this childhood friend the *Chronicle* had dug up, and nothing about Alex playing the violin. Charlie got out of the bed and started to dress. If he couldn't stop thinking about her, he could at least get some answers.

"Where are you going?" Simone asked, her voice sleepy now.

"I need to make a phone call."

"It's so late. Who are you possibly calling?"

"Just EmerSound business," Charlie said, and then pretending an easiness he didn't feel, added, "And it's not late. It's already early tomorrow."

She gave a little pout and arched her back, trying to get him back into bed, and when he ignored it, she sighed and rolled over—but she'd given him an idea. Maybe Clarence wasn't the only one who could get answers—Charlie could go to the source himself; seduction was a proven way to get a woman to talk, and he certainly knew how to seduce. It was part of his brand, after all.

Once in the hallway outside his bedroom, Charlie pulled out his phone and hit the button for Clarence. The private detective's voice came on the line after several rings, groggy and slow. "Hello?"

"Why didn't I know she could play like that?" Charlie asked.

"What? Who—what time is it?"

"It's five a.m. This is Charlie Emerson."

"Oh, Mr. Emerson! Hello. Who can play like what?" Clarence's voice regained some clarity and a lot of alarm.

"Alexandra Weiss. She's a goddamn violin player. How did you miss that?"

Clarence made a sound like a little cough. "I knew she wrote music—it was in the report, wasn't it? I... No one said she could play an instrument. I swear, Mr. Emerson."

"And why did the *City Chronicle* find her childhood friend and you didn't?"

"I...I'm sorry. I don't know. The *Chronicle,* you said? I'll look into it, of course.... But I did get some more information about her father and that murder David was asking for."

"What murder?"

"You know, the one at the institute. Let me get the file."

Charlie waited, leaning against the wall next to his bedroom door. How many details did Clarence miss on a regular basis? Was there something different about Alex, or was the man just incompetent?

"Okay, here it is." Clarence was back on the line. "There was some big scandal around the time she was at that Swiss clinic—you know, the second time for the heart transplant. It was right before she moved to the city. Um... Some crazy patient of her dad's at that psychiatric institute—the Greene Institute—murdered a doctor and then disappeared. There was a big investigation and a manhunt and the whole shebang, but they never found the killer, far as I can tell. Couldn't find much information on him either 'cause it was a kid—sealed records and such. But I think he's dead—got hurt trying to escape, someone said. Anyway, Old Man Weiss got a lot of flak for it—for not being around and whatnot, I guess. Then they put him on leave and eventually he retired. I can keep digging on the crazy killer patient, though."

"What does any of this have to do with Alex and the show?" Charlie asked.

"What do you mean? It's all about her dad."

Charlie wanted to reach through the phone and strangle the man. "I mean, did it affect Alex in some way that was documented? Depression, suicide attempt, anything like that?"

"Oh, well, she moved out right around then. You know, maybe they had some sort of fight over the thing. Or maybe the old man himself is crazy. How does a trained shrink not see that his patient is some psycho-killer? Maybe that's why your Alex is so weird. Like, inherited from the dad, you know what I'm saying? I think David could use this for the show, couldn't he? Isn't that what you're looking for? Some dirt for the show?"

"Yes, fine, for David—keep looking into the murder. But find this friend from the *Chronicle* article and get me something about her violin playing first," Charlie said.

"Will do. Listen, the dad wouldn't really tell me anything, just a lot of vague crap about her being sick and vulnerable and whatever. But maybe he'll tell you more, right? If you ambush him when he's in the cemetery he'll be caught off-guard, and he'll say stuff. He goes there every week like clockwork. Saturdays at eleven in the morning. And he stays exactly an hour and a half."

"I don't get involved with these things in person," Charlie said. "And I certainly don't ambush people. I don't need to."

"Right. Sorry. And sorry I didn't catch her violin thing. I—"

"Don't make excuses. Just do your job."

CHAPTER XV

One week later, at half past two in the afternoon, when the temperature had reached record highs, the grounds at Charlie Emerson's house in Connecticut were filling up as three hundred formally attired wedding guests arrived: celebrities, media executives, and journalists—both major and minor. Catering staff moved through the crowd with a stiff formality, balancing trays full of canapés or champagne glasses on fingertips, while a multitude of cameras ensured every corner of the wedding, down to the last detail of the Italian silk tablecloths, was recorded by at least one still photograph and several minutes of film.

Alex, dressed in a pink silk robe, stood at a bedroom window on the second floor and watched the gathering. She felt the heat coming off the glass, and the guests below looked as if they were wilting. The masses of white lilies crowding the cocktail tables, however, seemed impervious to the weather, their petals curling precisely and their stems standing at attention, as if they dared not cross Charlie Emerson. Alex couldn't decide if she really liked the air of sternness about Charlie or if she really hated it. Was it confidence or a need to control?

She was ambivalent about the property too—a sprawling estate on acres and acres of land with its own small lake, designed to be a secluded escape, and reminiscent of the Greene Institute. She could still remember in detail the vacant, staring eyes of the patients who'd wandered the lawns of the institute, lost and out of place in blue hospital pajamas. The guests today had a similar air of aimless wandering as those patients of long ago, evening gowns and tuxedos notwithstanding. If their apathy was so apparent to her, despite their careful disguises, did that mean they saw the incongruities in her as well?

"Okay, Alex, I'm ready for you," Grace called.

Alex turned away from the window to take her place in the salon chair placed in front of a full-length mirror, and Grace went to work on her hair. The camera crew had already set up near the door behind her, and someone called to start the recording. Alex hadn't realized just how much time she'd have to sit still while on camera in order to be made "beautiful"—that even after the makeover frenzy of the last few weeks, she'd still have to be carefully made up for every shoot. She was beginning to detest this chair. She fidgeted with her gloves just to have something to do.

"Close your eyes so I can do the eyeshadow," Grace instructed. "And stop moving."

Alex complied. She tried to relax by focusing her ears, deliberately narrowing in on individual sounds and separating out the colors they produced in her vision. She kept her eyes closed even after Grace had finished with the shadow, enjoying the chatter and chaos of the *Mrs. Music* crew as they set up, picking out the distinct voices, finding the familiar ones, and listening for the direction of their movements. The pale pink voice belonged to one of the lighting guys as he passed by in the hallway. The bright yellow tenor signaled Chris, the gaffer, coming to talk to David, whose answer buzzed a murky brown. And the deep blue baritone approaching—reverberating down her spine—was Charlie. Her eyes snapped open and she saw him through his reflection in the mirror, as he stopped just inside the door, a dozen feet behind her. She hadn't seen him since the night he'd interrupted her on the violin, a few weeks ago, and had somehow forgotten how imposing he was, with his broad shoulders and intense dark eyes. Maybe she'd made herself forget.

"They told me you were ready for the ceremony," he said to David, sounding slightly bored. "What's taking so long?"

"No, I said we were ready for you. I need you in this shot."

"I'm not wearing a microphone."

David waved a hand dismissively. "It's for a montage. We're not recording sound."

Grace noticed Charlie, too, and scurried over to him. "Mr. Emerson, do you need anything?"

Charlie shook his head, and then David leaned in close to him to whisper something, and they both looked at Alex. She dropped her eyes but strained to hear them through the background chatter. There was nothing for a few seconds, then: "Hello."

Alex drew in a sharp breath at Charlie's voice—intimate and too close. He was leaning over her, hands braced on the back of her chair, lips close to her ear, dark eyes mocking her through their reflections. She could smell the alcohol on his breath—maybe the same whiskey he'd been drinking during the proposal shoot. She swallowed, trying not to react any more than she already had. And what should her reaction be? What would Brandy do?

"Grace finally managed to get her hands on you, did she?" he asked. "You're quite striking."

Alex nodded. It was harder than it should be to channel her airhead alter-ego.

"Careful now. They're all watching and recording. Smile like you're happy to see me," Charlie said.

Indeed, the little red light on the camera behind her blinked with the agitating frequency of a recording in progress. She forced a smile.

"What's the matter, can't act when you're not in a clown costume?" Charlie asked, then slowly turned his face to kiss her cheek, his eyes continuing to watch her in the mirror. His lips didn't linger, barely brushing her skin, but a zing jolted through her anyway, and she lifted her hand, giving in to the impulse to touch the spot where she'd felt his lips.

"The gloves again," he said, his voice a shade too mocking. "I know your hands are not deformed—I saw them the other night. What are you hiding under there? Should I peel the gloves off and find out?"

She dropped her hand back onto the armrest. *It's for the cameras, it's not real*, she reminded herself. This was the Charlie Emerson of gossip—the flirt, the one who was so good at acting for the cameras—and he wasn't genuinely curious about her. The thought grounded her, allowing her to recapture her own on-camera persona. She gave him a toothy grin and blinked several times. "I'm the bride. I should, like, get to wear what I want to my own wedding."

Charlie lifted an eyebrow. "Why do you always wear them?"

"To protect my hands, silly."

"From what?"

"I'm delicate." She batted her lashes at him again.

He straightened, and as the cameraman approached to film them from the right, Charlie came around on Alex's left, facing her and resting his hands on the arms of the chair at either side, forcing hers to her lap lest she touch him again. It was harder to look at him without the shield and distance of the mirror between them.

"Take the gloves off," he said, voice a little too sharp for the sardonic expression accompanying it.

Maybe he meant to be threatening, Alex thought, but she heard only a challenge and felt something inside her tense that wasn't fear. "Okay," she said, her own voice upbeat, but she held his gaze, defiant even as she removed her gloves, pulling each fingertip in turn. When she was done and had laid the gloves in her lap, he straightened and grasped her wrists to examine her hands—first the backs and then her palms. He hesitated at the scar on the inner part of her left wrist, then traced a thumb over it. She shivered and hated herself for it.

"What happened?" he asked, more serious now, but still holding a faint smile.

"An accident."

"What kind of accident? Something at the coffee cart?"

"Before—I don't like to talk about it." She tried to pull her hands away, but he held on tight for an instant before letting go.

Then his smile dropped away. "Did you try to kill yourself?"

"What? No, of course not." Her voice cracked a little. She had to calm down.

The unsettling focus returned, his eyes sharpening as he bent over again, this time leaning lower on the arms of the chair to cage her in. "Things with your father must've been bad," he said, "for you to leave a comfortable home in the suburbs only to become a destitute coffee girl in the city."

Where was he going with this? Alex blinked and smiled, reaching again for her act, but she couldn't get the voice or the words right. "I wasn't destitute."

"Still, it must have been difficult to grow up with a father who worked at the Greene Institute."

"It was just his job." She could now feel the staccato rap of her pulse in her wrists and her neck. Why was he asking about this? What did he know?

"So you never visited the institute?" he asked.

"Why would I visit?"

"Kids visit their parents' workplaces. I used to hang out at the university where my dad taught all the time when I was a kid."

"Greene isn't that kind of place."

"That's right—there were violent patients there." He stretched the words out. "Didn't one of the patients kill a doctor there? One of your father's patients?"

She shrugged. "I was sick then."

"And at the Swiss clinic."

She nodded.

"So why did you leave home? If things were so great with your father?"

"I wanted to strike out on my own. See if I could make it without help."

"It seems to me like you've been through quite a lot already," he said, "with the heart trouble and all."

She thought he was getting closer to her, but he hadn't moved—it was more a suggestion of intimacy in his expression— and it made her want to lean into him, despite his incessant and probing questions. She shrank back into her seat. Not much of a movement, because there was no place to go, but he narrowed his eyes at her.

"Charlie, you need to do something other than just lean over talking," David yelled from somewhere. "Stand up or move around or something."

Charlie did stand up then, but he stepped back and walked around the chair and away toward the door, saying loudly, indifferently, and to no one in particular, "That's enough."

CHAPTER XVI

Charlie and Alex were to be married under a copse of trees, where delicate globes of white roses on ribbons were suspended from branches, to sway gently above their heads. Charlie waited with the officiant of the ceremony, a flamboyant young man in a sleeveless tuxedo that showed off his plethora of arm tattoos. He was the drummer from EmerSound's most popular band and never quite sober, but at Richard's insistence he had been ordained online the previous week. Charlie had picked him for his sensational fame, knowing he'd be one of the most photographed celebrities at the wedding, perhaps second only to Charlie himself.

Alex walked down the aisle in a wedding gown fit for royalty—chaste and intricately beaded, with a full skirt, long sheer sleeves, a high neckline, and uncharacteristically appropriate silk gloves. A veil hid her face, which Charlie lifted over her head for the ceremony, revealing a smile made phony by the ice in her eyes. She was prettier than he'd expected, maybe even beautiful, and though he'd noticed it earlier, he now decided that this was the reason he'd reacted so strangely to her violin playing, and it made his own smile almost genuine.

The drummer slurred his way through the brief exchange of vows—which involved no rings as Charlie didn't want a constant reminder of the show on his finger—and pronouncement, then Charlie took Alex's gloved right hand, turned it over, and bent to kiss the one bare spot below her wrist between her sleeve and the gloves, almost directly on her scar. The jagged line, from an injury that had needed, but not received stitches, seemed all the more severe against the delicate wrist. He paused with his lips on her skin, while staring up into her eyes, and watched with satisfaction the tightening of her lips and the slight widening of her blue eyes.

He did it for effect on both Alex and the audience. In this milieu of overstated flamboyance and advertised sex, an intimate kiss on the inside of a wrist was far more scandalous than if he'd taken her right there, in front of relatives, media, ordained rock star, and the entire world behind the streaming videos.

Charlie smiled his lopsided smile at Alex and then placed her veil back over her face and offered his arm, which she took while looking down and away from him, and they made their grand exit, back down the aisle.

Then, for an hour, he held her hand and they smiled for the cameras, pretending to be blissful—he more than her, he thought—as they spouted off their lines, though he found he had to control a flinch every time she delivered one of hers. She did it perfectly, saying the right words—"It's, like, such a dream come true," and "I, like, can't even believe he picked me"—affecting the right demeanor: too-high voice, dull eyes, exaggerated smile, and generally the embodying everyone's expectations for such a girl on such a show. It annoyed the hell out of him. *It's just the heat*, he told himself, pulling at his tie. *And because I haven't gotten all the answers I want out of her yet.*

Then it was time for their first dance. She wouldn't look at him, but when he slid his arm around her waist and felt her shudder, he knew it was the right time to ask her another question. Or maybe he should warm her up with a little more seduction? He'd already seen her reaction to him in the house earlier when he'd barely touched her. What would she do if he slipped his hand up her back, caressed her neck, kissed her hard? She'd have to take it, wouldn't she? In front of all these people. He'd like to—he went cold, cutting off the thought before it went any further. He shouldn't be liking any of this; that was a recipe for a loss of control.

He loosened his grip on Alex's waist and forced all thoughts of seducing her out of his mind. The questions would have to wait. When the music ended, he escorted her to the dinner table, posed with her for a few more pictures, and left without explanation to find the bar. Then, with another whiskey in hand, he walked the perimeter of the garden, taking measure of the event to ensure it was a success. That was his job, after all.

Groups of guests crowded the lawn, their chatter more animated than it had been earlier in the evening, probably because of the open bar, but a good sign either way. Outside the dinner tent several women vied for camera time, among them Simone, standing so one long leg was expertly exposed by the high slit of her gown. But something about her was off—the expression maybe, bright but empty, like a plastic doll's. Charlie winced a little because she hadn't always been like that. *It's your fault*, a little nagging voice in his head insisted. *And you're doing it again.* He knew that voice—it was the one he'd banished when he'd first started EmerSound. The one that kept asking him if he was sure this plan with EmerSound was right, kept insisting that what he was doing, the kind of non-talent he promoted, the pandering and the compromises, were against everything he stood for in science. The one that had tried to resurface when news of Zoe's suicide had broken.

This was just popular music and media, he'd reassured himself, and it had nothing to do with science or truth or progress. It was a tool—one that would allow him to actually do the science and find the truth without having to compromise and pander that work just to get funds. *But you haven't found any truths and your science is stalled,* the voice chimed. *That's not the fault of the plan,* he wanted to yell back.

"Glad I caught you alone—we've got to talk to you about the auditions," David said, turning up next to Charlie. He looked harassed, his forehead shiny with sweat and his hair sticking up in the back. Jennifer stood next to him, her face also beaded with sweat, but her expression and floor-length gown gave her an air of dignity.

Charlie drained his whiskey, though for once he was glad to be interrupted by EmerSound minutia. "What about the auditions?"

"Somehow, somebody let Alex put in the contract that she gets final approval over the musicians. I just assumed Jennifer could fix it but now she tells me she can't."

"I've looked into it," Jennifer said, "and I think we'd open up a real can of worms if we try to break that clause. She made sure the parts about her orchestra are iron-clad. I wasn't at the meeting, but she must've had her own lawyer handle it."

David shook his head a little wildly. "Do you know what we'll end up with? A bunch of boring, stick-up-the-ass nobodies. How do I make a sensational story from that? I've already vetted a bunch of people who are perfect—you know, volatile, camera-hungry, a little cuckoo. You need to fix this now, Charlie. The auditions start tomorrow."

"Who decided the auditions would be so soon?" Charlie asked.

"She did," David said. "It's in the damn contract!"

Charlie was not so glad anymore to be talking to David and worked hard to keep from rolling his eyes. When had his employees turned into children throwing tantrums, and how had he become the teacher on duty, entrusted to mediate their little squabbles and show them a reasonable way forward? He let the question go because it only took him a moment to find a solution. "The easiest way out," he told David, "is to let her have her musicians and hire your people to sit with hers as if they're part of the orchestra. If they're only pretending to play, they're not technically *in* the orchestra, and we're not in breach of contract. She'll have to let them be there. Edit it for the show so it looks like they're really playing."

David's eyes lit up. "Yeah, yeah, I get it. They're like orchestra extras but main show characters."

"Wait," Jennifer said, putting her hand on David's shoulder. "That doubles the cost—we'll have to pay two sets of people. It's money we really shouldn't be spending, Charlie."

"David doesn't need an orchestra-sized cast, do you? Maybe five or six people? And you don't have to pay them like the orchestra members. Anyway, I'm sure we'll make it all back when the show goes big." Charlie said it with a confidence he didn't necessarily feel, but they were at the end of their options. Either the show made it big or EmerSound was done for. "If that's all, I'd really like to—"

Simone grabbed Charlie's arm. "I need Charlie for a minute," she said, pulling him away from Jennifer and David. Charlie shrugged, allowing her to lead him to an isolated spot by a tree, hidden from the cameras and people.

"You're producing Alex?" she whispered, her face no longer a plastic mask but still contained enough that Charlie couldn't tell what the emotion was.

"Didn't Richard tell you?" he asked.

"He said something about producing music, but it's not really *her* music, right? It's some music you've had in the works and you decided she was the right person to take credit for it?"

"No, it's the project she's been working on—the concerto. You told me about it yourself." Charlie attempted to free his arm, but Simone wouldn't loosen her grip.

"None of the girls on your shows have ever been allowed to record their own music," she said.

"None of the other girls had written their own music."

An emotion—maybe anger?—flashed through her eyes, then she dropped his arm and laughed, though there was a bite to it. "A concerto is ambitious," she said. "Is it any good?"

A memory of Alex playing a tumultuous melody on her violin flickered in Charlie's mind, but he clamped it down, hard. "Whatever it is, it'll be good enough for us."

"What does that mean?"

"It means you don't have to worry about it."

Simone gave him one of her unhappy smiles, not seeming relieved. "Well, I hope you're right. Anyway, am I going to see you tonight? I told Richard I was staying out here with a friend."

"Have you changed something?" Charlie asked, noticing again that something wasn't quite right. "Your hair, maybe?"

"My hair?" She laughed, throwing her head back in a practiced gesture, though the mirth was genuine. "Charlie Emerson, you have never commented on my hair before. I haven't changed it in months. What's wrong with you?"

Charlie cocked his head. She was different, though, she really was—even without the plastic mask—but still he couldn't pinpoint it. He shrugged. "Forget it. I've just been drinking too much. I need to go."

"But Charlie"—she dropped her voice to finish—"about tonight?"

Maybe if he could hear her sing again, if he took her to bed, it would dispel whatever funk he was in. "Yes, tonight. But come to the city. I don't want to be out here anymore. I need to get back to my normal routine."

CHAPTER XVII

That night, Alex woke up in the dark, shivering and disoriented, straining to hear the blaring sirens that normally jarred her out of sleep, but found only a deep silence. Then her eyes adjusted to the low light and she recognized her room in Charlie Emerson's penthouse.

For the first time since moving here, she missed her tenement in the Bronx—missed the shouting and the honking horns that had lulled her to sleep for ten years, the sounds of life and movement. It was silence that disturbed her, silence that was blinding and dangerous. In her old place she'd been glad of the thin-glassed windows and their drafty panes that kept the silence at bay. Here, the windows were sealed shut, the triple-paned glass admitting no noise, and a sterility permeated all her senses, as if she were in a hospital or an institution. There was such a thin border between a refuge and a jail.

She got out of bed, nearly tripping when her foot caught on the stiff pile of her wedding dress, which she'd left in a heap on the floor, too exhausted to do anything with it after the previous day's sweaty, confusing mess of a wedding and Charlie's baffling behavior—his flirting, his drinking, his sudden coolness during the dance, and his early departure after sitting down to dinner just long enough to be in a few pictures and a single take for the show, then leaving without taking a bite of food or saying a single word to her.

Last night all she'd let herself feel was annoyance that she'd had to stay for hours, late into the night, while Charlie did not. But now, standing in the cool silence of her room, she acknowledged the full jumble of her emotions—the anxiety when he'd probed into her past, the rush when he'd pulled her close for the dance, the disappointment when he'd left early. Just how much did she actually like him?

But no, it didn't matter, she decided. Where there was no possibility of action and no future, there was no need for a decision, and so no need for deliberation. Besides, the auditions for her orchestra were today; what was a little boredom, a little acting, or even a mound of confusing emotions compared to the first day of a journey to give life to the *Red Concerto*?

Now wide awake, though the sun wasn't even up yet, Alex dressed in old jeans and a T-shirt. There were hours to wait until her day officially started—when the crew of *Mrs. Music* arrived at the penthouse to "record every damn thing from breakfast to dinner" in David's words—but she was restless. So without a clear intention of where she'd go, she opened her bedroom door and plunged into the dark corridor in bare feet. There was more silence and darkness out here, and having no idea where the light switches were, Alex felt her way along the walls, hands sliding against the rough linen paper, aimless until she heard it—a barely audible classical aria floating toward her, a hint of unseen brightness, like the scent of a flower on a breeze. She followed the music down a second hallway for a few seconds and stopped when she could hear it better, closing her eyes to listen and let her vision wander through the melody, almost tasting it, her mind filling in the gaps when she couldn't hear the notes.

The aria halted mid-measure on a giggle. Alex snapped her eyes open, unsettled and a little dizzy. She strained to hear but there was nothing now. Had she imagined the music? She'd never hallucinated, but she'd been told there was a small chance she could.

She was in Charlie's corridor, which she recognized by the dim nightlights that dotted the hallway every few feet. Up ahead of her, their glow reflected off a smooth silver surface set into the wall, which wasn't a surface at all, she realized as she neared it, but a door made of a shining metal, unlike the pale wood of all the other doors. It bore a keypad where the doorknob should have been, and it looked like a vault.

She listened, glanced behind her to make sure she was alone, then stepped to the door and gave it a push with both hands. She might have been pushing at the wall for the all the movement it made. It was a solid, steel barrier.

"What are you doing here?" Charlie's voice came from down the hall, low and severe.

She whirled toward him. "I couldn't sleep."

He stood at the door to his bedroom, and like her was barefoot and dressed in jeans, but he was shirtless—and somehow, he looked more threatening. Maybe because the lights were low. Maybe because his broad shoulders and toned muscles were on display. Or maybe because of the scar that ran diagonally down from his right shoulder to his hip.

Alex allowed herself a moment to enjoy the sight of him, trying to recapture the way she used to watch him from her coffee stand, but it was different now that she knew him. Instead of a Beethoven sonata, she thought of a statue she'd seen in a book once—a beautiful, sculpted angel, powerful but with one ankle chained and face tortured. The fallen angel of music.

Charlie's actual face, however, betrayed no torture, only austerity and a slight annoyance as he shut the door to his room. "You don't need to be in this part of the apartment," he said.

She wanted to ask about the secret room, if even just to see his reaction, but she saw the hint of a mocking smile on his face and the flex of his naked forearm as he pushed the door closed, and she flashed back to being in his arms yesterday. She reconsidered lingering here with him, in the dark. "I'll go," she said and turned to hurry away back down the hallway.

She ended up in the kitchen, which was lit by the glow of impending sunrise through the floor-to-ceiling windows, and Alex stood at the island to pour herself a glass of water without turning on the lights. She drank a few sips and concentrated on forgetting the image of Charlie as some sort of beautiful and tortured angel—but it was useless. The picture was seared in her mind, probably forever.

She heard that giggle again, this time much closer, and then a light flared. Alex shut her eyes and, for a harrowing second, she believed she was hallucinating, but she opened her eyes to find Simone Hawl holding on to one side of the door jamb while she put shoes on. She was still wearing the dress she'd worn to the wedding. This was technically Alex's house, but she felt like the intruder, and wished she hadn't come out of her room at all tonight.

"Oh, hi," Simone said, straightening her posture. "I'm glad you're here. I'd really hoped we'd get a chance to talk more at the wedding."

Alex placed her glass of water gently on a counter between them, for something to do, annoyed by her own reaction—disappointment again, but a little deeper this time. Not just that Charlie was sleeping with someone, but that it should be Simone. The woman was beautiful and had a raw kind of talent—if not properly developed—but there was something missing in her, like she had a hollow core. Was that the trick to being one of them? Did you need to hollow yourself out? Is that what Charlie wanted?

"Oh wait. Didn't he tell you about me?" Simone said, with that giggle again. "You should see your expression. Now don't get into a tiff, I know all about your so-called marriage. And the contract."

That same contract made a clear stipulation that Alex couldn't talk about the arrangement to anyone who was not specifically named, at the risk of forfeiting it all—and Simone was not on that list. So Alex said nothing, focusing instead on the cold of the glass between her hands, spinning it slowly.

"Oh, darling, don't worry. The whole damned thing was my idea!" Simone's laugh was a harsh, stark fluorescent yellow.

Was it true that Simone had picked her? Alex wondered. But then, it didn't matter, did it? Whosever idea it was, Charlie had accepted it, acted on it.

Simone moved closer to the counter and reached across, putting her hands on Alex's to stop the glass spinning. They felt rough and cold, but Alex didn't pull away. She lifted her gaze to meet Simone's full-on.

Simone sighed dramatically. "I just wanted to make sure you knew not to try to get into Charlie's bed, because I'm already there"—she waved an arm around indicating the room—"but I guess I don't need to tell you that part anymore. You be good and stick to your little show, okay?"

"Is that all?" Alex asked.

"Look," Simone said, "I picked you for the role because you seemed like you could use some money and a nice place to live for a while. It makes such a nice story, to save a girl like you. But there are lots of girls like you. So you should be thanking me, darling, not giving me that look. It's not nice at all. Besides, it's not like I'm threatening you, I'm just offering you some advice."

Alex reined in her temper; Charlie's private life had no bearing on her own, and she had to let go of her disappointment and whatever else she was feeling. The important thing was the music, the concerto. And for that she had to do the expected. So she gave the grin she should have affected when Simone had first appeared this morning—the grin of an idiot who'd go along with anything just to be famous. "Oh, like, I totally know what you mean," she said. "I just, like, didn't know you were in on it and everything. Right?" She blinked a few times for good measure.

"Good." Simone smoothed her skirt and nodded, but her expression was wary. "I'm glad we had this little chat."

CHAPTER XVIII

B y the time David and the crew arrived at the penthouse that morning, Alex felt more in control—she'd spent the time with her violin, and being immersed in her music always grounded her.

But David was not pleased. "How you doing, honey?" he asked when she met him in the foyer. "You look awful, didn't you sleep at all? Grace is setting up in the kitchen. Man, she's got her work cut out today. But you better get used to the long days."

The man treated her like a child, or a prop, and Alex actively disliked him. She'd heard herself referred to as Cinderella, and some sardonic part of her dubbed David an ugly stepsister. Or maybe he was the evil stepmother? The thought made the action of forcing a grin onto her face and nodding at him a little easier.

When Grace, the unlikely fairy godmother, was done fixing her—Alex hated the word *fixing*, as if there were something wrong with her face—David, two cameras, and three assistants of some sort were ready to start taping the inane details of her morning for the show. Or rather the inane details of someone's morning, because everything Alex did had to be doctored and re-taped. They took video of her drinking coffee and eating a croissant in the dining room—usually she liked to eat in the kitchen, but "princesses don't eat in the kitchen"—and video of her collecting her music scores, but not packing her backpack ("Someone get her one of the designer bags we brought"), and even video of her putting on shoes ("Wear the heels for the shoot and you can change into comfortable shoes later"). By the time she was ready to leave, Alex wanted to scream. It had taken her an extra hour to get ready, with them constantly in her way, and now she was late.

She pulled out her phone to book a car as she waited for the elevator in the foyer.

"What are you doing?" David asked.

"Getting a cab."

"No can do, honey. You're supposed to walk."

"I'm already late. I don't have time."

"I don't think that's in your contract," he said, leering at her. "Or should we wake Charlie up and ask him to mediate?"

No, not Charlie again. She couldn't afford distraction. And besides, this wasn't worth antagonizing David over. "Alright," she said and asked Murdoch, who had observed the morning quietly but astutely, to go ahead to Martin Hall and make sure everything was ready for the auditions.

∫ ₹

Martin Hall was a converted church, nestled at the end of a short, cramped street, with an aged but meticulously kept gray stone exterior, pristine concrete steps, and utilitarian steel double doors. Today the street was teeming with a huge crowd—long lines of people with instrument cases of all sizes, some chatting in small groups, a few already growing rowdy—here to audition on a scale beyond anything Alex had imagined. It seemed in the aftermath of all the publicity of a secret engagement followed by the reveal of the fiancée as an unknown, every musician in the city had come to get a glance at the unlikely bride, and as it turned out, many of them were not even classical musicians.

Inside, Alex sat in the front pew, where the light from the set of stained-glass windows at either wall streamed in, and took her time reviewing the pile of resumes to pick thirty candidates she hoped to audition before lunch. Then, she handed the list to Murdoch and settled into a seat in the sixth row—the best spot for listening to single instruments.

The footsteps of the first candidate clicked onto the low stage and behind a screen, where there was a small camera crew to tape each auditioner for the show. The screen would allow Alex to focus only on the music instead of the musicians themselves or all the crew. After the audition, she would ask a few questions of the auditioner to get a feel for their general personality. The person would then exit through the same door and be led into a little room in the back, where David was running the post-audition interviews. Alex had gotten lucky he wasn't observing her, because though cameras were trained on her, too, she wouldn't be acting today. With the small chat after the audition as her only opportunity to make an impression on her would-be orchestra, she couldn't afford to be anything less than she was, because when the first episode of *Mrs. Music* aired, the world would see her portrayed as the clueless airhead. Being herself now went against everything she'd done for years, but it was worth the risk.

The first audition began with a swirl of reds and purples pouring from a cello—a sonorous melody that filled all the empty spaces of the room in a beautiful testament to both the cellist and the superior acoustics of the hall. Alex knew this cellist—for certain musicians, the mix of colors and patterns were like a personal signature—and she'd heard Willem Salk perform a few years ago at the City Academy of Music, in his senior year there, and though she'd forgotten his name and hadn't recognized it from his resume, she'd never forgotten his musical signature. She'd found her first orchestra member.

The next nine candidates, however, were abysmal, their colors stilted and fading, and though she only needed to hear a few bars from each to make her decision, David had stipulated that every person was to play many more bars so the cameras could "get the right soundbite." By lunchtime three hours later, Alex was exhausted and irritable and had only identified two others to hire. Would everything be this torturous? Would she have to spend double, maybe triple, the time to get anything done because David had to get it all on camera in a particular way? He was definitely the evil stepmother, she decided.

After lunch—a sandwich she ate at her seat while reviewing more resumes—auditioner number sixteen took his turn. His resume claimed he was a a violinist, but the first couple of notes told her he'd probably only taken a few years of lessons, and those a long time ago. She looked more carefully at the resume and then asked Murdoch to come over. "I didn't pick this one from the pile," she told him, holding up the piece of paper. "This person doesn't have any formal musical training."

Murdoch gave her a sympathetic, maybe almost pitying, grimace. "David called in a group of people. I think there are about thirty here already. You'll need to audition them, too."

"But I'm supposed to be able to decide who I hire."

"That's correct. They won't play in your orchestra, but he still wants his people on the audition episode for extra drama."

"Every one of them?"

Murdoch nodded.

Damn. Alex hadn't put in any specifications in the contract about choosing whom to audition. "Alright."

Six more auditions—which yielded one probable violin hire—and then it was Richard's turn to harass her. He came in from the back, all ingratiating smile and effusive voice, and spoke in one long breath, not giving her a chance to answer. "Geez, it took me forever to find this place, I thought we were doing this at Bernak Hall, but never mind now, you're looking great, how's it all going? Good I hope, I think David's pretty happy with how the day is shaping up and everything, are you? Of course, you must be, a dream come true, I'm sure, okay, I need to know how long this Red song of yours is going to be, for planning and the media campaign and everything."

Alex had to fight hard against a smirk—he was an ugly stepsister for sure. Then she remembered this was Simone's husband and the morning came rushing back to her: Charlie looming in the dark, menacing and attractive, Simone's giggling revelation in the kitchen, her own disappointment. But she also felt a moment's sympathy for Richard, who didn't seem to fit with Simone at all, almost childlike in comparison to her deviousness. *It's none of my business.* She cleared her throat and told Richard, "The whole concerto is probably going to be between twenty-five and thirty-five minutes total."

"Which is it, twenty-five or thirty-five? I need to know exactly."

"I don't know yet. The fourth movement is a work in progress."

"You mean the damn thing's not even done?" Gone were the smile and pretense at civility, replaced by anger and a quaking sort of agitation.

Alex shook her head in answer, her sympathy for him dissipating. He may not belong with Simone, but he certainly belonged to the same erratic and obnoxious world that was EmerSound. Did Charlie belong there?

Richard continued to interrogate her. "But you'll finish it soon, right? When can I hear it? Next week?"

"If everything goes well, I think in three weeks you can hear a preliminary sample of the first movement."

"What?"

"If you want to hear it," she said, slower this time, "you'll have to wait until I've worked through it with the orchestra a few times at least, and I won't even have hired the whole group for another week."

Richard cursed, though compared to some of the things she'd heard in her old neighborhood—and even from David—he sounded like an eight-year-old who'd just learned how to do it. "Does Charlie know about this stuff?" he asked. "It doesn't matter, either way I've got to talk to him." He turned around and walked off, grumbling, "This is a disaster. I knew it was a bad idea. I told him, just hire Brandy and be done with it, and now..."

Alex should have lied to him, she realized. Having spent most of the day out of character, she'd actually forgotten to act, to choose her words while carefully considering their implications—for the show, for EmerSound, and especially for Charlie. The last thing she needed was for him to get involved. But it was done now. She'd have to deal with it later.

"Next," she called out.

CHAPTER XIX

Alex shivered against the autumn wind. Sometime during the last week, summer had given way to the new season and, too busy with auditions to notice it, she'd neglected to bring a coat. But she was not unhappy. The auditions had ended today and she'd had plenty of candidates to choose from. So much so that she'd spent an extra two hours at Martin Hall, reviewing resumes and notes to make the ultimate decisions on who to hire. She'd even had a full, blissful hour alone; a few days ago, David had reduced her evening camera crew down to one quiet, unobtrusive young man, because she was, apparently, "too damned boring," and David preferred his crew to spend their time poring over the hours of recordings they'd already made for the "Auditions" episode—and even that lone cameraman had gotten too bored and left early today.

She'd worried about walking home alone because people had started to recognize her; she'd noticed the stares and even some pointing several times this week, but she couldn't resist the opportunity to walk through the city on her own. The weeks of constant worry—was she saying the right thing to the right people, acting the right way for the cameras, switching between personalities appropriately—were starting to grate on her, and she'd actually been missing her coffee stand, which seemed peaceful and comfortable compared to her life now. She was exhausted and needed the time alone, if only to relax a little.

She came home to Murdoch, standing in the foyer, to tell her as she walked off the elevator, "Mr. Emerson has requested that you attend a benefit gala for the Humbolt Foundation for the Arts this evening. The show crew is there already, but Grace is here to get you prepared."

Then there were dresses to try on and powders to apply, and Grace complaining about Alex's tired complexion, and racing around to find "anything that brightens." All too soon, Alex was dressed in an evening gown of blush-colored silk—a floor-length sheath that revealed the delicate lines of her shoulders and collarbone and bared her back from neck to waist. She stood for a moment, a little taken aback by her own reflection: the way the dress highlighted the rose-flavored hues of her skin, the way her hair hung in loose golden waves down her back and glimmered with the slightest movement. She found herself liking it, even though it made her more the princess and theater prop than ever.

Then she was pulling on her white satin gloves, and Murdoch was hurrying her down in the elevator to usher her into a black limousine parked at the curb—an ostentatious car that Alex couldn't quite reconcile with Charlie. Even with all his money and all the talk of his extravagant lifestyle, the more she watched him, the less these exaggerated luxuries fit. But then the door closed behind her, and the sounds of the city receded to a pleasant hum, leaving the interior of the car so at odds with the frenetic pace of the previous hour and the chill she'd felt since leaving the hall that Alex felt like someone had plunged her into a warm bath. The leather seats cocooned her in soft comfort, and she closed her eyes, settling in. Perhaps this was one luxury that wasn't overrated.

She only got a few minutes of serenity. The opposite car door opened to admit a blast of cold air, the clamor of traffic, and Charlie Emerson. Alex sat up, back straight and hands in her lap, while he, smiling his lazy smile, took the rear-facing seat across a diagonal distance of a few feet from her and stretched his legs out in a casual, almost lethargic pose. His fingers, though, betrayed his tense energy, snapping and unsnapping the magnetic clasp of his watch band in a rhythmic *click-clack, click-clack, click-clack*— precise like a metronome.

"Nice dress," he said in the vague mocking tone she was becoming accustomed to, a deep blue tinged with green. His eyes were darker than usual—an effect of the dim light perhaps—making him more striking, the sharp outlines of cheeks and jaw standing in contrast to the black leather of the seats and his tuxedo.

Alex thought she could look at him for hours. She turned her head to the window, to stare absently at storefronts as the car crawled through Charlie's trendy neighborhood, slowed by the traffic and the slews of pedestrians out to enjoy a night out. Here was another place Charlie didn't seem to belong. Did he ever go out to the restaurants and shops in his neighborhood? Why live here and deal with this chaos?

After a moment, during which the *click-clack* of the watch clasp continued, Charlie said, "Has David talked to you about Bernak Hall?"

"What about it?" She turned to him again.

"Your rehearsals will be held there. Martin Hall is not grand enough."

She controlled herself not to panic and yell. *Stay calm.* In a low, flat voice, she asked, "What does that mean, 'not grand enough'? Bernak Hall is... I can't work there. It wasn't in the contract—"

"Screw the contract," he said, his manner so calm, his voice so steady that she didn't know why it should bother her, but it did.

"Have you ever heard the acoustics at Bernak?" she asked.

"Of course I have."

"So then you know how abysmal it is. From the third row on you can't even hear the cellos and—"

"How the music sounds is irrelevant." *Click-clack, click-clack, click-clack.*

"You're lying," she said.

He raised an eyebrow. "About what?"

"That the music doesn't matter. You responded to the music that night, when you heard me playing in my room. You felt something. I saw it in your eyes."

"Maybe. But why would it matter what I felt?"

"It's music. That's the point."

"No. I'm the boss—*that's* the point. I'm here to make sure the music sells. Not to feel anything."

"Fine, forget the feel of the music," Alex said. "You've done work in acoustics, so you know that the configuration and size of a room make a huge difference. When I read your paper on acoustic waves, the spot where you discuss wave interference and its dependence on—"

"You've read my paper?" The *click-clack* stopped. Alex, too, fell silent, and for a few seconds there was only the distant wail of car horns from the streets. Charlie added, "Or have you read *about* my paper?"

"Is there a difference?"

"Yes… And I think you know that." He stared at her openly, waiting, seeming almost interested, the corners of his eyes shifting slightly to suggest a smile, though his mouth remained a flat line. The car jerked to a stop, jolting them both and breaking Charlie's scrutiny of her.

Alex shrugged, trying for unconcerned and dismissive, while knowing she shouldn't have mentioned the paper—that was out of character again. Why couldn't she stay in character? Also, she felt a sort of danger in the topic of his old work, beyond what having read it meant about her, and it was like a loose thread she wanted to pull at, knowing that if she did, everything could unravel. She tried to shrink into herself, but found it difficult, as if she'd lost the habit.

The car started moving again, and after a minute, Charlie asked, "What do you know about the physics of acoustics?"

"I'm a musician. I know what I hear." She wished she'd read what had been said about his early papers so that she could quote those accounts and have him think she hadn't read or understood it for herself.

He raised an eyebrow, maybe surprised, maybe disbelieving, and the *click-clack* started again, though the rhythm was off—now a broken, agitated syncopation. Then he said, too casually, "Well, I'm a media executive and I know what works on a show. You'll start rehearsing at Bernak Hall next week."

"There are other halls, bigger and *grander* than Martin Hall, which have better acoustics. Maybe one of those—"

"No."

"But why not?" She almost screamed it.

"Because the decision has already been made," he said. "And please calm down. There's no need to get so upset." His voice was appeasing now, though still laced with mockery, and she thought that despite his words, he'd wanted specifically to upset her, except that was nonsensical—unless his aim was to shift the subject away from his old work.

This sensitivity about his work was the first vulnerability she'd seen in him. Could she use it to break him of his stoicism, the way he kept doing with her act? To make him feel something? She had to get him to change his mind, or this whole scheme was useless. The audio recording of the concerto would be made at the premiere so the hall mattered a great deal. And since she'd already outed herself about the paper, she might as well keep going with it. "How come you didn't finish your theory all those years go?"

The *click-clack* again halted, but this time Charlie didn't say anything—just shifted his eyes out the window and then didn't move at all, except for the slight shift back and forth as the car made a turn. Then, just when she thought he wouldn't answer, he said, "I was done with it."

"But it wasn't done. How could you just quit in the middle of something you loved so much?"

"How do you know I loved it?" he asked, and she heard his attempt to be dismissive, heard it not quite hit its mark.

"Because," she said, "you can't do something like that—integrate all wave phenomena into a grand scale theory—unless it's all you think about, all you do, for years. And to do that you have to love it."

The car turned again, putting them onto a wide two-way avenue that was clear of traffic, and as they accelerated, the intermittent lights from passing vehicles caressed Charlie's face, throwing his features alternately into focused relief and dark shadow. In one iteration of light, his expression grew intense, but by the next, he was smiling at her again—though this time it was sad and bitter. "Maybe I didn't do all that work. Maybe there is no grand scale wave theory. Maybe it was all made up. That's what everyone in the media said."

She held his gaze. "I don't trust the media. Is there a theory?"

"It doesn't matter either way. They didn't want it, and what I felt for the work wasn't love—it was obsession. And it was unhealthy. It's better left behind."

"What made it obsession and not love?" she asked, thinking of her concerto.

He seemed surprised by the question and frowned. Then the words came spilling out, edged with aggravation. "I couldn't think about anything else. Nothing mattered but the work, and everything I was and everything I had went into that damned theory. But I still had to depend on other people accepting it just so I could keep going with it. And when it…didn't work out…I had nothing left."

He didn't want to talk about it, she could tell, but he also couldn't help himself. How could he not recognize that as a hallmark of love? "That's not so different from love," she said. "Except the part about depending on other people accepting it, I suppose… So you quit because they didn't accept it, or because you didn't have the means to do it anymore when they didn't accept it?"

"Same thing."

"No, it's not. You have money now. If you don't care whether anyone accepts the ideas, you're free to do the work."

He laughed, and she didn't know why it would be funny.

"It doesn't quite work like that," he said.

"Why not? It's like what I was doing at the coffee stand, making money to support the real work."

"And how was that going for you? I seem to remember you were practically homeless when I found you." The smirk was back now and she tried to think of the right thing to say, but he was going on. "So you see, you've convinced us both. It's one or the other. The *money* is the reason you need to move to Bernak Hall. You'll have your music because I'll get the money."

And then she knew there were no right words to say tonight and that she'd lost him—because with his words, the clicking of the watchband had fallen into a steady rhythm again.

CHAPTER XX

Finally, the limousine pulled up to the side entrance of a hotel, whose main doors faced Central Park on its south side. The building was a grand affair covering an entire block, with gilded columns and uniformed doormen standing out in front of the palatial entrance. Most of the cameras and a large crowd had gathered to line either side of the red carpet from the curb to those main doors, and no one noticed Charlie's limousine—or the *Mrs. Music* cameramen—at the side entrance. Why, Alex wondered, had Charlie done this? Why show up in a ridiculous limousine only to hide?

The chauffeur opened the door and held a hand out to her, but Alex shook her head and got out of the car without his help, and coatless, she shivered a little in the cold. She paused on the sidewalk to straighten out her dress, then stilled; Charlie had rested his hand against her lower back, against her bare skin, and the touch enraptured her like the first whisper of some beautiful melody, warm and provocative, an invitation to lean in and submit.

Suddenly, someone from the crowd at the main entrance shouted, "It's Charlie and Mrs. Music!" and a mob of people and cameras turned and rushed them, one blinding flash followed by another, then another. The noise rose in a dark cacophony around Alex, and with her senses already overloaded from Charlie's touch, she struggled to keep herself steady as black and blue streaks raced across her vision, and then she had no choice but to cover her ears before she was blinded by the noise. Charlie's arm gripped her around the waist and pulled her past the wild fans into the hotel.

"I forget you're not used to this," he said, leaning into her. "You've garnered a lot of fans, you know. And Richard planted some extra excitement tonight. I should've warned you… Are you okay?"

Alex lowered her hands from her ears, and for one instant the expression in his eyes was like the continuance of that first touch of his hand on her back. Then he was pulling away, walking forward, but holding her hand, and she was grateful for her gloves and the barrier they formed between the naked skin of their hands. She'd be okay as long as he didn't touch her again.

But then they entered the ballroom. Alex gasped. The place was a crowded, twinkling chaos, and stepping inside was like stepping into fire; the glow from three enormous and elaborate chandeliers, each composed of hundreds of translucent orbs, reflected off the cut crystal tumblers and centerpieces of glass flowers set on dozens of tables. The people sparkled, too, because of jewelry, or expensive fabrics, or just the polish of their hair.

It was all getting to Alex now—the exhaustion, Charlie, the wild, unexpected crowd, and the cameras everywhere. And her supposed fans would be watching her every action, every stumble, every move in and out of character. *Fans are just people*, she reminded herself, *and people accept the expected. Give them nothing extraordinary and they'll forget.* And really it wasn't such a hard feat, because her so-called fame was ordinary at its base. The story of Cinderella was hundreds of years old, after all.

Charlie nodded at people and shook a few hands on the way to their table, and Alex managed a grin—convincingly, she thought—for the cameras. Charlie, too, had donned his adoring-husband act, and glanced at her with warmth to announce, "You know my friends, I think," and proceeded to introduce them all anyway, as the camera panned to each person: Simone, who gave Alex a sharp eyebrow lift but smiled sweetly on camera; Richard, grinning and clueless; David, who waved the cameras away; Brandy, who'd come as David's date and with whom Alex feigned an excited hug, air kisses, and over-the-top cooing; Jennifer Barnes and her husband; and finally Lawrence Berg, whom Alex knew from having taken his seminar at the City Academy, as well as his frequent trips to her coffee stand.

Alex ended up in a seat between David and Lawrence. David poured her a large glass of white wine, told her to drink up during dinner while the cameras were absent, then turned to Brandy on his other side. Lawrence grinned at her and she nodded back. She'd seen him with Charlie at the Academy a number of times, but his presence at this table, among these people, was baffling—he just didn't fit. He was dressed properly, in a pristine dark suit, and his posture was relaxed, but somehow, he still seemed to belong in oak-lined libraries and ivory towers, his slender form appearing too thin in the suit and his eyes too shrewd for such an event.

Alex stripped off her gloves and rubbed at her scar before remembering not to bring attention to it and instead picked up her glass to sip at the wine. It helped, so she drank a bit more.

"You're a musician, then?" Lawrence asked, leaning in a bit toward her.

"Yes," she said.

"Classical music, is it?"

"Yes," Alex said again, and leaned away a little, making room for a server who placed a salad in front of her. She caught Charlie watching her from across the table, but he'd put on his stoic, expressionless mask.

"I'd love to hear about your music," Lawrence said.

"It's a violin concerto," she said, keeping her voice crisp and then sipping her wine, trying to discourage the conversation.

"Yes, I know that part. I wanted to know how you came up with it, what it represents to you, that kind of thing." Lawrence gave her a sideways, good-natured smile, amused perhaps by her terseness, and she liked him for it, even though her purpose in being terse was to put him off. She rewarded him by smiling back. He continued, "I have heard a little about it from a musician in your orchestra—Willem Salk. He's a cellist."

"Oh! He's an extraordinary musician," she said.

"He says the same about your music."

There was a purposefulness to his statements somehow, and Alex went on guard, but still she asked, "How do you know Willem?"

"His cello is on loan from my collection—I have some antique strings. Do you play an instrument?"

"Violin," she said, stabbing a piece of salad around her

plate. She wouldn't be able to swallow any food now, not under Lawrence's interrogation. She tried to find another conversation at the table, something to distract Lawrence with, but all she could pick out was Brandy's high-pitch giggle among the din of other, undiscernible chatter.

Lawrence went on. "Willem called your style reminiscent of Beethoven. But a thoroughly modern version. He went so far as to call it revolutionary."

"Hmm," she said, noncommittal, though it was an astute observation—Beethoven was a major influence.

"I'd love to come to a rehearsal if you don't mind. Hear it for myself."

She took two more gulps of her wine. "You'd have to ask Charlie or David," she said, even though she really had no idea. She wanted to refuse him but feared raising his suspicion, and there was a chance that Charlie would say no, or that Lawrence would forget.

Jennifer Barnes leaned over to say something to Lawrence and he turned away from Alex, giving her a respite, though she still couldn't bring herself to eat. She drank some more instead and surreptitiously watched Charlie. He also didn't really belong here, but in a different way than Lawrence, and the distinction seemed important. Charlie did fit with the grace and splendor of the evening, but his demeanor—erect posture, blank face, distant eyes—all suggested something darker, quieter. In the car she'd thought he wore his tuxedo with ease, but here, the severe, immaculate lines over his tight form made it more like a uniform.

Charlie had called the people at this table his friends, but while watching him Alex wondered at the description, because this wasn't how you faced friends, this was how you met enemies. People talked at him, smiled at him, moved around him, but he was still, occasionally nodding, as if his armor of control and indifference were up—and yet this was just a party, and one he'd presumably paid a lot of money to attend. Why, she wondered again, was he doing all this?

Then the lights and voices dimmed, someone took the podium, and as the salad course was replaced with a plated chicken dish, the speeches began—mostly people congratulating each other for supporting the arts before asking for donations. She poked at her chicken, drank some more wine, and wondered why her glass was still mostly full. Then she glanced at Lawrence. He seemed like a person who could be a real friend to Charlie. "Do you know Charlie very well?" she asked, sotto voce, leaning over to Lawrence this time.

He gave her a delighted smile. "I do. We were at university together," he whispered back. "These days we meet for coffee at my office...at the City Academy."

He'd put a peculiar emphasis on "City Academy." Did he remember her? From the coffee stand or his class? "I audited your class on advanced theory once," she said.

"Ah, so you do remember me."

Alex smiled and added, "Coffee, two sugars and *a lot* of cream."

He gave a guffaw that was a bit too loud, and several people from other tables turned to them. Lawrence mouthed a "sorry" to them, then raised his eyebrows at Alex and said, "I hate coffee, but it's a concession I make for the cream and sugar. It would hardly be professorial to walk around campus with a cone of ice cream or the like."

Somebody behind Alex gave an irate, "Hush!"

Alex laughed softly, and as someone reached over again, replacing their dinner plates with bowls of pink sorbet, Lawrence put a finger to his lips. Then he attacked his sorbet.

Alex stirred hers idly for a bit, deciding she liked him and that he was perhaps the first person whose presence in Charlie's life made any sense. And if Lawrence had heard about her music and knew Willem, it probably made no difference if she acted like she understood things or not—he likely already had a good idea about that part of her. So she sipped at her wine and took a chance, waiting for him to finish his sorbet, then whispering, "Do you know why Charlie comes to these things? He obviously hates being here."

They both glanced at Charlie, who hadn't touched his dessert, but who had been delivered several glasses of whiskey, one of which he was just finishing.

Lawrence opened his mouth, then closed it again with a frown. "That's true," he said. "Charlie does hate it. I suppose he does it because it sells something he calls his 'EmerSound brand.' I don't suppose he cares if he's happy or not."

She put down her wine glass and leaned in a little closer, just to suggest a bit of privacy, and asked, "And do you know why he quit graduate school?"

Now Lawrence's gaze sharpened on her. "The situation surrounding his theory…disillusioned him with the academic establishment."

"What was the situation, exactly?"

"As I understood it, his advisor wanted to publish Charlie's findings before Charlie was ready. They quarreled and Charlie said he couldn't work in science after that. So he quit."

"So he didn't fake data—then why not fight back with the truth? Why not go somewhere else? Or fight to publish his way?"

Lawrence smiled at her, a gentle expression she'd never seen on his face in the many months she'd stared at him while taking his course. "You should ask him sometime," he said. "It's rather complicated."

That's when the room exploded in applause.

CHAPTER XXI

The lights came up and a jazz trio started playing a swing tune, galvanizing couples toward the dance floor. Then the *Mrs. Music* cameramen were back and someone came over to attach a microphone to Alex's dress.

"I supposed we have to behave now," Lawrence said, winking at her.

Alex felt a little lightheaded and forced down a few spoonfuls of sorbet, trying at the same time to recapture her sense of the Brandy persona. But even with the girl gabbing incessantly a few seats down from her, it was difficult. She kept thinking about Charlie and his theory, and his astounding turns of mathematical creativity. How she'd love to see his mind in action.

"Alexandra?"

"What?" Her head snapped up. It took a minute to determine who'd called her name: Richard.

He was leaning in toward the table, a few seats on the other side of Lawrence. He said, slowly, "I take it your music is finished by now?"

"It's…close," she lied. She hadn't had time to think about her concerto's final movement, much less write anything new.

Next to Charlie, Simone sniggered, then waved her miniature sorbet spoon around in a graceful casualness. "See now, I know you're done, because one of the musicians told me there are four movements in his version of sheet music."

"Which musician?" Alex asked. She'd provided copies of the full concerto to some of the musicians—the ones she'd known she was going to hire right away, like Willem—but she'd also told them the fourth movement was not final.

"Preston something or other," Simone said.

"I haven't hired anyone named Preston."

Brandy gave a loud titter and Simone, in turn, gave her a cutting look, then said, "Well, I must have the name wrong. But I did see the sheet music."

"That's an old version and it's not working. I'm rewriting it."

"There's no time for something like that!" Richard said, livid, eyes wide.

No one answered, and the silence at the table was filled with the steady reverberation of the music around them. Both Alex and Simone now had cameras trained on them, and Alex had the distinct impression they'd zoomed in on her face. She looked down at the napkin in her lap, twisting it into a tight coil. *Concentrate and be Brandy.*

David stood up abruptly. "People, we're on camera. I need something to happen. Alex, talk about how the auditions went." He refilled her wineglass, then turned to the crew. "Stop filming me, you morons. I'm not on the show. We need her."

Alex, finally recapturing the right persona, grinned as the focus turned to her. "The auditions were, like, so awesome. So many, like, totally great musicians came, and I didn't even know who to choose…"

She blathered on for a while, sipping her wine whenever Brandy joined in with comments—nuggets like: "Are any of them hot? You've gotta get some hotties," and "I mean, I don't even know how you can just like sit there and listen to people playing, like, the same music over and over and over. I'd be, like, so bored."

Eventually David was satisfied. "Okay, cut," he called. "That'll do for now. Charlie, you and Alex go dance. Look in love and all that crap."

"I'm not miked," Charlie said, his expression flat and making no move to get up.

David waved him off. "It doesn't matter. We have to get Alex's microphone off her anyway so we don't get it in the shot. I just need some footage of the dancing. People want to see you guys together. And I'll get everyone in order here. Brandy has some friends who'll come join our table so we can get something interesting."

As a crew member detached Alex's microphone, Charlie stood up and came over—reluctantly, she thought. But then she was reluctant, too, not wanting to be so close to Charlie. Or maybe wanting it too much. She carefully unwound her napkin and placed it on the table, then put her hand in his outstretched one. She startled a little at the heat of his skin against hers— belatedly realizing she was still gloveless—and she flashed to the memory of his hand on her back earlier. She wouldn't be able to stand it if he did that again, she thought, a little unsteady on her feet, as they navigated around tables to the edge of the dance floor, where the cameras were waiting for them. But when Charlie slid his arm around her back, he held her without the use of his hand, exerting pressure with his arm, so she felt only the rough fabric of his coat. Their hands, though, were still clasped, now raised in dance position.

"Do you know how to waltz?" Charlie asked.

She shook her head no, and the movement made her a little dizzy. How much wine had she drunk?

"It'll help me lead if your body is closer to mine," he said. "And if you surrender a little control."

No one was actually waltzing, though the music had the right beat. Still, she consciously relaxed her body and allowed him to lead her through a lazy waltz, moving her gently, with small steps. She kept her gaze averted from his, but could feel him watching her and knew he wore his mocking smile again.

"Where did you learn to ballroom dance? No one does this anymore," she said, trying to distract herself from the way his body moved. She should either say as little as possible or say something completely inane, but all of that was beyond her now.

"I made it a point to take lessons precisely because no one does this," he said, his voice a lovely low, pure blue. "To be famous you have to be different, stand out."

"And that was your goal, to be famous?"

"No, the goal was to make money." He gave his light laugh— the one she liked. "Haven't we been over this? The fame is an important part of it."

"Isn't it boring, though?"

"What? Being famous?"

"No, all the pretending so you can be famous. With your kind of mind...Doesn't it make you feel like you're in some sort of prison?"

There was a pause in his step, a fraction of a second—something she wouldn't have noticed had she not been in his arms—but his voice was smooth when he answered, "Sometimes you have to do things you don't enjoy to get to the things you do."

"But what things are those? What do you enjoy? Because I know it's not the money." She was talking too freely and was almost definitely drunk—on wine or Charlie, she wasn't sure.

"I enjoy the money," he said, but it was unconvincing, almost rote, and he stopped moving.

She pulled back to see his expression. It was that intense one from the car again, serious and searching, but this time aimed at her and it jolted her, as if he'd suddenly stripped naked, or stripped her naked.

She swallowed, cleared her throat. "And you don't find any of this boring?"

"It used to be boring, but I'm mostly accustomed to it now," he said, his voice flat with control.

He tried to move again, to lead her back into the dance, but she wouldn't budge. She was getting somewhere with him and wanted to pull an answer out of him. "That's worse than being forced. You voluntarily shut down your brain and you're used to it? It's like you're always in the prison now."

"It's not a prison. It's just a little slowing down. And it keeps me in control."

"Sounds like torture to me."

"It's not like that for me. I don't run away with emotions." This time when he pushed her, she followed the movement and they were dancing again. She felt no tension in him, not in his hands or his arms, but she knew he was unbalanced by her questions through some strained manner in his movement. And that controlled, flat voice.

"So you don't feel anything?" she asked.

"Not anymore."

"Is that why the music doesn't matter then? You don't like to feel anything?"

A few beats of silence passed. Then he changed, pulling her in a little closer and repositioning their clasped hand so he could caress her wrist—her scar—with his thumb. He bent his head to put his lips by her ear and said hoarsely, "I like to feel *some* things."

His breath was hot against her skin, and for a moment all she could focus on was the whooshing sound of her blood, pulsing hard through her ears, her neck, her whole body. But she thought she'd also heard the timbre of his voice slip back to the mocking blue-green—was he trying to change the topic again or was the seduction real? Maybe she'd just had too many glasses of wine.

Then the music stopped and David was there with someone to clip microphones on them again, and Charlie released his hold on her, turning away.

She watched him go and, inebriated or not, she was coming to understand something about him, because she knew what it was like when you lost the music, when you couldn't feel the joy of it anymore, and life became a gray, dull, and faded thing. And she was stuck with Bernak Hall unless and until she could find a way to break him out of it.

CHAPTER XXII

The keypad beeped three times, then the little light in the corner turned green. Charlie pushed the heavy silver door open and reached up with both hands to grip the top of the doorframe, leaning forward slightly, though not committing himself to enter. He hadn't been in his private laboratory—a specially designed five hundred square feet of space—in two years, three months, and five days.

Today, the room was hazy, the early morning light tempered by a fine veil of dust that covered the wall of windows and shrouded the view beyond, making the city seem like a dream not quite remembered, lacking the vibrancy and detail of reality. The staff wasn't permitted to enter this room, so the dust had buried everything. The racks of audio hardware lining the walls, the mass of wires cluttering the corner of the worktable, and the rolling chalkboard bearing half-solved equations were all blanketed by a layer of soft white powder, like a frost that had yet to thaw.

This particular space was the reason Charlie had bought the penthouse long before he could properly afford to buy such a sprawling condo in the middle of the city. The building was new, allowing the two rooms that became the lab to be more easily fitted with weighted floors and heavy, vibration-proof walls, and the high floor isolated the apartment from the din of the city—a low-level hum that interfered with experiments on the minutia of air and sound waves.

For five years Charlie had spent every morning in this lab, waking up at 4:00 a.m. so he could have several uninterrupted hours with his scientific work before he needed to be at EmerSound. But he'd quit doing that a long time ago. Yet, this morning, he'd jerked awake to the feeling of anticipation, as if he needed to do something important. Not yet fully awake, enacting the dead habit of a half-decade, he'd left his bed, grabbed his phone and a shirt, and hurried down the hall to the lab.

But now he remembered that this could not be the thing he had to do today. What was it then? Why had he felt he needed to be here? He let go of the doorframe and went in, walking around the room aimlessly, the way he used to do in that last year before he gave it up, touching the instruments, gliding his hands over dials and screens. He opened drawers and pulled out tools to turn them over in his palm, feeling their texture and their weight. Then, not having used them, he put them carefully back. These, he knew, were the gestures of a man in mourning, as if he were mulling over the possessions of a dead lover. He'd told himself when he stopped coming here that it was a good thing—he was finally free of the obsession—but he now knew there was no joy to be found in this kind of freedom, only an impulse to return again and again to the grave of his dead theory.

Was it freedom or a prison? he wondered. Realizing the thought came from Alex's words during their dance the previous night, he cut it off. He shouldn't have gotten himself caught up in a conversation with that girl. He certainly shouldn't be worrying about it now.

There was a ringing and Charlie startled, disoriented and with a screwdriver still in his hand. Then, recognizing the sound, he dropped the tool back into its drawer and fished his phone out of his pocket. "Yes?"

"Charlie? It's Richard. You left so early last night. What happened? I was waiting until you finished dancing and suddenly you were gone. Simone wanted to talk to you, too, and, man, was she annoyed she couldn't find you. Don't even get me started on David. You've got to stop leaving the shoots early."

"I needed to clear my head," Charlie said. "I went for a ride."

"You and that damned bike. Anyway, you need to make Alex use whatever she's got for her concerto. No more of this writing-the-music-over-again thing. Who knows how long that'll take? She needs to hire a soloist now. Apparently, no one's been good enough for her so far. How long can this take?"

"I'll look into it."

Richard was going on. "And David says he tried to get her drunk last night and nothing! No big blowup, no crazy dancing, so that's a bust. He's thinking instead to lean into the Brandy storyline—you know, have her perform at the dinner thing. I know, I know, you hate her, but she's got fans. I really think we should sign her."

"You think she'll sell?"

"My gut says yes."

"Fine, let her perform at the dinner and we'll see," Charlie said. The idea of signing Brandy did irk him, but he agreed partly to get Richard off the phone and partly because EmerSound's profits were still hurting, and despite the publicity the show had generated, they'd yet to see much profit. Charlie, having never had the knack or patience to untangle the tastes of the lowest common denominator himself, had always depended on Richard's gut feelings—they were right roughly 65 percent of the time. "Just give me the talent," he used to tell Richard, his ironic use of the word *talent* lost on the man, "and I'll determine how much to spend on it." That way Charlie only had to deal with spreadsheets of data— numbers on the likelihood of music sales, merchandise, and ads. He crunched these numbers brilliantly, as he'd always done, and never had to think much beyond that. There were no principles to work out or run afoul of. No truth to seek or to fake. No new ideas to come up with. Nothing new at all.

Looking at the lab now, Charlie remembered how he liked to think his brain was divided into two processors: one to run the EmerSound world—its calculations, finances, and meetings; one to run his work in the lab—experiments, equations, and theories. He'd tried not to adulterate the lab processor with the mundane tasks of EmerSound, keeping the practicalities of the company separate.

But it hadn't worked. Maybe the size of the processor—or the space given to it—grew or shrank, not in proportion to its difficulty or his preference for it but in proportion to the amount of time it was running. What was that cliché? *Use it or lose it.* He remembered now, back in those early days, if he was too busy with EmerSound and went a month without doing his lab work and thinking about those kinds of problems or reading papers and books in physics and math, it took days to be able to think properly again; concepts he'd had a good grasp on turned murky somehow, the connections between ideas seemingly less dense, less far-reaching. It had been subtle but definitely present. But he'd also used his mind differently for the different tasks, hadn't he? Was that detail important?

The phone rang again and Charlie groaned, determined to ignore it, until he saw the name of the caller: *Glen Clarence, private investigator.* The possibility of information about Alex could not be ignored, especially given their conversations last night. She was clearly far from what she was pretending to be, and he hadn't even begun to properly consider all the things she'd said.

"You wouldn't believe it," Clarence yelled from the other end of the line. "The old man hasn't touched Alex's room. It's all pink lacy comforter and heart paintings on the walls, and knickknacks everywhere. Little girl things—teddy bears and dolls and books."

"And?" Charlie said.

"There were diaries, too. From when she was living there. And are you ready for this? I have them."

"He gave them to you?"

"Who?"

"Dennis Weiss."

"Uh, no. I didn't talk to him so much as take a look around, if you know what I mean."

"You mean you broke in and stole them."

"You could call it that. I call it borrowing."

"I didn't hire you to go steal things from people."

"This is how it's done, boss. You want damning info you gotta be willing to stretch your principles, you know? Besides, it ain't like there's state secrets in them. They're mostly the rantings of a little girl."

Charlie stilled. "You've already read them?"

"Just the beginning parts really. I think she might be crazy. She makes up stuff and believes it, you know? But if you want, I could put them back."

Charlie dropped his head and pressed his forehead against a wall. Clarence was right. He had to read the diaries if he wanted ammunition against Alex. No, not ammunition—what a strange word to use. He just needed some more information. Did that excuse his reading of her private thoughts from stolen diaries? He needed time to think, to consider. "Just hang onto them," he told Clarence, "but don't read any more. I may want them eventually."

Charlie remained in the lab, leaning against the wall, for many minutes after the phone had gone dead, thinking about the lifeless tundra of his old work. His mind was like that, too—frozen over—except the ice that kept him together was melting, slowly dripping away under the heat of some unchecked emotion. He was headed for disaster and it was *her* fault; Alex had done this to him. Perhaps *ammunition* was the right word after all. She may have seemed to understand him last night, but he couldn't let himself get tangled up with her. He couldn't let her play him. She'd already driven him back to this torture chamber of a lab, and if he let her, she'd destroy him, because destruction was inevitable in this scenario—the only question was which one of them would it be: Charlie or Alex. And he wasn't going down.

Decision made, he took a few minutes to choose a course of action, then pressed the button on the wall-mounted intercom. When Murdoch came on the line, Charlie told him: "Please confirm with Jennifer that in Alex's contract the soloist isn't technically part of the orchestra. Then let David know right away that he should hire the soloist. It can be anyone he wants who can generate large audiences for the show."

There was a pause from Murdoch before his terse, "Yes."

Charlie felt the impulse to explain that it was only self-defense, that he needed to distract Alex—and they'd see how much energy she had left to ask him about his theory or tell him he was in prison once she had to deal with whatever monstrosity of a musician David hired. But he didn't explain. He merely jabbed the button to disable the intercom and strode out of the lab, pressing in the code to seal off the room without glancing inside again. The door shut with a low thump and the sound reverberated down the empty corridor, hollow and final. He waited an instant longer to hear the click of the electronic locking mechanism, then turned and walked away.

CHAPTER XXIII

lex's weekend was a miserable duo of failures. First, she'd woken up with a mild hangover the morning after the gala. Then, she'd tried working on the final movement of her concerto, taping sheets of staff paper to the wall in her room—her favorite way to compose—but the pages remained blank, even after the many hours she stood staring at them. She groped for some new, fitting idea, but everything she came up with was wrong, and the explanation for it eluded her. It was like being stuck in some surrealist painting where the path looked to be rising but ended up back at its own beginning. It was horrifying to her both in abstract drawing and in real life. Those paths led to nowhere and no one, dooming you to repeat the same actions over and over again without result.

She also wanted to convince Charlie to let her remain at Martin Hall, but he'd locked himself in his library office and would not see her. What was Charlie's problem? Every time she thought she was making progress he'd swing to a new mood; at the gala he'd gone from cold and a bit hostile to pretending interest in her. But he'd still disappeared early. It was just like the wedding. At a loss, she appealed to Murdoch for help in changing Charlie's mind about the hall, but he shook his head sadly and told her that once Charlie made a decision, it was final.

So by the time Alex arrived at Bernak Hall on Monday morning for her first rehearsal, she was seething, and David kept prodding her to smile more. "No one wants to watch a morose princess," he told her, which only added to her annoyance. But she pasted on a grin for the cameras as she walked into Bernak.

Her path took her down a luxuriously carpeted center aisle, past rows and rows of velvet-lined seats with intricately carved wooden armrests. So much money and design had gone into these details, but no thought had gone into the acoustics, and Alex could hear it even now. The orchestra, a group of thirty people, was already seated in chairs on stage, and some had begun to play, tuning their instruments or warming up with exercises. The sound would be—and should be—a cacophonous mess in any other hall, but here, through the back half of the room, the sounds were so muted and thin that Alex felt like she needed to dial up the volume. The place was all pomp and circumstance, no substance. Fitting for EmerSound, actually, if not for Charlie himself.

Once on stage, she placed her score and baton on the conductor's podium and dropped her bag on the ground.

"Welcome," she said, and waited until the sounds of instruments had died away and heads turned to her. "I hope you all read my email with instructions about the concerto and what I'm looking for. You'll have the new version of the final movement by the time we're ready for it in a few weeks. I haven't hired a soloist yet, but that will be taken care of, too, by the time we're ready.

This morning, I'd like to dive straight into the first movement, and we can get to know each other through the music. Anyone have a question?"

No one did, so she raised her baton and the musicians raised their instruments, but as soon as she moved her arm to give them the beat, from somewhere offstage David yelled, "Hang on!"

Alex sighed and waited silently—he'd continue whether acknowledged or not.

He appeared in front of her. "What the hell was that?"

"What do you mean?"

"Why are you acting so weirdly? Be yourself."

Alex wanted to laugh in his face. In the tumult of anger over the hall, she'd forgotten her act. But she didn't laugh. She merely nodded at him and tried to recapture her sense of Brandy. It was like pulling on an itchy sweater in too-hot weather, and she hated it, but she did it. *I can do anything if it's for the* Red Concerto, she told herself.

She grinned, and when David moved away and called action, she said, "Okay, you guys, like, let's get ready to play!" She couldn't bring herself to look at any of the musicians' faces, though. *I can do anything for the* Red Concerto, she repeated silently, then she raised the baton again. This time, a door clattered loudly behind her.

"Sorry! Are we late?" someone called from the back of the hall.

Alex whirled around. Seven people—three men and four women, all in their twenties—had entered the hall, with an assortment of stringed instruments. She thought the group had gotten their rehearsal time wrong, but they kept walking toward the stage, unperturbed, and David, now in a seat in the frontmost row, smiled deviously at her.

"What's going on?" she asked him.

He affected an innocent expression. "What's going on with what?"

"Who are these people?"

"Just some actors I hired for the show. Don't worry, they're not going to play their instruments or anything. They'll just sit with the orchestra and pretend. I need them to make the show interesting."

She stared at him, wanting to shout and deny and throw the actors out. But she couldn't—it was a clever ploy around her contract stipulations. The actors weren't technically part of the orchestra if they weren't playing. And she recognized them all—David's people, the ones she'd auditioned and rejected. This had been his plan all along. She might have underestimated him. "Fine," she said.

Once the actors had taken their places and pulled out their instruments, and once the cameras were rolling again, Alex smiled apologetically at the orchestra, still not really looking at the faces of her own musicians, then raised her baton. "From the beginning of movement one, please."

The orchestra played through four measures, all of fifteen seconds, before David shouted, "Cut!"

Alex paused, baton in the air, and the music died. "Yes?" she asked, keeping her voice flat, though she wanted to scream.

"Take a small step to your right so the light is better," he said.

She did, then started the orchestra playing, but again, a few minutes later David interrupted. "You need to turn your face to camera three every once in a while—the one to your left behind the big violins."

"The violas, you mean," she said, through gritted teeth. "Alright."

The third time he intervened, Alex lost her temper. "I cannot have you interrupting me every two minutes. Tell me everything you need from me and then stay quiet," she said, then added a calmer "Please."

David smiled and raised his arms, palms open by his ears in a "hands-off" motion. "Nothing else. Carry on." The smile didn't fit, as if he were happy that she was upset. First, Charlie at the gala and now David? Was she being paranoid? She pushed it all aside. It was a distraction she didn't need.

David didn't interrupt again, but they had to stop the music several times anyway because of the actors: a violinist, whose pretend-bowing was particularly spastic and not at all genuine, got his bow tangled up with the real musician sitting next to him; then, a few minutes later, a fake cellist dropped his instrument with a loud clang; and throughout the day, the two planted viola players kept chatting loudly. Alex actually had to separate them as if they were children. The whole thing was like being in a group therapy session at the Greene Institute. Maybe worse—because at least the therapy patients couldn't help their tics and spasms and outbursts.

Alex persisted. It had to get better as they all got used to it.

But every day in the weeks that followed, it was the same. Cameras with her in the morning; David again interrupting her constantly during the rehearsals, no matter what she said to him; the actors disrupting the music; and Alex getting more and more frustrated. All of it meant that not only were they not making progress on the music, but Alex couldn't keep in character, and David would make her wait in the hall after all the musicians—but not the actors—had gone home, saying he needed more interesting footage of her: "What happened to the fun girl who danced with Brandy at the club? The one who loves to talk about her hair? The conducting stuff is boring." Then she'd have to get into character for video diaries and scenes where the actors played out what could only be scripted love triangles.

The real musicians, too, were frazzled and distracted. Several weeks into rehearsals, Alex still couldn't see the fierce burst of bright reds that a properly performed first movement should create. Even accounting for Bernak Hall's terrible acoustics, the orchestra had barely made progress, and Alex went from frustration to anger.

So when David approached her at the end of rehearsal on a Friday afternoon as she was still on the stage making notes on her manuscript, she held up one hand and shook her head. "I won't stay late today. And next week, either you don't interrupt me or I'll make sure you can't be here at all anymore. We'll never be ready at this rate." She'd said it more loudly than she should have, and a couple of the musicians turned to watch as they filed down the stairs and off the stage.

"Relax," David said. "Jesus, you're worked up. I think it's going fine."

"It is not going fine," Alex said, stacking her manuscript pages together maybe a little too violently. But only the actors were left on stage, and they were standing together in a group, chatting loudly, so it didn't matter.

"Well, you'd better find a way to deal with it. Especially since I just hired the soloist."

"What do you mean, *you* hired a soloist?" Alex asked, dread knotting in her gut and her hand frozen in the act of shoving her papers into her backpack.

David shrugged. "A soloist is not technically part of the orchestra, or so I'm told."

"And who told you that?"

"Jennifer Barnes. She's got a law degree, you know. Though I think it was Charlie's idea. You were just taking too damn long to decide. Things in this business move fast." He snapped his fingers twice. "Don't worry. The guy can play violin. He said your piece would be no problem for him."

Alex looked away from David and concentrated on zipping her bag closed. Maybe it wasn't so bad. Maybe the guy could actually play. "Does he have a name?"

"Oh, I think we'll wait until next week when he gets here to tell you that part." The sly smile was back.

"You're going to completely destroy my music," Alex said, unable to rein herself in—she'd had it with David. "I can't work like this. If it continues, I'll quit." She meant it, she realized.

"Hey, I've got an idea, let's do a video diary right now," David said, without apparent relevance.

"What are you talking about?" Alex almost screamed it.

"You're so worked up, it'll be great. People are going to love your spunk."

"I'm not a little dog doing tricks."

He lifted his hands in surrender—a gesture Alex was beginning to detest. "That's good enough for now," he said.

She wanted to kick herself. The cameras were still running, of course, but she barely registered them anymore, they were so ubiquitous. And David had been purposefully riling her up. She hadn't been paranoid before—this was his job. Hadn't he complained that she was too boring? He just might pose the most danger to her, not only because he had the cameras rolling constantly but because he wanted her unguarded and emotional.

She forced a bland smile, slung her backpack on, and walked away from him, slowly off the stage and down the hall toward the exit.

"See you tomorrow night at the dinner party, honey!" he yelled after her.

The hall had mostly emptied of the real musicians, and with the lights dimmed everywhere but on stage, Alex almost didn't recognize Willem Salk waving at her by the back row and was about to stomp past him when his very unique silhouette—specifically his mass of curly hair and the cello strapped to his back—caught her attention. She could see better as she neared and returned his smile.

"Some of us are going out to this jazz bar downtown tonight," he said. "Want to go? I wasn't eavesdropping but I heard the thing about the soloist—you guys were kind of loud—and I thought it might make you feel better to go out. You know, blow off some steam."

Willem was younger than her by a few years and had a fiery, intense glance that matched the way he played music. Their friendship, her best one of the few she'd made among the musicians in her orchestra, was initially triggered by their mutual acquaintance with Lawrence Berg and sealed by their passion for music. But she had to be careful. "I can't. I have a bunch of work to do."

Willem's shoulders slumped a little in disappointment and it made her wish she had time to go out with them. But already, Willem knew too much about her, and he'd eventually want her stories and her history—things friends wanted that she could never give. But, not wanting to alienate him either, she grasped for another topic. Her eyes caught on his cello. "Have you been bringing a different cello to rehearsals?" she asked. "I thought it sounded different this week."

He laughed, then looked at her ruefully. "Yeah… I was worried—the other one's an antique, on loan from Lawrence. With all the chaos and the cameras and so many extra people, I was worried it would get stolen or damaged. That's why I have multiple cellos. Different cellos for different purposes, you know? I hope you're not offended."

"No, I understand…" Different instruments for different rehearsals. And she'd always thought of music halls as instruments. "But it gives me an idea."

"Yeah?"

"Do you think the orchestra members would be willing to go to extra rehearsals in the afternoon at Martin Hall? If I paid them for it?" She'd have to work it out, but she could use the money from the sale of the coffee stand to begin with, at least.

One of the doors opened, letting in a blast of bright light from the anteroom. "Hey, Willem, you coming?" a woman called in.

"In a minute, Ellise," Willem called back, then turned to Alex. "Martin Hall is amazing. I don't think anyone would mind doing that—any serious musician would follow you into hell to play this piece. It's…it's really a once-in-a-lifetime opportunity. And just think, we haven't even done it with a soloist yet. And if you're making the fourth movement even better…"

"Thank you," she said, smiling. This is what she liked about Willem, his openness, his willingness to be affected by the music and to show it. She could always know what someone was about from the way they responded to her music. Her thoughts tried to skitter to Charlie and his response to music, but she caught them and wrestled them back. No more thoughts of Charlie.

CHAPTER XXIV

Alex stared at the black silk dress Grace had left on her bed for tonight's dinner party. A dress she'd refused to wear because of the deep V cut into the front, situated exactly to expose a scar from heart surgery. They argued about it.

"David said...he wanted..." Grace had stammered, but even she wasn't callous enough to admit outright that a display of such scars was the point of the dress. Instead, she went off and found a piece of black lace—intricate enough to hide the details of anything underneath it, while giving the impression of baring naked skin. In exchange, Alex agreed to leave the gloves off until after dinner.

Now the dress lay there, and even though it was flowing and delicate and beautiful, all Alex could see was an empty shell, as if the woman who'd been wearing it had melted into the bed and vanished, leaving behind only that shadow of a dress. Alex was the ghost who'd replace the woman, an ideal media princess and vapid wife. A persona she was having more and more trouble forcing on herself. *I'm just acting*, she told herself, *which I always do*—and which she was beginning to see she hated. The more time she spent on her music, the less able she was to be anyone but herself, and yet, somehow, she still couldn't finish her concerto. Why? Why now, when she almost had what she wanted, was she failing herself like this?

She thought of the abysmal weeks of rehearsal, Bernak Hall's lackluster acoustics, and the prospect of a terrible soloist, and felt a weight descending on her—a heaviness that foretold failure, if not something worse, and had her considering if it was time to retrieve the papers for her new identity from her safe deposit box and disappear. No, not yet, she thought. It's not that bad yet. Besides, tonight's party was here, at Charlie's place, and it would be easy to sneak back to her room if she needed to. So she put on the dress and the straitjacket of her fake persona and forced herself out of her room, just as the din of arriving guests began.

David found her immediately—in the hallway, a few steps from her room. "Come on," he said. "I need a shot with you and Charlie."

Charlie was alone in the living room, leaning by the fireplace opposite the entertainment center, drink in hand, his tall form accentuated by the cut of his slim jeans and navy shirt. His eyes flickered down her body as she approached. David walked right up to him, but Alex, unnerved by that glance, stopped to lean against a high-backed chair a little way from them.

David looked back at her and sighed. "Come over here."

She moved to stand behind and to the right of David, still keeping her distance from Charlie. David shook his head, annoyed, but he let it go.

Instead, he said, "I need some PDA from you two. We'll do it right here, by the fireplace. You'll start and the cameras will come in like they've caught you in the act."

"What are you talking about?" Charlie asked, voice and expression inscrutable.

"You know, public display of affection," David said. "Hold hands, kiss, that kind of thing."

"No," Charlie said, and the word fell like a stone, heavy and final.

Strange, Alex thought, since Charlie'd had no compunction about doing it before. But then she was ambivalent herself, simultaneously disappointed and relieved by his refusal.

David sighed, running a hand through already disheveled hair. "Look, people really like you guys as a couple but they're starting to wonder if it's fake. There are way too many posts about it. Let them see some affection."

"To hell with the people," Charlie said. "I don't do public displays of anything."

This was stranger still. Alex had come to see that most of his actions in public were calculated for effect—the limousine, the gala, the whole show itself.

David looked to Alex, maybe to appeal for help, but whatever he saw on her face made him reconsider and he rolled his eyes. "Just think about it, Charlie."

"It's final." Charlie walked away, out of the room. He hadn't spoken to Alex at all.

"Stay here," David told Alex, and left her standing in the living room alone.

The hubbub in the apartment was increasing as more guests arrived. Alex had no idea how many people were coming and was already considering sneaking back to her room before anyone noticed her when Willem peeked in from the hallway and, seeing her, came in.

Alex was surprised and delighted to see an actual friend here. The actors from the orchestra were always at these things, but the real musicians were never invited. And in his standard khaki pants and blue button-down shirt, Willem was refreshingly normal. "What are you doing here?" she asked.

"What, you mean you didn't think I'd rate with all the B-list celebrities on the guest list?" Willem asked, laughing. "Well, you're right, I didn't. Lawrence brought me as his plus one. I kind of made him."

"Lawrence is here?"

"Somewhere. Anyway…" He pulled out his phone from a back pocket. "I needed to see you, because I found out who David hired to be the soloist."

She didn't like the tone of his voice—the usual color was light orange, but it had turned a sort of sour hue. "Tell me," she said.

"I'll show you." He kept talking as he tapped his phone to bring up whatever it was he wanted her to see. "It's a guy named Michael Chap, and he's been posting videos for a while—maybe five years?—and he's got almost a hundred thousand followers. His first posts aren't so bad, he talks about violin technique and life after music conservatory, that kind of thing. I mean, he's trained and he can play, but the more recent stuff… I don't know. Here, I've bookmarked a few for you to see."

They huddled together by the fireplace, backs to the door of the living room, to watch a series of five-minute videos, which consisted exclusively of Michael Chap, young and unremarkable-looking, pointing out flaws with other violin players—people of all ages who'd posted their own videos of recitals, or public performances, or just themselves playing in their bedrooms. Alex didn't have a problem judging other people's—or her own—performances. But Michael Chap had a cutting style that wasn't exactly wit, and his focus was on things mostly not relevant to music at all, like what the performers were wearing ("Oh my God, can you believe those pants? Like, is he waiting for a flood or what?"), or how they were standing ("This girl stands like a drunk duck."), or their appearance ("Dude, put on some makeup or use a filter. Don't make us have to look at you like that!"), and even in one instance someone's bedspread in the background ("What the hell is that pattern, anyway? That is a lot of flowers. Looks like his mom's garden threw up all over his room.").

And his followers loved it—their comments echoing the caustic and pointless ridicule. But Willem was also right that Michael had violin training. His technical proficiency was evident in the first few videos, though without the kind of artistry Alex wanted in a soloist. But he hadn't played in a video for almost four years, so he may not have kept up even his technical skills.

"This isn't going to work," Alex said, mumbling a bit to herself.

Willem put his phone away. "What are you going to do?"

"I don't know. I—"

"Brandy is here!" David, more chipper than Alex had ever seen him, strode into the living room, camera crew and Brandy, in sequined red skirt and tube top, in tow.

Alex grinned and exchanged her usual hug, air kiss, and inanities with her so-called best friend, then David led the girl off to meet some other guests, switching his—and the camera's—attention to Brandy exclusively.

"Thank God that's over." Alex relaxed onto the couch. Then, while looking at the entertainment center, she said, "I never noticed how many speakers are in here. I wonder how it sounds."

Willem sat in a chair next to her. "You're so different from the footage they edit for the show," he said with an edge to his voice she couldn't quite classify.

She laughed in spite of it. "You watch the show?"

"Of course," he said, then, understanding, his eyes widened, and he leaned toward her. "You mean you don't?"

"I don't."

"How can you stand not to know what they're doing? The whole show is about you!"

"No, it's about a fictional character. You know I'm mostly acting on camera."

"But everyone else thinks it's real. And you don't even know how they're showing you to the world?" he said. "You come off…I don't know…dumb, unlikeable, untalented. And not just from the way you act but the way they edit the scenes. It's maddening. I thought you knew at least." He was furious, dark eyes blazing and voice harsh.

"I don't really care what the world thinks of me," she said, though it wasn't quite true—she cared about the information she needed to control, and in that sense, it was better they think her untalented and unlikeable, because then they'd leave her alone.

His eyes narrowed. "It's true what they say, isn't it, about the marriage being a publicity ploy? You and Charlie aren't in love at all. Some of the other musicians and I have been wondering."

"I can't talk about it."

Willem's eyes held hers and they had a look of the unfinished, as if he wanted to say more, but he glanced away and said only, "Alright. But I don't like it. Not any of it."

∫ ℓ

Dinner was a sit-down affair at the long white table in the dining room, with Alex at one end, Charlie at the other, and the slew of celebrities—none of whom Alex recognized—between them. Willem was placed at a table set up in the kitchen with crew and other non-celebrities, so after David pointed Alex to her place, no one paid any attention to her, the guests too wrapped up in their own importance and celebrity. The cameras and producers focused on Brandy and Charlie.

Charlie sat with his face hard, frown kept in check for the benefit of the guests and cameras, and posture unforgiving—reminiscent of his attitude at the gala—and Simone and Brandy flanked him on either side. Despite herself, Alex felt a stab of annoyance whenever Simone leaned over to whisper something to him or whenever Brandy touched him, which was often. And even though David constantly gestured and directed him to engage, Charlie didn't react to the women except to nod and give terse answers.

It was strange to see these other people in the penthouse, in this setting, with their pretense at colorful gaiety among the white austerity of Charlie's home, and it struck Alex that what he'd constructed here was a cell, but was it a jail cell forced on him, or was it a self-imposed monk's cell? Was there a difference? Either one was a dissociation from life, severing him from the joy of living. She knew that firsthand.

Before she'd learned how to ignore her sound visions in her late teens, Alex had been given medication to control them—but the drugs had been too strong, eliminating her sound vision completely, and she'd felt like she'd lost a limb or become blind. What was it like for Charlie, giving up his theory? Alex had at least maintained music as her solace during that dark time, studying it and listening to it, even if it had lost a vital dimension. What would she have done if she hadn't had that to pull her through, to remind her there was something beautiful and worthwhile to strive for? Would she have ended up like Charlie, bereft and tormented?

That's when the new melody insinuated itself and began insisting on attention. It was only in her mind, she knew, but she heard it as though the cello were right next to her, playing a desolate, somber melody, tinged with the same blue as Charlie's voice. She was intoxicated, her thoughts completely taken over, and she barely noticed the rest of dinner—except when, during dessert, she saw Charlie smile ever so slightly as Lawrence came up behind him to say something, and a violin joined the cello in counterpoint, a new variation on the melody, a lighter happier sound, all yellows and oranges on top of the blues of the cello. Alex wanted to close her eyes and lean back in her seat, to concentrate on the light and dark tones of the two instruments playing against each other, to savor the taste of this new theme, to see what it would grow into.

No, she couldn't be that person now—she had to be what they expected here. But the Brandy persona, somehow too thin and substance-less, wouldn't come. Simone's demeanor, from the schooled expression of boredom and flat eyes to the taut uncomfortable posture and occasional empty smile, was less demanding, and Alex squeezed herself into a copy of it, all while the persistent sounds and sights of her new piece shrouded her awareness.

Then dinner was over and all the guests were hustled to the ballroom, which was set up for Brandy's performance, a stage at one end where the band was already waiting and a handful of tall cocktail tables throughout. Again, David and one of the cameras spent a perfunctory few moments with Alex, leading her to one of the tables in the front, through the crowded, noisy room—even more people had arrived just for Brandy's performance—but for once Alex wasn't bothered by the chaos. She stood at her table, leaning forward with her arms on the table, relaxed, still floating on her melody, buffered by it from everything around her.

Charlie was again placed far away from her, across the room at another table, though he stood back, closer to the wall than the table, another drink in hand. Without warning, his head snapped toward Alex and his eyes changed from their tortured boredom to something fierce. Alex's table rattled, confusing her, until she understood that her hands were shaking as they gripped the edge. She let go but then didn't know where to put her hands, or what to do, only that she couldn't look away from him. He seemed to know it, too, smiling in that way he had of narrowed eyes and slightly curving lips—and leaning back against the wall, one hand in his pocket, the other bringing his glass to his lips for a lingering sip. The gesture highlighted the width of his shoulders and triggered the memory of his lips hovering at her ear, whispering, "I like to feel some things," and of that vicious scar down his torso, under his clothes.

The music in Alex's head stopped. The melody that had haunted her for hours just…disappeared, and she wanted to scream, because now, when she needed a diversion, when she would take anything to dilute Charlie's power and release her from his gaze, she had only silence in her mind.

Then, his eyes flashed and he turned away, and Alex became aware of Simone standing next to her.

"What do you think of Brandy performing tonight?" Simone asked, without preamble.

Alex clenched and unclenched her hands, trying to siphon her emotions into the movement so she could regain the context of the evening and parse Simone's words—and stop herself from remembering that this woman was sleeping with Charlie. David had appeared again with a cameraman and did his finger twirling gesture to indicate the camera was rolling.

"Oh," Alex said. "Um, yeah, it's…um…like, I'm so happy for Brandy…right?"

Simone lifted an eyebrow and smiled—a cunning, unhappy expression.

Alex overcompensated for her lackluster Brandy imperson-ation and ended up grinning too widely, almost maniacally. "I mean, she's, like, wanted this for so long, you know, like, to be noticed and stuff?"

"So you don't mind that she's stealing your thunder tonight?" Simone asked, pouting as if to empathize with a terrible situation.

Don't look at Charlie again. "Oh, like, no way. She's totally my bestie, you know? We, like, share everything."

"Not really everything? Though she would probably love that."

Alex caught the meaning and knew she was supposed to be jealous—and was, but not because she believed Charlie was interested in Brandy, or even because he was sleeping with Simone. She groped for the reason and flinched at her own answer: It was because Brandy and Simone could both try to seduce Charlie, could have an actual relationship with him, maybe even be themselves with him, whereas Alex could not. She swallowed hard, tried to grin again, and knew she'd failed to hide her dismay, because she could see Simone's satisfaction at having hit her target.

CHAPTER XXV

Charlie wasn't sure how many drinks he'd had since the dinner party started, but he wasn't going to be able to get through Brandy's performance without another one. He deposited his empty glass on the table reserved for him, signaled to one of the waitstaff for another drink, then slouched back against the ballroom wall again. A few yards away, Murdoch and the minions he'd hired for the evening headed off several people who tried to approach his table—not that anyone could have a real conversation above the echoing din in the room. Still, no one even tried. This was the great advantage of Charlie's position: he was untouchable. Well, mostly anyway. The dinner had been a dismal affair, but whiskey was helping—another one appeared in front of him—and soon he'd be back to that state of indifference where nothing touched him and nothing mattered.

For now, he returned to observing Alex, as he had surreptitiously done most of the night. The dress riveted him, from the V that plunged down between her breasts almost to her navel and the lace underscoring her naked skin beneath, to the juxtaposition of the ashy black fabric against her paleness. It gave her an ethereal look, as if she didn't belong here in this setting. Or in his life. Or almost even on earth. He'd taken a special pleasure in rattling her from across the room—she'd been watching him, also, a little too intently. He figured it was out of anger, because he'd heard of her reaction to the actors they'd forced into her orchestra and to the prospect of a soloist she hadn't hired. Then someone blocked his view.

Here we go again. Jennifer strode toward him—when had she arrived?—with David's unkempt form following close behind. Why did these two always accost him at parties just when he'd managed to relax a little?

"Turn your mic off," David said, cupping his hands around his mouth and leaning into Charlie's ear. "We need to talk to you."

Charlie sighed and reached behind him to the little black microphone transmitter box attached to his belt and felt around for the switch. He nodded when he'd clicked it to the off position.

David glanced around dramatically, as though searching for spies—who was going to be able to hear them in this racket, Charlie didn't know—and again used his hands to focus his voice. "Listen," he said, "if you don't want to be affectionate with Alex on camera, fine. I get it. People don't like to kiss and touch on screen or whatever. But we need something to make up for it. I'm thinking we could lean in harder to the love triangle, make everyone think you're cheating on Alex with Brandy."

Charlie grimaced at the thought of being with Brandy, but before he could refuse, Jennifer put her hand on his elbow and said something too low for Charlie to make out.

"What?" he asked, pointing to his ear.

"Did you read the financial reports I sent?" she repeated slowly, almost yelling. "The opening share price for EmerSound's IPO is now projected to be lower than before *Mrs. Music* aired."

"We've only aired a couple of episodes so far," Charlie said, projecting his own voice. "You can't predict where it will go from a few sets of preliminary numbers." It was technically true, and though he didn't really believe it himself, he had to allay Jennifer's fears somehow. *But why do you always have to do that*, a little voice whispered. *Because that's my job.*

"But we're bleeding cash," Jennifer yelled. "And we need to do something to stem it. It's like you don't care anymore. What's happened to you?"

That reached him—what had happened to him? EmerSound was sick, possibly terminal, and he still couldn't stomach doing what needed to be done.

David chimed in. "Come on, Charlie, all you need to do is spend some time flirting with Brandy. No PDA. Maybe we do a shoot where you guys meet up for lunch. Real easy. Just give the audience a teaser and I'll take it from there."

This was why he'd hired the man, Charlie reminded himself. David was an expert at generating audiences and riling them up, and this was a viable plan. He could do it, even if it made him queasy. "Fine," he told David. "Tell me when and where." Then he thought for a second, took out his phone, and motioned to Jennifer to read as he typed: *Take everything that's underperforming—below twenty percent of predictions—and stop all spending related to it. Marketing, upcoming concerts, merchandise, all of it. If that's not enough, go to thirty percent and so on, until we're breaking even. Put Richard on finding new sponsors for the show, too.*

Jennifer's eyes went distant for a minute—calculating how much Charlie's idea would help, probably, then nodded, saying, "It's risky, but it could work."

Appeased, and probably because it was too hard to carry on a conversation without losing their voices, Jennifer and David finally left Charlie to his drinking, and for a few minutes he had peace, if not quiet. Then the lights went down, and with much fanfare, Brandy came on stage to perform. The ballroom was not an acoustically appropriate place for so many people talking at once, much less for a rock band, complete with electric guitars and drum set, plus someone had dialed the gain on the speakers too high. The music pulsated relentlessly around the room on top of the conversations—no one had really come to hear Brandy; they'd come to be seen and to network. Charlie turned to Alex and felt a sort of macabre satisfaction when he saw her grimace and put her hands to her ears. Then he returned his attention to the show.

He tried to be objective about Brandy—the music was typical pop-style, and she was an average singer and pretty enough, if tacky. Though Charlie hadn't wanted her in the role of "wife" on *Mrs. Music*, she was exactly the kind of act that would sell and sell well. He'd sign her, and someone at EmerSound would take her in hand and make her a superstar, and she'd earn piles of money, keeping EmerSound afloat long enough to drive the share prices up. Afloat, like a rotting log in the middle of the ocean—something to hold on to, but not for long, and without the hope of forward progress or salvation.

He stopped short at that word—why think of salvation? EmerSound had always been this way, had always hired this kind of not-quite-talent. Maybe because tonight, no matter what he told himself, it turned his stomach. He kept picturing Brandy next to Alex—nothing specific from the show, just Brandy Starr singing side by side with Alex playing violin—a mental image he couldn't shake or make sense of, and which persisted until the music ended and the lights came up and someone called for his attention from across the room.

"Charlie! Over here," yelled Richard, looking a little ridiculous wearing a suit to a rock concert. But it helped that he was between the two stunning women, his right arm wrapped around Alex's waist and his left slung over Simone's shoulders, who Charlie noticed for the first time was wearing a black dress similar to Alex's. They came over, but since David and his cameras were still busy with Brandy, Charlie left his mic off, pushing off the wall to step forward and lean over the table in front of him, arms and elbows flush against the top. He glanced at Alex long enough to see that her face was blank—no anger, no discomfort, no nervousness, nothing. Maybe because with the end of the music, many people had left the ballroom and the place was at a more reasonable decibel level.

"What do you think of the show, Charlie?" Richard asked, releasing the women as the three of them reached the table. "I want to sign Brandy for a release this Christmas. It's soon, but it's possible."

We can do better, Charlie thought, but it was a fact that he never signed any artists with excessive talent or original ideas—never knowingly signed them, in any case. And there was no point in starting now. Mediocrity was what sold and what people wanted. Mediocrity was easy, safe. "Sign her," he said.

Richard beamed and clapped his hands. "You won't regret it. She's got her own fanbase and she's been received really well by the audience whenever she's on *Mrs. Music*. Best of all, she'll do anything. We can change her looks, her music, her lifestyle—whatever we need. She's ours to groom. She's great."

"She's not great," Charlie said and, looking at Alex, added, "But Brandy *is* perfect for EmerSound."

Alex's face betrayed only a watchful interest, but it was as if she were seeing something beyond what was being said.

One of the waitstaff brought glasses of wine for them, and they fell silent while the man placed the drinks on the table one by one, then left.

Simone cleared her throat. "The cameras are coming," she said, glancing meaningfully over Charlie's shoulder. Charlie straightened and switched his microphone on. When David and the cameras reached them and set up their boom microphone over the table, Simone smiled sweetly and said, "So, Alex, I hear you're finally getting a soloist."

"That's what they tell me." Alex gripped the stem of a wineglass and held it on the table without drinking. Her gloves—made of a black silk that reached up to her elbows—gleamed with the movement.

"Alex…" David said, warning in his voice.

Her eyes flicked to him, then went blank, and she grinned, blinking several times. "Yeah, like, we totally hired Michael Chap for the solo part."

"Oh," Simone said, genuine surprise on her face. Charlie understood why—Alex wasn't supposed to know who it was yet.

"Isn't he really famous online?" Simone asked. "Does all those videos of himself playing."

"Totally," Alex said and lowered her gaze to her wineglass, which she was now spinning with the thumb and forefinger of one hand. But Charlie saw a spark of anger pass through her expression and it made him want to look away, too. No, it made him want to leave. *Coward,* he chided himself. *You can't run away from consequences of your own decisions.*

Simone, voice now smooth and saccharine, said, "Are you going to make him play a regular violin, or let him do his electric thing?"

"Electric violin sounds intriguing," Charlie said and added, for the benefit of the cameras, "Don't you think so, Alex, my darling?"

Alex's eyes snapped to him, an icy expression solidifying on her face, and he forced a smile, then picked up the full glass of wine in front of him and swallowed three long gulps. He barely tasted it.

"Hi-hi!" Brandy said, teetering up to the table. She gave Charlie a particularly lascivious smile, which he returned without flinching at the shrillness in her voice, though his smile didn't quite have the same degree of innuendo.

Brandy went on. "Were you guys, like, talking about Michael Chap? He's so awesome!"

"He's going to be the soloist for Alex's little orchestra," Simone said.

Brandy entwined her arm with Simone's and giggled. "Oh my God, that's, like, so great. His last video got like a million views or something, and he's all, like, making fun of this one guy who plays the violin, because he's, like, really awkward and stuff."

Her voice continued to grate on Charlie, and he swallowed back a wave of distaste at the prospect of flirting with her. And then he saw it—the way Brandy's sentences all ended by pitching upward, as if asking a question, the particular cadence of the speech, even the words—Alex had been doing an almost exact impression of it since the very first taping of the show. He'd done this to her. He'd turned her into Brandy. Something hard and heavy settled in his gut, but he swallowed and worked to eye Brandy as if he were interested in her. She noticed and grinned at him again.

"We were just discussing if Michael should play the electric violin for the concerto," Richard said. "What do you think, Brandy?"

The girl clapped her hands enthusiastically. "Oh yay! That would be so cool. Like, make it less old-people-y and stuff?"

"Exactly," Richard said.

This time, Charlie could not make himself look for Alex's reaction.

"Cut," David said. "Thanks, everyone." Then to Brandy, he added, "It's time for your video diary, honey. And I have something to tell you." Then he led her—and the cameras—off toward the back of the room.

Charlie gulped his wine until the glass was empty, then slammed it down on the table. "I'll be back. Maybe."

As he pushed his way through the crowd to the door out of the ballroom, he caught a glimpse of Brandy cooing to the camera about being signed to EmerSound. Well, why not? She'd save the company—for a little while, anyway. This is what Charlie had always done. They had a roster full of people exactly like Brandy. What was one more? What did it matter? What did anything matter?

CHAPTER XXVI

Finally, near midnight, David sent the camera crew home, and taping for *Mrs. Music* ended. The guests, too, were mostly gone—but Willem had lingered and asked Alex to meet him and Lawrence in the library when she was free. Alex was exhausted and needed time to rest and time to consider Charlie's actions and reactions tonight, certain that they were a key to him, and maybe to changing his mind about Bernak and Chap. But Willem had said it was important, so she'd accepted.

She'd never ventured into the library because it was Charlie's office, and usually the desk was cluttered with files and papers. Tonight, though, the room had been cleared for the party, and she found Willem and Lawrence sitting together on the couch. They both stood up when she came in.

"Have you managed to give David the slip, then?" Lawrence asked.

"They're done taping," she said.

"Marvelous. Then I can stop hiding."

This made Alex and Willem both laugh, though Willem sobered quickly. "Have you figured out what to do about Michael Chap? I mean, is there anything you can do?"

She thought of Charlie's expressions of distaste throughout the night whenever Brandy was involved—when she'd sung, when she'd spoken, when Richard had mentioned signing her. Each reaction was fleeting, but taken together they meant something. Charlie did know good music and he did care, whether he admitted it or not. Maybe if she could just show him Chap's videos, he'd recognize the unsuitability and reconsider. "Maybe if I talk to Charlie?"

"I was hoping to speak with you about him, actually," Lawrence said and gestured to the sitting area. "Come sit with me for a moment, won't you?"

She nodded, and Willem clapped his hands together once in a gesture of finality. "And that's my cue to go home."

They said their goodbyes, and after he left Alex sat down on the couch, enjoying the silence that had fallen throughout the apartment. She relaxed a little.

"You asked me a while back about Charlie's past—do you remember?" Lawrence said, taking a chair opposite Alex. "About why he quit his graduate work."

"I remember."

"Have you figured out anything else about him since then? Had any of your questions answered?"

She shook her head. "I only have more questions now. I don't think he really wanted to quit, but it seems like he got pushed out. And I don't understand why he hasn't gone back to it now that he has all this. Surely he can afford to fund it himself."

"That was his plan," Lawrence said with a slight and approving smile. "He has a lab—right here in the penthouse. He built it so he could continue the work."

"Really?" she asked, leaning forward. Maybe Charlie hadn't given up on himself.

But Lawrence stood up and started to pace silently, his hands clasped behind his back, much the way he did when he was lecturing and trying to formulate a complex idea in simple terms. Even his accent grew a little thicker the way it did when he taught. "Charlie was different when he built the lab. No, no, it was before that—when he was at university—he was...less guarded, I suppose, more hopeful. I don't quite know how to explain it. He was angry as hell when he quit Asher, but the idea was to make loads of money and then retire and return to the theory. That way, he could work on his science without being chained to grants and institutions—as you suggested.

"And for a while he did do that work. He had the lab and it was going rather well, I think. But when it came time to retire from EmerSound—I think he could've done it several years ago—he wouldn't. At first he said it was too early. Then he said it was too late. And now this show—your show—is supposed to get the company to the right place, whatever that is, so that he can retire."

"So his continuing the work depends on me?" she asked. Would she have to choose between Charlie's work and her own?

Lawrence stopped pacing to study her, his own face inscrutable, only his eyes narrowing. "I don't truly know. It could be just another way to put off something he doesn't think he can do anymore.... But I've been thinking—perhaps you're the one to get through to him. If you can really understand his work, that is. It's quite difficult."

He was probing her, she realized—either because he genuinely didn't know if she could understand, or he did know and was gauging her willingness to admit to it. Could she admit this to him?

Alex's final violin teacher, Gustav, had told her, the very last time she'd seen him, that he couldn't really teach her any more in technique or musicality. "You're a fully formed artist now," he'd said. "But in order to make music with the kind of passion that will connect with people, you have to learn to trust them. If you want someone to be open to your art, you must be open to them. Let them see *you*." Gustav had been almost eighty years old then. A man with a shock of white hair and a gentle, serious manner, who approached his work as if it were sacred. Nothing mattered to him but the music, and so her pretenses hadn't mattered either—allowing her to drop her guard. This had changed her music, made it blossom in directions she hadn't imagined it could. Lawrence had something of Gustav's attitude in his refusal to see her pretenses, taking her seriously despite the show. She had the sense there was something else important about Gustav's words, but she couldn't quite grasp it. Right now, Lawrence was offering to help her, and she had to give him a chance.

"I've read what I could find of Charlie's work," she said. "I mostly get it."

"And what did you think?"

What an absurd question. "It's brilliant."

Lawrence's expression hinted at relief and pride. "I have all the papers. The hard-to-find ones and the never-published ones.

He finished the theory, you know. And I could dig that up for you, too—if you're interested?"

"Yes," Alex said, "I'm definitely interested."

CHAPTER XXVII

Charlie came into the library in search of a drink and found Lawrence and Alex in the sitting area, deep in discussion. Their low voices and resolute expressions suggested a serious topic, and normally he would have avoided getting caught up in that, but he was drunk enough—disconnected enough—to approach them. Nothing could rattle him now. "Hello," he said, looking at Lawrence. He thought he saw, in his peripheral vision, Alex flinch at his voice.

Lawrence stood up. "We were just talking about you, Charlie," he said. "Well, about your scientific work, anyway."

"Were you?" Charlie asked, with a skeptical laugh. Most people, when they approached the topic, merely talked around it.

"Yes," Lawrence said, smiling. "Alex was curious about your wave theory."

Charlie finally had to look at her. "I never said there was a theory."

"No, you said *maybe* there was no theory and that it didn't matter either way. But it does matter," she said.

"To whom?"

"To me."

Charlie laughed, now genuinely amused—though even he could hear the edge in his own laughter—as if she could understand it enough for it to actually matter.

"How is that funny?" Lawrence asked.

Charlie shook his head. "Never mind."

"I'd like to give her my copy of the paper you wrote, if that's alright with you," Lawrence said.

Charlie shrugged. "Fine." Why not? It made no difference now.

Alex smiled at him, triumphant, and it occurred to him again that she was beautiful. He'd watched her, admired her dress, her figure, yet he'd not thought those words tonight. He smiled down at her.

Abruptly, she stood up and went through one of her shifts in mien, smile vanishing and eyes dropping. It seemed to Charlie, though, that this time it was involuntary, because she was wobbling, unsteady on her feet—so much so that he almost stepped forward to catch her. Almost.

"Something the matter?" Lawrence asked her.

"No…I just…I remembered something I need to do. Excuse me."

Charlie and Lawrence watched her hurry from the room, but neither of them commented on it, and after a moment, Lawrence folded his lanky frame back onto the couch. "So you have talked to her about your work."

"Not really. She's hassled me about it a little—though not as much as you do."

"You should tell her more."

"Why would I do that?"

"At university you were constantly looking for an opportunity to show your work to someone with the potential to understand it. I remember because my lack of knowledge about maths was always a little disappointing to you."

Charlie stuck his hands into his pockets. He remembered it, too. There had never been many people with that potential. "And you think Alex has that potential?" he asked wryly.

"Wouldn't hurt to find out."

Charlie shook his head. "No. I'm sure she can't do it. And besides, that was all such a long time ago. I was a child. I don't need anything like that anymore."

"What do you need?"

"A drink, probably."

Lawrence grinned. "Well let's do it."

Charlie poured out two glasses of scotch from the cabinet behind the desk that opened to a full bar. He held a glass out to Lawrence. "You seem to think you know Alex pretty well."

"I'm observant is all. You've noticed certain things about her, too, I'm sure," Lawrence said, taking the glass and sipping it, thoughtful for a moment. Then he said, "Though I've noticed one thing I know you haven't."

"What's that?"

"The way she bows her violin is very particular. Something about her arm position—it's strange but familiar. I don't know quite how to explain it. It just struck me, the last time I saw her play. There was a woman at the Academy—a student— who bowed that way. It was rather before my time there, but I've seen recordings."

"When have you seen Alex play?"

"I've been to a few rehearsals. She demonstrates sometimes if the orchestra isn't getting what she wants."

Charlie longed to ask about the music—what was the concerto like, how did she talk about it, was it any good—but he resisted. The tenor of his curiosity felt too close to what he felt when he was on the verge of some new obsession, and he did not want to feed it. So he threw back the rest of his scotch and turned instead to a tangential, and safer, curiosity—Alex's violin education. "Maybe this woman at the Academy was one of Alex's instructors. I don't know about them."

"Maybe. Teaching is certainly one of the ways students earn money on the side. But I've already asked around and nobody seems to know what's happened to the woman…which is rather strange, too, because she was on her way to becoming a serious force as a violinist. She's just…disappeared."

"Send whatever information you have to Murdoch, will you?" Charlie said. "I'll have Glen Clarence—he's my investigator—look into it."

Lawrence frowned. "This wasn't meant as something for you to dig into, Charlie. It was just an observation."

"Look, I have noticed some things about Alex and they're not all positive. She's too secretive, has too many idiosyncrasies. And Clarence…he's gotten hold of these old diaries of hers. He says she may be not quite right," Charlie said.

"Not quite right?"

"Mentally, I guess. I haven't read the things—haven't decided if I should or not. I probably should."

Lawrence laughed. "You don't believe she's mentally unstable any more than I do. And it's not like you to start stealing."

"I need to protect myself—and the company. Too much is riding on this show, on her. People are digging into her past all the time and someone might find something damaging. We have to beat them to it."

"But diaries—"

"Whose diaries?" Simone's voice echoed in the library, followed by the clicking of her high heels. In this light, her dress, coated with tiny sequins, glittered, and it annoyed Charlie with all its striking ostentation.

"You really ought not eavesdrop," Lawrence said with only a faint hint of mocking.

Simone rolled her eyes and clicked up to them. "Come on, you guys, tell me the gossip. I might be able to help."

"Help with what?" Charlie asked.

"Protecting you and the company."

"It's not necessary," Charlie said, voice cold.

"Don't be so sure. Everyone needs help whether they ask for it or not."

"And what can you do?" Charlie asked.

"Oh, I know lots of people and I have all kinds of influence. I can make or break anyone. Even you, Charlie." She said it with a laugh calculated to make her words sound like a joke, but Charlie wondered if she wasn't trying to threaten him.

Then he laughed, too, because no one could touch him. Especially her.

CHAPTER XXVIII

Sometime in the middle of the night Alex woke up to her new melody, an array of sounds and sights—sights that weren't just colors but full images: a ship caught in a raging sea, its fight to stay afloat, dark waves, a tempestuous wind. But there were images of Charlie mixed in, too: Charlie leaning against the wall, Charlie looking tortured, Charlie smiling at her in the library.

It was the smile that had brought her melody exploding back, as if it had uncorked a bottle to drench her mind. She hadn't been able to stay there, so close to him, in the wake of the maelstrom, and had escaped to her room, stumbling to change into her old T-shirt and lying down in bed exhausted, drifting into sleep on the melody.

But a few hours later, she was awake and alert, knowing the music would drive her until she'd poured it all onto paper, and there was no point in trying to do anything else until that was done.

The dawn found Alex standing at one end of her bedroom, her staff paper taped in tidy rows to cover half the wall, starting just above her head and reaching down to knee level. She wrote furiously, her hand extended to reach the top row or kneeling down for the bottom, filling the neat pattern of grouped horizontal lines on the paper with slashes of notes. She wrote like that for the next thirty-six hours.

Through the intercom she told Murdoch to send word that rehearsals were canceled for Monday and that she was not to be disturbed—no David, no Grace, no cameras. He assented but did disturb her: several times to bring food, once to give her a package from Lawrence Berg—Charlie's papers—and once to tell her that David wanted to speak with her. She accepted the food and the package gratefully but declined David's request. She would see no one, she told Murdoch, except for Charlie—who did not come. She hadn't expected him to.

She worked, adding variation after variation on the original theme, then orchestrations to each variation, the music swelling and falling like the ocean. Whenever the wall of paper was completely written, she carefully took the pieces of paper down and laid them on a stack at her feet. Then she taped up fresh paper and continued, carried along on an endless river of music, caught in its current, unable and unwilling to stop.

Then she was done—the story was told and the concerto complete—and she stood in the middle of the room, breathing hard as if she'd run a long way.

But whose story was it? *It's my own story*, she told herself, *and Charlie is the thing I'm fighting—he's the storm.* Thoughts of him brought thoughts of his papers—his theory—and she longed to read them. But her thinking was muddled, swallowed up in the exhaustion of not having slept more than a few hours for almost two days. It was early evening on Monday, though, and if she went to bed now, she could be up early to read at least some of it before rehearsal on Tuesday.

She lay down in bed and closed her eyes, again wondering about the story in her music, and again telling herself Charlie was the storm. But she knew she was trying too hard to convince herself and that it might not be her own war in the music at all. There was a roiling of emotions beneath the surface of the music—in the thumping staccato of the bass tones and the lilting melody on top fighting to force the bass down—that reminded her of Charlie and the face he put on to hide his turmoil. No, not to hide but to extinguish.

Then, as she fell asleep, she wondered if he'd realized that because he couldn't destroy his emotions, he'd turned instead to destroying the things that aroused the emotions in the first place.

CHAPTER XXIX

t had been a week since the dinner party. A week in which Charlie had thrown himself into work at EmerSound, determined to save the company and ignore everything else. He'd even skipped his rides, spending many hours at the office, reviewing the company financials with painstaking care, rereading every report from the past six months, and helping Jennifer make the requisite budget cuts. The rest of his time he'd spent doing shoots for the show—with Brandy. He was finally back to his old self, the one who could do the necessary and distasteful tasks required to run EmerSound, the one who had control of his feelings.

And then Richard had shown up to his office this morning, and instead of giving his latest report on *Mrs. Music's* reception with audiences, he was standing there across the desk from Charlie, ranting about Michael Chap. The whining quality to his voice—the high nasal pitch of a pouting toddler—made Charlie want to throw him out. Or punch him in the face. All of his careful control was slowly melting to reveal a growing jagged edge of anger underneath—disturbing because he had never before wanted to beat down on someone so obviously weak. And yet, an aspect of the violent tendency felt well-worn and accepted, as if it had been around a long time, which was absurd. After all, Richard was an innocuous and necessary part of the business, like the building where EmerSound's offices were, or the recording studio where they cut albums. You couldn't be enraged by a permanent fixture.

"It's a disaster, Charlie," Richard was saying. "I just talked to Michael Chap and he's threatening to post a video he just made… and it's bad for us. I'm just glad I caught him before he actually put it up—luckily, Simone heard about it and told me. But anyway, Michael says the show is overworking the musicians with double rehearsals or something, making them go from one place to another every day, and I don't know what he's talking about. I asked David and he doesn't know either, but there it is, Michael is accusing us. I got him to give us three days to work it out before he posts his video, but I don't know what to do."

Charlie pulled from whatever patience remained in him to keep his outward cool. "Did you talk to anyone else in the orchestra about these double rehearsals?"

Richard's eyes widened as if this were some remarkable new idea. "No…but yeah, that would help. They could tell us if it's true or not."

"Do that and let me know how it goes. Now, what about the report on *Mrs. Music*?"

"Right. Let's see." He sat down and opened the folder he'd brought. "Um…people are really engaging with the Brandy storyline. David worked some footage into the episode we released this week and they're already posting about a possible affair between you guys, so that's been great for the ratings. And once the dinner party episode airs, it'll blow up.... A couple of the other stories about the cast are doing okay, too. There's a catfight that went viral last week. The girls pretending to be violinists... or was it violists? It doesn't matter. Anyway, they're fighting over some guy, pulling hair, all of it—and that spiked our viewership. Alex finally finished her music, so that's good, but she isn't really trending with the audiences anymore, and it's going to be a huge problem since she's supposed to be the focus of the finale. I mean, we've got to get the viewers to watch that episode live for the sponsors, you know? They're expecting it. I think I need to start her posting about the show or your relationship or something. Do you think she'd do that?"

"Post? No, but it doesn't matter. Don't bother asking her. Just have someone write the posts for her. This type of thing is covered in our standard contracts and—"

One of the double doors of Charlie's office swung open, crashed against the wall, and bounced back to be caught by the arm of the man who entered. "Charlie, what in hell are you doing?" Lawrence said, glowering with a severity Charlie had seen from him only once—when his best antique viola had been stolen while on loan.

Richard's eyes widened and he stood up, grabbing clumsily at his folder and papers, catching them just before they slid onto the ground.

Charlie leaned back in his seat. "Richard, I think we're done here?"

The man nodded vigorously, placed the now-messy stack of reports on Charlie's desk, and almost tiptoed around Lawrence to escape the office.

Charlie smiled at Lawrence and pointed to the chair Richard had just vacated. "Sit down. Want a coffee? Or a whiskey?"

Lawrence didn't sit down. "Have you heard it? Do you have any inkling of what she's done?"

"I have no idea what you're talking about."

"I'm talking about the *Red Concerto.* It's…I've never heard anything like it. Even with that Chap idiot as soloist. The entire concerto—it's written as a fugue, but the variations on the theme and the way the three voices harmonize…and the drama! It's the mathematical precision of Bach mixed with the emotional intensity of Beethoven. Where Beethoven himself would've gone if he hadn't become slightly batty at the end and—"

"Slow down," Charlie said, forcing a nonchalance he didn't feel. He'd have to hear about Alex's music now—there was no way to stop it—but he needed a moment to prepare. "I think you definitely need a whiskey. I know I do."

"It's ten o'clock in the morning."

"And?"

Lawrence sighed and sat down. "Fine, I'll have a coffee," he said. "And we are going to talk about Alex."

On a cart against one of the walls adjacent to his desk, Charlie kept the implements for making the variety of drinks that got him through the day—namely coffee and liquor. He sauntered over, placed a cup under the coffee machine spout, and pressed the brew button. Then for a moment he splayed his hands on the glass surface of the cart and dropped his head, the position putting his back to Lawrence, and that, together with the clamor of the grinder as it pulverized coffee beans, gave him the space to settle his thoughts. But all he felt was an immense weariness, one that was deep and very old, as if it had taken root a long time ago, had grown unchecked for many years, and was now reaching out to strangle him.

When the grinding gave way to a low whirring hum and the aroma of coffee filled the air, Charlie straightened his posture, poured whiskey from a decanter into a second cup, and took a long sip. Then, still without turning back to his friend, he said, "I don't know what we need to talk about. So Alex can write music. I gave her an orchestra. What else does she need? What am I doing to her?"

"We'll talk about the orchestra—and Michael Chap—later. But right now, Bernak Hall."

"Bernak?"

"You know quite well what I mean," Lawrence said.

Charlie turned and brought the drinks back to the desk, where he set them down, then took his own seat. "She knew what she was signing up for. We always do the show finales at Bernak."

"Have you heard the concerto performed at Martin Hall? It doesn't compare. I hadn't thought about the performance venues very much before this. But now I've heard it…" Lawrence leaned forward on his chair and braced a hand on the desk. His eyes blazed. "I don't know anything about the science of acoustics but—my God, Charlie!—this was practically your field. You're an expert on waves. Not to mention the fact that you own a music label. What you're doing is practically criminal."

"Wait," Charlie said, beginning to make sense of Richard's rant. "Go back for a moment. You're saying you've heard the concerto rehearsed at Martin Hall—recently?"

"Yesterday afternoon, in fact."

"How did you know where and when to go?"

"Willem Salk told me. Remember my cellist friend who's in the orchestra?" Lawrence said, then frowned. "Do you have a problem with me going? I told you the other night I've gone to rehearsals. Or is it that you didn't want me to hear it at Martin Hall?"

"She has two rehearsals," Charlie said.

It was not a question, but Lawrence answered anyway, "Well, yes. Didn't you know?"

Charlie stood up—a hasty, almost involuntary movement—and turned his back to Lawrence again, now to stare blindly out the window, hands in his pockets. "She was serious about the acoustics. And she found a way around Bernak," he murmured. What would it take to stop this girl? And how was she paying for it?

"Charlie? What's the matter?"

"I haven't heard it."

"The concerto? You mean you haven't heard it at all?" Lawrence asked, astonishment in his voice. "Why ever not?"

"There was no need. She was supposed to be mediocre, like all the rest of them. I thought she had no talent."

"I don't understand."

Charlie pivoted again, wanting to pace or to hit something, but he held himself steady and leaned his back on the window instead, gritting his teeth against the thing that was roiling up inside him. "I wanted to hire someone we could mold, someone who'd fit with the rest of EmerSound. Who could be what the show needed her to be. We'd make whatever music she was doing passable like we always do—you know that's all anyone ever wants. They don't know the difference between passable and good anyway. That way the girl would be thrilled because she'd being doing better than she could have imagined. And I wouldn't have to worry about strangling another talent." *Or getting involved with someone I admire, and then strangling her talent—purposefully or not.*

Lawrence opened his mouth but closed it again without speaking, his brows furrowed. Then he picked up his coffee, leaned back in his chair, and sipped it a few times. Charlie waited, because somehow Lawrence's response seemed important.

After a minute, Lawrence nodded to himself, replacing the cup on the desk, and with a low, almost gentle voice he said, "You need to hear the concerto." He glanced at his watch. "Today. You still have a little over an hour before they start rehearsals at Martin Hall. Clear your afternoon and go. Please. If for no other reason than it's an experience not to be missed. Then we'll talk."

CHAPTER XXX

An hour and a half later, Charlie arrived at Martin Hall. The rehearsal had already started and Charlie stomped up the front stairs two at a time and threw open one of the double doors and entered a small anteroom. A second set of double doors leading into the main space had been left a few inches ajar, and he stopped upon hearing a stern voice floating through: "I need to hear it speed up gradually until it reaches the peak. Up, up, up! Don't wimp out." Alex's voice, but strong and confident. "And you...you'll never be able to get it to tempo and in tune without more practice. Every other note is flat."

"No one can play it that fast—it's impossible," a man answered.

Charlie pushed the door wider to peer inside. The converted hall was small by modern standards of concert halls and would hold only a few hundred people in the audience, but it had soaring ceilings and acoustic paneling that looked haphazardly placed, though were actually the work of some expert sound engineer.

"Let me hear the first two bars of the violin solo again. Just Michael this time," Alex was saying. She wore jeans and a simple sweater and was standing next to Michael Chap on a low stage, surrounded by a semicircle of thirty people in chairs—her orchestra—each holding a stringed instrument: two dozen violins and violas and several cellos and double basses.

The sight of her jolted Charlie. All week he'd pretended she didn't really exist, not as an actual person anyway, but as a line item in the company financials, or a character he had heard about in the context of the show, even refusing to meet with her though she'd asked several times—because if he had, he'd have to think of her in that black dress, think of her pale skin and delicate arms...think of her as a woman. Just like he was doing now.

Alex started clapping rhythmically. "Here's the tempo," she said. "I'll keep the beat while you play."

Michael Chap shrugged and lifted the violin to his chin, then stroked his bow across the strings. He played the first few notes, but then, unable to keep up with Alex's tempo, his fingers stuttered on the neck of the instrument and his shoulders hunched a bit. The notes took on a horrific, squawky texture—a cacophonous noise that no longer resembled music. The whole performance lasted only a handful of seconds, but it felt much longer, and Charlie understood why Alex had asked Chap to play only the first two bars of music.

There was a brief silence, then Alex sighed and said, "Let me show you... Maybe if I...give me the violin." Michael shrugged again and handed his instrument to her, and she fiddled with it for a moment, tuning it.

Charlie stilled, acknowledging his own almost-desperate desire to hear her play again, hear this music that had sent Lawrence to yell at him in a rage. And then knowing he shouldn't, knowing it wouldn't end well for him and was a path into hell, he entered the hall, keeping his footsteps light. He took a position in the back, hidden among the shadows, and leaned against the wall, arms folded across his chest.

On stage, Alex lifted the violin to her chin and looked up at the orchestra. "From the beginning of the fourth movement, please."

She stood straight now, head raised, voice commanding, with all the ease of a born leader. With her right hand she swept the violin bow up, then from side to side, conducting a measure of silence.

On the next upsweep, it began.

For all the warning he'd had, Charlie was not prepared. The blast of music startled him like a slap in the face as the concerto exploded into the hall. The notes burst out like spurts of lava choreographed in an intricate dance, coalescing into three lines of melody that moved in parallel and battled for supremacy; each line poured out and dissipated into the next in a complex cascade that should've been chaos, but the harmony progressed so logically that it created a sense of control—the sense of a powerful force keeping the fury at bay, smoothing it, shaping it, directing it.

Alex began to play on the third measure. Her fingers raced over the neck of the violin, her bow moving in violent, jagged angles. Her slight body moved with the same precision and severity as her bow, simultaneously graceful and furious. Out of that turbulence every note rose precisely in tune.

Then, while she continued to play, Alex began to yell over the music. "Crescendo! Crescendo! Now *prestissimo*! Keep up!"

A few violinists dropped out of the ensemble and sat watching her, eyes wide. Others kept playing for a while longer but eventually gave up, and were followed in succession by the rest of the orchestra sections. Alex's eyes closed and her voice fell off as she continued to play—now a soloist without accompaniment—and the violence and control of the piece became a haunting, lonely thing, like the wind raging through a vacant desert, a struggle against emptiness.

The struggle settled on a triumphant note, but without the grounding deep tones of the cellos and double basses and the complementing high tones of violins and violas, the victory sounded hollow. The last note rang through the hall, its gradual dissipation accentuating the stillness that followed.

Charlie opened his eyes, surprised, not knowing when he'd closed them. He blinked, almost feeling like he needed to remember himself, where he was and who he was.

On stage, Alex stood as if still playing, violin held to her chin, bowing arm raised to the strings. She was motionless but for the minute tremor of the bow, which stilled in the next moment when she lowered the instrument and held it out to Michael. He nodded, staring, and took the violin.

"See if you can get it up to that tempo," she said. Then she looked around at the orchestra and nodded. "Everyone, please have this movement up to speed by next Monday. Then we'll worry about the dynamics and expression."

There was a pause of silence after she'd finished speaking, then the orchestra exploded in applause and cheers—everyone but

Michael Chap, who tromped off stage and out a side door. Alex laughed, putting her hands up to stop them. "Thank you," she yelled over the clapping and then again when it stopped. "Thank you for that and your hard work. Let's adjourn for the day. I'll see you at Bernak tomorrow morning."

As the orchestra's chatter began to fill the room, Alex gathered her score off the podium and stuffed it into a backpack, which she slung over one shoulder as she walked off stage. When she was halfway down the aisle, Charlie stepped out from the shadows. She halted, her hand frozen in the gesture of pulling on a glove, but for once her first action wasn't to look away. Though her face remained blank, her eyes were bright and sharp, and he saw again what he'd seen that day he first heard her play the violin—but now she was not only the brilliant violinist, she was also the genius composer.

She was the one to break the silence. "Who told you we were here?"

"Lawrence. Was it a secret?"

"No," she said simply. Then when he didn't respond, she asked, "Is there something you wanted?"

Yes, he thought, his eyes roaming down her figure, thinking of her in the black dress. But he hadn't come here for that. Something else, then. He fought to remember. "I came to tell you these extra rehearsals have to stop."

"Why? I'm paying for all of it myself. It's not doing you or your stupid show any harm."

"That's not how Michael Chap sees it. He says you're working everyone too hard."

"I've been trying all week to talk to you about him. He's lazy. He refuses to put in enough hours to practice, and he's barely

squeaking by technically—well, he was until the fourth movement, which he's not even close to getting technically or otherwise. And his artistry is nonexistent. Why did you even hire him?
Why not someone better?"

Someone like you? He smiled without amusement. "That's not
what we do at EmerSound."

"What, exactly, do you do?"

"We hire and promote mediocrity. That's all we do and it's
all I want to do. So you don't have to go thinking that you can
convince me to hear something in your music that I can't." *I don't
want that responsibility.*

As if she'd heard his silent thought, she smiled—a slow
movement that started from a flash in her eyes and moved to her
lips. "No, it's not that you can't see what's in my music, but that
you would prefer it weren't there. It would be easier, wouldn't it?"

"Easier?"

"Easier. Because you're trying to kill the part of you that
wants more from life than this, and you have to convince yourself
that more doesn't exist."

"More?" He gave a mirthless chuckle. "It's as if you don't
understand the situation here. I am the man who runs EmerSound,
the company that's making all this"—he waved a hand to indicate
the room—"and so much more possible. I control every aspect of
your life. Of many lives. This is what most people aspire to."

"You're not most people."

Charlie felt something leaden drop in his gut, something
familiar, and it made him want to punch a wall again. "You've
picked up some armchair analysis techniques from your father,
have you? You don't know me at all."

"I know that doing what you hate—or even what you're not proud of—can only make you feel guilty. And that the guilt keeps your mind in a vise, like there are places you can't go, thoughts you can't have, or you'll have to face the guilt. So you reduce your thoughts, or you try to make yourself believe that you have no choice in doing what you're doing. Both, probably. Can't you feel the difference between who you are now and who you were before you became this? How it felt to succeed at something you loved?"

He didn't want to consider her words, wanted to continue to fight remembering what it was like—the exhilaration, the pure joy he'd felt while working on his theory, all those years ago. And the night he'd finished the theory, how he'd felt like he'd reached a peak after a long climb and could look out from that vantage point to see all the roads now open, all the solutions his theory made possible; he hadn't been able to sleep for all the applications that kept coming to him. From sound engineering to supersonic flight. It had all been there, and he could see and plan the lab he would have one day—all its various arms, with physicists and engineers and musicians.

"No," he said, shaking his head at her words, and his own thoughts, and the conversation as a whole. "None of this is relevant…. You can't have two rehearsals."

Her eyes narrowed in frustration. "You can't stop me. All the musicians except Michael are happy to do it. And I can have my rehearsals here without him."

She moved to walk past him and out of the hall, and he didn't follow her or turn to watch her leave, telling himself he didn't have to chase her to tell her she was wrong—she'd find out soon enough. He was Charlie Emerson, after all, and he only had to put a little pressure on Martin Hall's owner to have them stop Alex from rehearsing there.

Michael Chap's threats to destroy EmerSound weren't idle—he could do it, and he would if he didn't get his way—if the double rehearsals continued, even if he wasn't required to attend them. And Charlie couldn't allow EmerSound be destroyed. Whether he was glad about it or not, he wouldn't let himself find out.

But a question popped into his head that he couldn't ignore: *Was he losing control of EmerSound along with everything else?*

CHAPTER XXXI

Willem was waiting for Alex at the bottom of the stairs when she came out of Martin Hall. "What did Charlie want?" he asked, looking worried and a little guilty.

She walked past him to the edge of the sidewalk, gazing down the street for a taxi. "It's not a big deal. He just wanted us to stop the Martin Hall rehearsals. But he can't."

"I'm sorry, it was my fault he found out. I told Lawrence and—"

"It's okay, really," she said, turning to him. "I knew he'd find out. We're not doing anything wrong."

"Okay," he said. She was about to turn back to the street when he grinned and his eyes lit up. "The fourth movement and your playing today were incredible. Isn't there any way you can do the solo yourself?"

She sighed. "I may have to."

"That makes you sad?"

"No. I just…it's a long story. Look, I have to meet…my dad uptown. Can we talk later?"

Willem nodded, not seeming overly concerned, which was a relief, and she quickly hailed a cab and got in, pulling out a hat and sunglasses from her bag to disguise herself. It would be an expensive ride all the way up to the Bronx, but even with her disguise, there were too many people on the subway with too much time to stare at her, and she feared being recognized. The show was doing well enough and had a high enough viewership that her face was becoming known. This was a concern in itself, but she'd known it would happen from the beginning.

She wished she could avoid this meeting, but Dennis Weiss called her early in the morning and insisted on seeing her. She tried to refuse—for one thing, she didn't have the time. She'd barely managed to get a few hours off from the cameras in the afternoons for the Martin Hall rehearsals, and then dealing with Michael Chap's lackluster playing on top of all the other show drama left her with little psychological stamina to countenance Weiss's disapproval. And he'd never disapproved of anything as much as her contract with Charlie Emerson. But he'd said it was important. To save some of her stamina for the conversation, she kept strict control over her thoughts now—she would not think about her run-in with Charlie, or the fact that he'd seen her play, or the things he'd said. That would go in a vault to be considered later.

Weiss sat in their usual corner booth at the diner, and on seeing him an unexpected pang shot through Alex—the pang of loss for the familiar comfort she'd known in his care. She'd missed him more than she'd realized.

And maybe because it had been so long since the last time they'd met in person, she saw the changes in him. He was so different now than he'd been ten years ago, in the "before" time:

before the culmination of the heart trouble and the mess at the institute, before she left for the city. He seemed so worn out now. But then he looked at her and she saw the fire still there in his eyes—a fire she hoped wouldn't be directed at her. She pulled her sunglasses off and sat down across from him.

"You look tired," he said.

That made two of them. "I'm not sleeping too well."

"Why not? What's wrong?"

"Nothing. Just wired from all the work."

"I see." He paused as if to choose his next words carefully. "But you're taking your medication regularly?"

She nodded.

"And it's keeping your vision clear?"

She nodded again.

He lifted a small paper bag from the seat beside him and put it on the table. "I brought you more. This should last you through the next four months."

She took the bag, about to put it into her backpack, but, remembering she should show an interest, she stopped to open it first, to glance inside as if making sure everything was right with the pills, and as if she weren't going to take them home and stick them under her mattress…then not look at them again except to flush them when they eventually expired. Was there anyone, she wondered, she didn't have to put on a show for? And it was strange to realize, after all these years, that she never stopped acting, was never just herself with anybody. Strange and a little painful.

A waitress appeared, placing thick white mugs on the table between them and filling each with coffee. When she'd taken their order and left, Weiss said, "There's a problem."

Alex paused with her coffee cup lifted halfway to her mouth. "What is it?"

"I kept some diaries," he whispered. "The childhood ones up until the trip to Müller. They were there on the shelf in the bedroom and…and now they're gone. They've been stolen."

Alex just shook her head. "I don't…I don't understand."

"There have been so many people around, asking questions, trying to talk to me. All sorts of journalists and people claiming to be old friends. And well, one of them broke in and took a bunch of stuff from the bedroom. And the diaries…"

Alex closed her eyes, her mind working through the implications, trying to remember what might be in those notebooks.

"They are…revealing," Weiss said. "If someone knew what to look for."

"You were supposed to burn them," she said, her voice low and hoarse. She hadn't had the right to ask him to burn those things. Not really. But she'd asked anyway and he'd said he would.

His eyes wouldn't meet hers, but his tone when he answered was hard. "I burned most of them—the later ones. But I couldn't part with everything."

The early entries couldn't be so bad. Nothing had really even happened yet. Alex swallowed a gulp of coffee—it went down with difficulty.

"His private investigator came to see me, too, not so long ago," Weiss said, more softly now. "He had a lot of questions that went way past a normal background check."

"Charlie's private investigator? When exactly?"

He gave her the date and she thought it an ominous sign, the investigator going to see him soon after the gala, where she'd given so much of herself away to Charlie. Really, it was a bad sign if the investigator was still asking questions at all, because didn't they run the background check on her before Charlie even proposed? Could someone put it all together? Depended on what questions they asked. But she didn't ask Weiss what words had been exchanged between him and the investigator, unwilling to betray her alarm—maybe unwilling to feel her alarm. Not just yet. She sipped her coffee and waited for him to continue.

But he was a good psychiatrist with an astute eye. "Too scared to ask what happened? I'll tell you anyway. He had a lot of questions: 'Who were Alex's violin teachers? When did she start playing? How was her mental state when her heart was bad?' He even asked about Chris Donnelly—that kid from next door. I handled it, but the investigator himself didn't strike me as too clever, so I'm sure all those questions were spurred by Charlie." Alex nodded, trying to process it all, and Weiss added, "That man is too interested. I think he's become fixated on you. It's time to end this thing and leave."

She put her coffee cup down. She was too close to having her concerto recorded—she couldn't leave yet. She had to take the chance. "Charlie is not fixated. He likes to understand things and I don't fit whatever idea he had of me. I just need to try harder to fit. Isn't that what you've always said?"

"Yes, and you never have. If he's the one who has these diaries…he'll figure it out. For a man who has the ability to reinvent a whole field in physics, a strong curiosity about anything becomes a fixation. He won't stop until he finds out what he thinks he doesn't know."

"He didn't reinvent the field, he just hinted that he might be able to, then quit before he actually did it." Well, quit before he ever told anyone he did it. She didn't know why she was lying, why she felt she needed to convince Weiss.

"That might be even worse. His—"

The waitress came back with plates of sandwiches and Weiss halted, waiting until she'd placed the food and left, before he leaned forward to continue, voice lowered. "His detective has already dug up the mess with Shaylan. And those records were sealed."

Shaylan. The name hit her like a punch in the stomach. Would they never be free of that damn doctor and the way he'd ruined their lives? Alex swallowed hard. "What does he know about it?"

"So far as I can tell, just that it happened. And I told him that the trauma of the investigation into my involvement was the reason you left."

"Okay." This was alright. She could work with this. "Someone was bound to find it sooner or later. At least we know so there's a chance to control it."

"You can't control Charlie Emerson—that's what I'm trying to tell you!"

Alex flinched at his loss of composure but managed to keep her own cool. "Not to control him, but the situation. The way the information comes out."

He stared at her for a moment. "You're going to get caught," he said, and now he was relaxed again, but some subtle shift in his eyes, a coldness, or a distance, appeared.

Alex made a deliberate show of picking up her sandwich and taking a bite, of refusing to answer him. The heater kicked on somewhere above them and filled the air with a whirring sound. He bit into a potato chip. They ate for a while, both silent, but the distance that had formed between them grew.

After a long while Weiss said, "I'm worried you'll try to make a connection with him and reveal too much."

She might have done that already. "But maybe a connection is the thing that'll assuage him."

"And then what?" The slap of his hand on the table was followed by the tinkling rattle of silverware on plates. "After everything that's happened, how have you not learned that your actions have consequences?"

She closed her eyes, not in surrender, but as a veil to keep him from seeing the emotions there—her anguish and the hint of contempt for the man across the table from her. Contempt because he shouldn't have said it, because of course she knew her actions had consequences—hadn't she been living with them almost her whole life? And because he was responsible, too. "This is different," she ground out. "Don't use guilt to get me to—"

"How the hell am I supposed to save you from another tragedy? So many damned deaths in your life! If I'd known the music would lead you astray like this… Do not fall in love with Charlie Emerson. He's going to destroy you." He was thoroughly agitated now, his voice dropping to a cold monotone, which, for him, was worse than yelling.

Alex let her disdain swallow her pain and her guilt, and she opened her eyes to let him see the defiance. "I'm not going to fall in love with Charlie Emerson." And anyway, it didn't matter, because he was already sleeping with Simone.

"I've seen the way you look at him on that show."

"It's called acting," she said.

"Damn it, why won't you let me help you?" he asked.

"I would if there were something you could do. But there isn't. Not anymore."

CHAPTER XXXII

That evening Charlie was intent on going for a ride on his motorcycle, even though he'd been drinking steadily and heavily since his Martin Hall visit—well, since just after he'd made the call to the owners of the hall—and even though he knew he shouldn't be riding. He simply didn't care. Neither did he bother changing out of his jeans and long-sleeved polo shirt, forgoing the heavier and more protective clothes he usually wore.

Down in the garage, he donned his helmet, mounted his motorcycle, and pulled out of his spot, revving the motor to speed up the ramped aisle and taking the first turn without slowing down, then accelerating further into the second turn. But the alcohol had diminished his reaction time and he didn't turn at the proper angle—or came out of the turn too early; he wasn't sure—and he skidded into one of the garage's broad concrete columns, hitting it hard, his left shoulder, arm, and leg smashing and scraping against the rough surface. The impact didn't knock him down but left him disoriented, and he stood precariously for a moment, balanced on his right leg, fighting to keep the motorcycle upright.

When the disequilibrium finally subsided, he dismounted—which caused a stabbing pain to shoot up his leg—and pushed the motorcycle to its parking spot, his gait heavy with a limp. The shock of the crash and the resulting pain had sobered him enough that by the time he made it back upstairs to the foyer of his apartment he was exasperated again and threw his helmet to the ground with a loud crash, cursing loudly when the movement sent a burning pain up his left arm. He'd really needed a long ride to numb himself, and he'd been stupid to try it when he knew he'd had too much to drink—because he might not care if he lived or died, but if he'd made it out of that garage, he might have killed someone else.

"What happened?" Murdoch asked, running into the foyer.

Charlie sighed, pressing his right index finger down his left forearm, searching for the source of the shooting pain—which he found just above his wrist. He flinched and glanced up at Murdoch. "What are you still doing up?"

"Waiting for you, actually," Murdoch said. "I wanted to see how things went at Martin Hall, and you haven't been answering your calls or texts…. Did you crash?"

Charlie shrugged and shuffled past him down the central hallway. "Just a little, in the garage."

"Not that little—your sleeve and jeans are torn, and your arm is bleeding. A lot." There was definite disapproval in Murdoch's manner as he followed Charlie down the hall. "Why weren't you in Kevlar, or leathers at least?"

"Too confining," Charlie said. He paused at the door to the living room to examine his left arm again, finding that he was, in fact, bleeding from a gash just above his elbow, the red now soaking through his torn sleeve. He stripped off the shirt, crushed it into a tight ball, and pressed it to the wound. "Ow…"

"I'll get the first aid kit," Murdoch said with a sigh, and by the time he came back with it, Charlie had managed to hobble to the couch, a bottle of whiskey open and in hand, his bloody shirt discarded somewhere along the way.

Murdoch sat down next to him, examined the arm, and declared that no stitches were needed, but several layers of skin had been scraped off. Then he went to work cleaning the wound. Charlie hissed at the burn of peroxide, but Murdoch remained totally unperturbed, despite the ugly scrape and the profusion of blood dripping down Charlie's arm.

"How do you stay so impervious to everything?" Charlie asked him.

"I'm not impervious. If I were, I wouldn't care about anything." Murdoch glanced up for a moment before going back to his work. "It's a bit of an act—part of the training: Feel it but don't show it."

Charlie didn't want an act; he wanted control. He wanted to stop caring so much about everything. That would solve a lot of his problems. "Did you learn it in the army? To ignore what you feel?"

Murdoch dug in the bag for more supplies. "In the army— yes, but I don't ignore my feelings. My commanding officer drilled that into us: You need to have mastery over your emotions; acknowledge them, but don't let them dictate your actions. That's different from ignoring them. It's when you ignore them that they really get you." He pulled out more gauze, a roll of medical tape, and a pair of scissors and started to wrap the wound.

Charlie guzzled straight from his whiskey bottle, thinking about how Alex had pitched him off balance all day with her… music—how he'd headed straight for a bar after their encounter to dull everything he thought and felt with whiskey. How it had ended with the crash. "So it's like ignoring your enemy, then, if you ignore your emotions?"

"Worse than that. It's like ignoring your allies and turning them into enemies. All because you didn't listen to what they were alerting you to." He taped off the gauze, then cut the tape from its roll before continuing. "You have to feel the fear in order to know what scares you. And only then can you go deeper to see if it's a justified fear. Then the emotion itself can't surprise you and get the better of you in battle—you'll already be in control of it."

What battle was Charlie fighting, he wondered, and what would control look like? Was the key really what Murdoch thought it was—to feel it all, to delve down into the depth of his emotions? He shuddered at the thought.

Murdoch closed up the first aid kit and stood up. "Can I get you anything else before I go to bed? A doctor maybe?"

Charlie snorted. "No doctor. But you could turn on the stereo on your way." He gestured toward the entertainment system with his whiskey bottle. "The record that's already on the turntable is fine."

There was only ever one record there, though Charlie hadn't listened to it in a long time—an album of his favorite arias, sung by Simone per his request in the first year of their relationship, sound-engineered and perfected by himself and only for his own ears. He could give the feel-everything tactic a try, could withstand it for a little while.

Murdoch switched the system on and grumbled under his breath—something about motorcycles being worse than boxing—as he left.

"Thank you for patching me up," Charlie called, placing the bottle on the side table nearest him, then leaned back, eyes closed, as the music filled the space around him with a perfect swirl of tones. Alex would love this room, he thought idly. It was his own design, every inch acoustically measured and outfitted with custom equipment to deliver a flawless audio experience. He'd have to keep her away from it. If she knew the real depth of his expertise, she'd never stop harassing him about Bernak Hall and its abysmal acoustics. No, he was supposed to be listening to the music, not thinking about Alex.

He sighed and tried to relax, to recapture something of his joy in this music. But all he felt was the tight ache in his neck and the throb developing in his knee. Then the sixth track came on—the piece Simone had sung the evening he'd met her, the one that had captivated him—but tonight, far from being mesmerizing, the aria was disturbing. It irritated and unsettled him, as if his skin were too tight, and he longed again for his motorcycle, to be riding at the edge of a precipice, in control of himself and his life.

This was not the thing he'd wanted to feel. This was the thing he'd wanted to stamp out. He couldn't imagine how delving into this muck of torture would help him. He got up violently, ignoring the stabs of pain now spreading along the entire left side of his body, and lurched to the turntable to tug the record off. A loud screech echoed through the room, then flattened to empty static as the turntable continued to spin and the needle found nothing but air.

Record in hand, Charlie hobbled to the lab, frustration growing at his own awkwardly slow gait, and punched in his code to enter the room, where he laid the record down on the scarred surface of the workbench. Then, he rummaged in a drawer, pulled out a hammer, and stood rotating the tool in his good hand, considering the record. With the lights off and the door open, the only illumination came from the hallway, a strip of light that didn't quite reach the workbench and left the record in shadow—a black circle, ominous and taunting, like a portal into the abyss. Charlie didn't know when the things he used to enjoy had become a source of such vitriol in him, or why the only feelings left to him were rancorous, but he'd had enough of it—the music and Simone and Alex and Brandy and EmerSound. He'd had enough of all of it.

He lifted the hammer and, in one sweeping motion, brought it down as hard as he could. The record shattered with a satisfying crunch. *Yes.* This was what he wanted. Destruction upon destruction. Now, he wouldn't have to hear the evidence of what he'd destroyed ever again. He wouldn't have to remember how Simone had been almost perfect, how he'd let her give it all up to be on one of his shows, knowing she'd never come back to it—knowing that once she'd stepped away to something less meaningful, it was impossible to return. The way he hadn't been able to go back to his theory and his science.

He lifted his head to look around him. Maybe he should destroy this room, too. He stopped, sensing a shadow cross the doorway. Alex stood just beyond the opening, visible in the light, wearing jeans as she had earlier, but instead of the sweater, her top was a black T-shirt—it's V-shaped collar reminiscent of the black dress from the party. Charlie's first thought was: *We're alone.* His second: *This is bad*—bad because he was a little out of control and he really wanted to touch her. He thumped the hammer down on the bench and gave her his best smile of condescension, the one calculated to make his victims self-conscious and a little scared.

But Alex didn't scurry away. She stood up straighter, and the flicker in her eyes was more determination than fear. "That was Simone on the record," she said.

Of course she'd recognized the voice. But also: "You've been stalking me since I was in the living room?"

She shrugged. "I heard the music earlier, and then I heard you rip it out of the player. And when I saw that"—she pointed to the table—"I guessed it was the same record. So what happened to Simone? She doesn't sing like that anymore."

He looked down at the shattered pieces of the record and put his hands over them, palms flat down, to feel the jagged sharpness press into his skin. "I happened. EmerSound happened."

She frowned and moved into the room and out of the light, and Charlie shook himself mentally. He couldn't get into a conversation with her. He shouldn't be alone with her. *Make her go away. Press on her points of weakness.* "What are you hiding?" he asked.

She froze. "What?"

"It's like you're two different people," he said. "Sometimes you're this person—the one you are now—confident, intelligent. But other times you pretend to be some victimized little girl, as if any moment someone's going to strike you. As if you don't understand everything that's going on around you—which I know you do."

"I'm acting for the show," she said.

"Oh, I know that. But I'm not talking about your Brandy-inspired personality. I'm talking about what you do when no one is taping—like at your coffee stand or when we met at the diner. Or now." He pulled his hands away from the debris, dusting his palms of the tiny bits of plastic, then pushed away from the table.

"I have no idea what you're talking about," she said, her eyes roaming down his body, hesitating at his still-shirtless chest. Her neck bobbed in a forced swallow.

This was going in the wrong direction and he should stop it, but he'd become interested in his own question—wanted her answer, wanted to know who she really was. So he gave her a heated smile and started walking around the workbench toward her. Then he faltered, his leg screaming in pain, forcing him to stop and lean against the table.

"You're hurt," she said with a measure of alarm. "What happened?"

"Crashed...my bike." He had to grind out the words through the pain.

"You look like you need to go to the hospital."

"I'm fine—don't change the subject. What are you afraid of?" He'd fought off the pain and his words came out easily, smoothly.

Alex didn't answer right away, but her face was still in shadow and Charlie couldn't tell what expression she wore. Finally she asked, "What are *you* afraid of?"

"Me?"

"Yes, you. Here you are with a carefully designed lab space you don't seem to use." She gestured to the room. "And I can tell you want to do this work—is it related to your theory?—but you won't let yourself. Instead you go out and crash your motorcycle."

He wanted to protest but the words stunned him a little. Was he keeping himself from doing the work?

"You're afraid to do this work," she said.

"And you're afraid to do anything but your work." The realization came to him in time with the statement, and for a moment they just looked at each other, maybe both a little astonished now.

Then, forgetting about the pain, Charlie took another step toward her, but this time his left leg gave out completely and he stumbled. He saw her move almost immediately, running to him—did she think she'd stop his fall with her tiny body?—while he reached out for the workbench with his right hand, turning to fall forward against it, and somehow she got caught in the middle, between him and the waist-high table.

They froze. She stood looking up at him, her hands gripping the edge of the bench behind her while his arms, also braced on the table, caged her in. Both of them were breathing harder than their movements had called for, and though not quite touching, every inhale, whether his or hers, gave them an instant's worth of feather-light contact, the pinpoints of intermittent sensation on the bare skin of his chest simultaneously too much and not enough.

He had to touch her; there was no help for it. He lifted his left hand and slowly traced the edge of her V-neck shirt, from collarbone to just above her breast and then back again, the pad of his finger grazing both the shirt and her skin. She shivered but didn't move away.

"This shirt reminds of your dress last week at the party," he whispered, hand lingering at her collarbone. In the dim light, the pale blue of her eyes seemed otherworldly, as if she were some fantastical character come to life. *I should kiss her to make sure she's real.*

Alex dropped her gaze so she was staring at his chest, and now he expected her to pull back, but she lifted a hand and, just as slowly as he had, traced the jagged scar on his chest. "How did you get this?" she whispered.

He closed his eyes to savor her touch and his voice rasped as he answered, pushing the words out in spurts, between breaths. "Motorcycle accident...car cut me off...didn't have time to slow down...hit him pretty hard...broke three ribs...punctured a lung...got this gash...and a concussion."

She dropped her hand and he looked down to see her head lifted to him again, eyes concerned, maybe a little angry.

"How can you be so calm about something that almost killed you?" she asked. "Did you want to die?"

"Not that night."

"But other nights?"

Yes. He didn't answer out loud, but her eyes widened as if she'd heard the silent word.

"Why?" she asked.

He lowered his hand from her collar and put it back on the table, pulling away a little but still keeping her caged in. He had to be careful with how much he touched her, but he wanted to hold her here, to keep this bit of contact a little longer, so he gave her the truth. "EmerSound," he said. "It requires a sacrifice any time you want it to pay out. Like those stories where the characters turn to dark magic and then have to make offerings to get what they want. I offer people—musicians, mostly—as sacrifices, and we all make a ton of money and get famous. But the musicians always pay. Stunted music, compromised principles, eating disorders, addictions…death. Some sort of…destruction. Sometimes, I get tired of it.”

“That’s why you don’t want good talent?”

He nodded, just barely.

“And you consider Simone one of your offerings?”

He started, the mention of Simone shattering the spell and bringing reality hurtling back—a bigger shock than when he’d crashed into the concrete column earlier. His thoughts came on top of each other: *He couldn’t do to Alex what he’d done to Simone; he couldn’t add to it by sleeping with her; he shouldn’t have confessed to her; he wouldn’t get dragged into another obsession.*

He pulled back all the way and let his arms fall. Then he stepped aside.

She remained standing against the table, her unearthly eyes stormy with indignation, but when she spoke, her voice was steady. “People make their own choices. Are you sure you bear all the responsibility for Simone? Maybe she wasn’t—”

“Please leave.” He cut her off before she could say the words that might absolve him, before she could forgive him. No good lay in that path. He looked straight in front of him, above her head, and forced all expression from his face.

She hesitated for a minute longer but then did as he’d asked…and left him alone.

CHAPTER XXXIII

Charlie woke up but kept his eyes closed because his head was pounding. He couldn't stand the aftermath of heavy drinking—the headache and the groggy dry feeling like he was pulling himself out of quicksand. Today everything hurt. His leg, back, and arm were throbbing, and he wasn't in his bed; he was on something solid and cold. He cracked his eyes open and recognized the flat gray of the ceiling above him. He was on the floor in the lab.

Then he remembered—the *Red Concerto*, the accident, the record, the lab, Alex... And then after she'd left—his body hurting and his mind churning, running too fast. He'd called Glen Clarence to demand he bring Alex's diaries to him as soon as he could, and Clarence had promised to do it today. And then Charlie had started drinking. After two double whiskies, his thoughts hadn't slowed at all. The alcohol had only added a sheath of murkiness over them, making him feel as though he were lying at the bottom of a lake, looking up to see the world through the distorting surface of the water, and longing for a breath he couldn't take.

Is this what he'd been doing to himself for the years he'd been drinking? Did he do it to make himself fuzzy? And maybe it wasn't just the alcohol—maybe some part of him, of his own mind, resisted focus. *The guilt keeps your mind in a vise.* Was he so much a coward that he couldn't bear to look at the details of his own life and had to smudge them out?

He sat up—an angry and too-swift motion that made his neck scream in pain and then made him so dizzy he had to lie back down again for another five minutes. He needed a good painkiller, a shower, and some food. Then he'd be okay.

∫ ℓ

Adequately medicated so he was numb to the pain from his accident, his night of overdrinking, and his rampant emotions, Charlie was eating breakfast at his desk in the library and reviewing EmerSound's most recent—and harrowing—financial reports, when the intercom buzzed.

"Simone Hawl is here to see you," Murdoch announced.

Charlie stilled. He never saw Simone during the day for sex…and it wasn't even their usual day to meet. But he couldn't recall the last time he'd kept a date with her. Weeks ago, probably. He'd been coming up with excuses not to see her for a while, and he couldn't really refuse her now. "Alright, ask her to wait in the living room, please, but let me know the minute Clarence is here."

"I'm sorry, but Simone insisted on waiting in your bedroom… I think you'd better meet her there," Murdoch said, sounding strained. "She said to tell you she's here to have a little fun."

Charlie laughed a mirthless laugh, realizing he wouldn't have called what they were doing fun. But if he wasn't having fun with Simone, what exactly was he doing with her? She numbed his pain, he thought. His nights with her were an anesthetic, like the drinking or the motorcycle rides.

The reason for Murdoch's dismay became clear when Charlie walked into his bedroom and saw Simone; she was standing next to a small table by the window—completely naked. He stopped cold.

"Well, you don't have to frown quite so hard, dear," Simone said in her fake-casual voice.

"What are you doing here now?" Charlie asked, and the weariness bearing down on him had nothing to do with his hangover.

"Can't a girl just show up to see her beau spontaneously?"

"Not when she's married to someone else and there are journalists camped out in front of the building. You're supposed to wait until later, when they're gone."

"Oh, it's fine. I know how to avoid them." Her eyes were a little wild, but she leaned against the edge of the table in a deliberate gesture calculated to be graceful and enticing.

But he wasn't enticed—not the way he used to be. When had he stopped desiring her in that compulsory way? And why hadn't he realized it? Because he'd forgotten what it was supposed to feel like—until last night when the compulsion had returned, but for a different woman. "Please put your clothes back on," he said.

She tilted her head and pouted very slightly. "But I've come for my reward. Didn't Richard tell you how I helped with Michael Chap? I've been working pretty hard for you, and you've been ignoring me. A girl might get the wrong idea. But listen, I have a great plan for the show. It's so good even David was impressed."

She spoke with an insistent lilt in her voice, as if to be quiet would acknowledge his rebuff, and her voice was the barrier between her and that knowledge. "First, you need to put me on the show. I mean, just the other day, the *Music News Daily* website did a spread about the best singers, and they mentioned me. It was so amazing. Plus, I need a new pop album so I can take advantage of all the publicity. EmerSound can—"

"Glen Clarence is here." Murdoch's voice from the intercom interrupted Simone's rant.

She straightened, staring at Charlie. "Why is Clarence here?"

"Just routine stuff."

"Is it about Alex?"

"Why would it be about Alex?" Charlie asked, both to deflect and because it seemed strange, her guessing it right away.

"Just a thought. Never mind," she said, and then crossed the room slowly, swaying her hips.

It struck him, as it had before, that her movements were always like this: affected, rehearsed. But today—maybe because in those weeks away from her, he hadn't thought of her sexually even once—Charlie suddenly saw Simone, really saw her, for what she was now, as a separate entity from the girl on stage all those years ago. That girl had possessed a real potential, but it had never been reached, had maybe never even been sought, and this had been the real Simone for a long time. In fact, all her incessant chatter had always been about fame and money, never about the music. Alex's words came back to him: *People make their own choices. Are you sure you bear all the responsibility?* Maybe he hadn't destroyed Simone. Maybe she'd never really existed.

"I think we should end this," he said to Simone, almost gently.

"Exactly." She slipped her arms around his neck and moved in close. "That's what I'm getting at. Once we get rid of Alex, things can go back to the way they were. David's already set the stage for a nasty fight between you and Alex about Brandy and then—divorce. A real scandal. We can make some of it about Alex's bad behavior, too. I have all sorts of things you can use. People will eat it up."

This close, Simone looked less lucid than she sounded and he could see that her eyes were dilated—she was probably high. He tensed, wanting to push her away violently but didn't, afraid he'd hurt her. "No," he said. "I mean end us."

"Charlie…" she whispered against his lips. "What are you talking about?"

"I don't want to sleep with you anymore." He grasped her wrists to try to pull her arms away from him, but she clamped her fingers into his hair. He tugged harder but softened his voice. "I'm sorry," he said.

She let go and stepped back, laughing. "Stop playing."

"I'm serious."

"No." She shook her head several times. "What about everything I've done for you? You can't just send me away."

He waited—to feel the guilt, or the anger that usually followed the guilt, but those feelings didn't resurface with full force. Neither did any affection. There was a remnant of all those things, but they were like the resonance of an echo—an old wave, fading away.

"I'm sorry," he said again, taking a blanket off the bed to drape around her. She accepted it, but when he tried to usher her to sit down on a chair, she pushed away from him.

"You're just going through another phase, Charlie. You've never been able to keep away from me for long. Even when I married someone else, you accepted it. You need me." She walked a little unsteadily to the bed, where she'd left her clothes, and began to dress.

Why had he stayed with her after her marriage? Because she was safe. He'd already ruined her, and he wasn't vulnerable to her anymore. Something was wrong with that plan, though, because he'd still needed her—he could see that now, because as he watched her, a new and curious feeling took root. It wasn't detachment exactly, but the sort of remoteness that develops after the initial mourning for the dead is over. He didn't need her, not anymore. He was free of his dependence on her. But more crucially, he was on the verge of something else, something about his theory and his quitting it all those years ago, and about how he'd never really been free of his dependence on those things. There was an important connection, but it was still vague, and he couldn't quite grasp it.

∫ ℓ

The dining room was the easiest place in the penthouse to barricade against the outside world—easiest aside from the lab, anyway. Charlie sat at the head of the table, and behind him the balcony doors were closed and sealed, obscured by pale blue curtains that hung heavily to the floor. The set of double doors at the opposite end of the room were made of oak and several inches thick, and were soundproof when shut.

Those doors stood open now, and Murdoch came in behind Glen Clarence, who held a stack of twenty notebooks—the kind used for grade-school composition, with marbled black-and-white covers and dark strips of tape for binding.

"I brought the diaries," Clarence said.

Charlie gave a single nod. "Good. Leave them and come back in two days, then put them back where you found them."

Clarence dropped the pile of diaries on the end of the table and grinned with a conspiratorial air—which made Charlie a little sick—then said, "I found the friend, that Donnelly guy from the news article. You know the neighbor guy who said his mom took care of Alex when she was young and whatnot? He said he's got nothing else, only he made sure to mention the newspaper paid him for his story, you know? I think there's got to be more that he knows and he just wants a payout."

"Fine, see how much he wants. I'm sure we can pay him for his time," Charlie said, his glance moving to the diaries again. He felt a pressure on his jaw from an involuntary clenching of his teeth. Was it because reading the diaries was wrong or because he was so impatient to do it? Both maybe.

But Clarence wouldn't leave. He kept talking. "I got some other news for you, too. Real cloak and dagger stuff. I know this guy who used to be a cop—got canned for bending the rules—but anyway I asked him to get me files on that murder, where the patient killed the doc, and he says the files are gone. It's a cold case and all, so he had to have a friend of his dig into storage, but this guy swore that the files are missing. There's a box with the label, but it's empty. He says maybe the hospital still has some of the backup tapes of therapy sessions or something, though, and I thought—"

Charlie held up his hand to silence him. "I don't care about the murder. It's got nothing to do with Alex."

"But you said to get dirt; you know maybe we can blackmail her dad into telling us something."

"Just leave the diaries and get the hell out."

The entirety of Clarence's face and bald head reddened, and he bumped into Murdoch, nearly tripping as he made his retreat. Murdoch gave Charlie a raised-eyebrow look, then walked out, too, carefully shutting the double doors behind him.

Charlie checked his watch and decided that it had been long enough since his last pain pill that he could have a drink without too much extra liver damage. He could drink a little without getting murky again. He poured himself a whiskey and stood sipping it, eyeing the diaries on the table, forcing himself to wait to read them—to prove that he could wait. Then, when he'd emptied the glass, he fanned out the notebooks on the table's surface and perched on the edge of a chair in preparation to read—as if somehow not fully committing to the chair meant he wasn't fully committing the betrayal of reading Alex's diaries. He knew this but did it anyway.

The notebooks' covers weren't labeled, but inside each one, a meticulous hand had titled every entry with the day of the week and the date. She had written weekly, sometimes daily, since the age of seven, which, by Charlie's calculations, was a year or so after her mother's death. The first few years were childish and sparse, and these he skimmed over.

She was almost thirteen when the entries began to get longer and more in depth, and also when the oddities began. In particular, a girl named Katia appeared in many entries. Katia, Alex had written, was a patient of her father's at the Greene Institute and one year younger. Alex at that time was mostly confined to her house because of her heart condition, often under the care of an older next-door neighbor—whom she described as "nice but not someone I can talk to about anything." This must have been the mother of Chris Donnelly.

Aside from the neighbor, Alex spent most of her time alone during the day, but she wrote: *Daddy tells me stories every night when he comes home from work and I really love it.* Many of these were stories of Katia, a twelve-year-old wunderkind, who was full of energy and loved music and books, *just like I do.*

The Katia character became a major influence: Katia was reading a series of mystery books, and Alex asked to read them, too. Katia was learning calculus, and Alex worked to catch up. Katia played the violin very well, and Alex begged for lessons.

Had this been Weiss's method of encouraging his daughter to try new things? In a way, this would've given Alex a friend she could identify with, someone to keep her company, someone who was also sick—though Weiss hadn't told Alex why Katia was at the institute.

Then things took a turn that, especially given that he was a psychiatrist, Weiss should've anticipated: Alex longed to meet Katia.

Daddy says we have to keep Katia a secret. We can't tell other people the stories about her because she's his patient at the hospital where he works. They're supposed to be our secret stories. I said I wanted to meet her and to be like her and asked him how come I couldn't be that great at everything, but he said those kinds of talents come with problems and it's better to be normal. Her problems are even worse than mine, because she thinks so differently from everybody else and she might have to be locked up forever, but I have a chance to get better.

From there, the entries about Katia increased in tension and emotion. It was a difficult thing to read; Charlie was certain Katia was an imaginary girl, or at least the stories about her were very exaggerated, and her status as his "patient" meant Weiss could get out of ever producing her for a meeting with Alex.

But Charlie also felt a pang of sadness for Alex. Over and over again she lamented the fact that she couldn't meet with Katia, couldn't hang out with her, and some of the entries were angry, agitated: *I hate Daddy for not letting me meet Katia. He gets to be with her all the time.* In some entries she made elaborate plans for sneaking out and going to the institute to find Katia. Other entries were jumbled and the handwriting was illegible, the pages smeared with round stains, as if she'd been crying.

And then one day, a year or so after the initial mention of Katia, a diary entry reported: *I finally met Katia in person! But it's an even bigger secret now. I can't talk about it out loud even, in case someone hears.*

Charlie flinched in shock. Had fourteen-year-old Alex had some sort of break with reality? Up to this point, he hadn't been able to reconcile the girl of the diaries with the Alex he knew now, but something like this might explain it. In her desperate desire for a friend and within the confines of her illness, she'd brought the imaginary girl to life. Would Weiss have exposed his daughter to a patient whom he'd described as "needing to be locked up forever"?

Alex made no mention of Weiss's reaction to this new development, whether he even knew about it. In fact, Weiss all but disappeared from the diaries, except for a few mentions of him logistically: *Daddy brought me a book,* or *Daddy took me to the doctor,* or *Daddy got me a new violin teacher.*

Charlie got up and paced. He poured another whiskey, which he swallowed without tasting. Was Katia real, or had Alex been hallucinating—was she schizophrenic? Or worse? It could be anything. After all, he hadn't known her for very long—he maybe didn't know her at all.

He thought back to his interactions with Alex and the details he'd learned from Clarence and Alex herself. So far, none of it was contradictory with what he'd read in the diaries, not in the sense of what had happened: Alex had been very sick, she'd had violin lessons, Donnelly's mother had taken care of her, and Weiss was very protective of her. Maybe the estrangement between Alex and her father had to do with the fact that he'd fabricated Katia and precipitated Alex's break with reality. Maybe Alex had recovered and, recognizing that the stories were lies, was upset with him.

Charlie returned to reading, though he remained on his feet, leaning over, propped up by his arms, elbows straight and hands grasping the edges of the table.

The Katia dream continued, both in space devoted to it and in its elaborate details. Katia "visited" on the weekends and went with Alex to the park, or out shopping, or swimming when Alex "was up to it."

She wrote that Katia worked with her on the violin and occasionally transcribed some of their lessons, but these entries were mostly incomprehensible—with passages about colors and patterns rather than sounds—and Alex seemed herself not to understand exactly what was going on. "Katia says this piece is blue, but I don't see that. I can't seem to make it blue for her."

She wrote at one point that she sometimes recorded *Katia's thoughts as best as I can, but I don't always understand them right away. I write them down and reread them and sometimes I get what she means. But sometimes not.*

The entries about Katia were almost always about music and the most striking to Charlie, and he found himself looking forward to them. At fifteen, Alex wrote: *Katia brought me a book she said a friend of hers got from a music library, and it's all about fugues. She said it could help me understand how the fugue structure works, but it's really hard.* And there followed a discussion of fugues, complete with their mathematical structures, surprisingly dense and mature. *Each fugue has a main subject and different voices expressing it.... Using combinatorics you can see how the voices and their different permutations interact, overlap, and complement each other. You can also break up the different parts of a piece and model their relationships using graph theory...then map the nodes to the different emotional colors created by the different segments....* Then there were a series of complicated equations with their derivations, written in painstaking detail. Charlie had never known anyone, besides himself, capable of and serious about that kind of thought at that age—and for a moment he felt a pang for the loneliness Alex must have experienced.

Speckled throughout the entries was also evidence of Alex's growing physical illness, her bouts with fatigue, her longing to be a normal girl, her deepening depression. And as she grew older, the illness took over and her entries changed, often becoming terse recordings, always mentioning her health: *Feel tired today. Daddy says my heartbeat is high. Read* Catcher in the Rye. *Holden is an idiot. Katia agreed.* Or: *I was well enough to practice the Bach partitas on the violin today and go for a walk. I can't wait to show Katia how much better I am at the trills.* Day after day, entry after entry, of just a few sentences each.

The Katia dream remained her salvation, though: When Katia visited, Alex's joy and love of living returned. She practiced violin, she wrote, *because Katia loves it so much. She loves to see the music.* Could a psychosis really help someone in this way? Charlie wondered. Had the invented friend sustained Alex, saved her life?

Throughout all the entries, Charlie tracked Alex's intellectual development through Katia, who, Alex claimed, progressed faster and better. Alex sometimes celebrated her friend's genius and sometimes lamented her own lack of it, writing, *She's surpassed me again,* and then gave the subject or particular areas where Katia had done so.

Once she wrote, *I think Katia pretends to know less than she does so I can understand and we can still be friends. Daddy reminded me that Katia has to be in the hospital because of it, and I can't decide which is worse—being stuck at home so much because I'm so tired or being locked up like her just for a certain kind of thinking.*

These passages where Alex explicitly gave credit to Katia for advanced thinking made Charlie pause. Why had she done that? Why had she ascribed her best qualities to someone else? And how had she even been able to do it? What was Weiss's role in this?

Then he thought of the way Alex changed when she was off-guard, how her confidence would suddenly appear and her eyes would be shrewd and full of understanding, and how she'd almost vibrate with tension and vitality. He thought of her with her orchestra—how she spoke to them, how she played the violin. Maybe it was in those early years, when she'd needed a friend, that she'd learned to separate parts of herself in order to make one part a "friend." Had she done it so thoroughly she didn't even know she was doing it—even in the privacy of her own journals? At one point she wrote, *Katia looks like me. Well, her hair is different, but otherwise we could be sisters. I wish I had a sister. I'd be a lot less lonely, I think.* And could someone come back from something like that? Charlie hadn't even been able to switch between his work at EmerSound and the lab fully—and he'd been consciously trying. And here she was, seamlessly going back and forth without knowing it.

And then, finally, Charlie reached the end—an entry dated from when Alex was sixteen years old:

My heart is failing and Daddy says we're going to a center in Switzerland where they're going to give me a new heart and do an experimental therapy to make sure that my body doesn't reject it, because the other therapies don't work on me. We don't have time to tell Katia in person because we have to leave right away. I've decided that I'm glad she's the smart one. She's the one who'll get to live and use all that knowledge. Even if she has to do it from Daddy's hospital. It would be wasted on me—I don't think I'll live long.

But Alex didn't die. Charlie remembered from Clarence's original report that she'd come home from Switzerland after three months, a little improved, and then returned to Switzerland again a year later for the final cure. Another transplant, Clarence had assumed, but he hadn't been able to get any of those medical documents. And now thinking of it, Charlie wondered if it were normal to give someone two new hearts within the span of a year and a half. Was it because the special therapy—which Charlie had never heard of—hadn't worked that they'd given her another new heart so shortly after? Was it worth trying to get the medical records?

But maybe that wasn't important because Alex's health was fine now. What might be important was that somehow, over the years, she seemed to have reconciled her dream character Katia back into her own self, perhaps becoming that other girl altogether, because those talents and the genius that she'd ascribed to Katia as a child were part of her, and she obviously knew it now.

So the question remained: Was she still unstable? Charlie should be glad if she were—it would make it a lot easier to do what he had to do—but all he felt was a sinking, drowning sensation, a lot like the one he'd felt when faced with the choice that had ended his public career as a scientist—and eventually his private one, too.

CHAPTER XXXIV

On Monday, Martin Hall called to cancel Alex's contract for her rehearsals, stating only that extenuating circumstances had forced their hand. She assumed Charlie was the circumstance—he'd worked quickly. And she didn't know how to reach the man. In the lab, he'd been so honest, and she'd thought she was about to succeed, but in the end, it hadn't helped. Just left her confused, wanting him in a way she could never have, and now angry too—not just because he was insisting on destroying her music but, more generally, because he'd resigned himself to such a life and constructed the monstrosity that was EmerSound to intentionally produce mediocre art. But another part of her saw that he'd taken blame for things that weren't his fault, and maybe it was this guilt that kept him mired in a life he didn't find worth living anymore—kept him ensnared because he'd accepted it as his punishment, and she thought if he could face that, see that he could redeem himself if he stopped doing what he hated rather than punishing himself with it, he could help both of them. But how could she make him see that?

She had no answers and so was back to putting real effort into the Bernak Hall rehearsals again, and it hurt—a sharp pain, like a jab at an open wound—because her music was almost unrecognizable, garbled and lost in the place, and she had no ideas, could see no way to fix it. Every day that week, she left rehearsals shaking and furious, asking herself if there was a point in continuing—and so far, the answer was always yes. Yes, because she refused to give in to David and Charlie, or to give up when there was a chance to make the *Red Concerto* what she had imagined. Yes, because it was better to be taken down fighting than to surrender. She thought she might know what it was like to be a general at war, to lose battle after battle and still gear up every day, wounded or not, to face one more battle, because the war wasn't lost. Not yet. She had to find a way to fix the Bernak Hall problem; that was all. And when she found the solution, she'd approach Charlie with it. *Anything for the concerto.*

But she couldn't do much about David's interruptions and all the fake drama for the show—again a torment now that she had to take the rehearsals seriously, and especially because she continued to struggle with Michael Chap, trying to nurture some musicality out of him. She'd made changes to the solo part for him, to make the piece easier, to take advantage of his strengths and hide his weaknesses, but it wasn't helping. He could mostly handle the piece technically now, but he still wouldn't follow her directions on the emotional tone she wanted from the piece.

Finally, at the end of the week, when the orchestra had been held up on the same four bars for many minutes, Alex held up her hand to stop the music.

"Your timing is off again, Michael," she said.

He lowered his violin to his side and gave her a petulant expression, as if he'd expected to be called out and was looking to be offended. "I'm reading what's on the page," he said.

"Yes, but you also have to play with the rest of the orchestra. You have to listen to what's going on around you and look at me sometimes. When I motion to slow down, you need to slow down," she said.

"I'm doing the best I can with what I've got to work with. It isn't my fault if this crap makes no sense."

The rudeness was new, but not unexpected—this was what he did on his videos. Still, it irked Alex. "You think the music is bad?" she asked.

He shrugged.

"Don't you know whether you like it or not?" she asked again, not confrontationally, but the way she might inquire if he liked some particular food.

"Everyone says it's no good." His manner was confrontational. Maybe this was his problem—he didn't even know what he liked. Alex might hide her preferences, but she knew what she liked and why she liked it.

"What do you think of it personally?" she asked.

He glanced around, looking for support, as if waiting for people to join him in insulting her the way they did online. He met only silence. Not even the actors said anything. "I should be able to express my opinion," he said, his eyes darting everywhere—at the orchestra, the cameras, the walls, but never at her. "You can't discriminate against me."

"I'm not going to discriminate against you for your opinion. You haven't expressed one. But I am going to fire you," she said.

"You can't do that!"

"Of course I can."

Michael stomped to one edge of the stage. "David, tell her she can't do that!"

Alex only then thought about the cameras—noticing that several had switched positions to better record Michael from different angles—and the show she was giving them. Of course, David would never let her fire Michael, she lamented, but he'd let her get angry on camera. Then the man shocked her: from his corner offstage, he answered Michael by smiling and holding up his hands, his eyebrows raised, radiating helplessness. He mouthed, "Out of my hands."

"What the hell?" Michael sputtered but pulled his violin case out from under a chair and started to pack his instrument away. No one else spoke or moved. There was only the sound of Michael clicking his case closed and stomping to the stairs. He turned at the last minute, before stepping off the stage, to add, "Wait till my followers hear about this."

Alex waited until he was almost at the door, then turned back to the musicians, ignoring the grins and the satisfaction on their faces. They may have enjoyed Michael's humiliation, but she'd found no joy in it—only annoyance and distraction.

"Excuse the interruption," she said evenly. "We'll work the sections without a soloist for the rest of today. Let's take it from bar three-twenty again and remember to come in pianissimo, from almost nothing."

It was with some difficulty that she led them through the remaining hour of rehearsal, but by its end, she'd forgotten all about Michael and David and the cameras. She was even able to see the colors with the music a little now—she just had to stand in a particular spot for any particular color she wanted to see. Finally, she called an end to the day and knelt down by the conductor's podium to put the *Red Concerto* score back in her backpack, thinking of the way she'd moved around to see the colors she wanted and how it reminded her of one of Charlie's unpublished papers that Lawrence had sent her, and his example of—

"That was great," David said, coming up to her. "Man, did you screw Michael. He's so pissed off. We did a sort of video diary with him outside already, to fully get his reaction and all. Now we need one with you."

Alex didn't answer. She'd just figured out a way to fix the hall.

"Oh, come on," David said, pointing to the cameraman he'd brought over with him. "This is your chance to make your case against Michael."

"I'm sorry," she said with a grin. "I really need to go. There's something...something I need to read."

She dashed off the stage and heard David yelling behind her, "Who the hell leaves a shoot to read?"

CHAPTER XXXV

The double doors of the dining room were open, spilling a stream of morning sunlight into the hallway, contained within a bright yellow rectangle. Sundays were designated camera-free days at the penthouse, so Charlie knew he could enjoy his breakfast in the dining room without being disturbed. It was strange to find himself in a good mood. Probably because the pain from his accident had finally subsided.

In the room, though, he found Alex sitting catty-corner to the head of the dining table, face turned toward the window, where the curtains were open, and beyond which the city sparkled, cold and impersonal. He walked to the opposite end of the table, nearest to the door where he'd entered, and braced his hands on the back of a chair—the same one he'd sat on the previous week while reading her childhood thoughts. She hadn't seen him yet and so he watched her for a moment. Her hair was pulled back in a sleek ponytail, exposing her neck, and she wore a tightly fitted navy sweater, a combination that stressed the lines of her throat and torso and made her seem almost naked.

He almost didn't want to go in. He wasn't prepared to see her and had a vague feeling that he needed a plan or some sort of a fortification, at least. He tried for a moment to convince himself that she was only his employee, no different from any of the other girls who'd been on his shows over the past six years. He thought of the diaries; she was so innocent, seeming to care only about her music and wanting nothing else from him. How could someone like that—someone he could squash so easily—feel threatening to him?

She turned her head slowly, and it seemed like at first she didn't recognize him, so distant was her expression. Then she smiled—an unselfconscious and easy smile—one that tempted Charlie to reciprocate.

Which he did. "Good morning," he said.

"Good morning." Her expression faded, but only in increments, as if she were slowly returning to the present.

"Murdoch told me you never eat breakfast here unless it's for a shoot," Charlie said.

"I've been waiting to talk to you about a couple of things."

"Oh?" He raised an eyebrow.

"I fired Michael Chap. And I need a new soloist."

He'd already heard the news of the firing from David, who was thrilled about the drama, but it was brave of her to confront him like this. He liked her direct glance, her lifted head, the straight line of her shoulders. This was the personality she usually hid from everyone else but revealed to him often, as if she trusted him. But she shouldn't trust him at all. He was going to destroy her, like he did all of them. Wasn't he?

"It is completely pointless to try to perform the concerto with Michael as the soloist," she said firmly, loudly.

"I haven't said no to a new soloist."

"You looked like you were going to."

"I was thinking about something else."

"So I can replace Michael?" she asked warily.

He smiled, but before answering he ambled to the intercom mounted by the door, ordered his breakfast, and then finally leaned back against the wall, arms crossed. "Yes," Charlie said, "You can replace him."

"I'll start auditioning right away and—"

"No, I meant *you* can replace him. As in you can be the soloist."

She shook her head. "I can't. I can't play and conduct at the same time."

"I saw you do it at Martin Hall just last week."

She had no retort for that and sat in silent, almost wide-eyed, shock.

Charlie laughed. He liked seeing her shocked. "What else? You said you had a couple of things to talk to me about."

A housekeeper walked in with Charlie's breakfast on a tray—plates of eggs, toast, fruit, and coffee in a pot—and he nodded for her to lay it out at his usual spot, the seat at the head of the table, catty-corner to Alex. He watched but didn't move from his spot against the wall just yet. He could tell Alex was picking her words out with care.

Finally, when they were alone again, she said, almost hesitantly, "I wanted to ask about your theory."

He pushed away from the wall. "You need help with the paper?"

"No, I finished it. But I was thinking of how to extend unified wave theory—"

"That's fine that you read it, but I don't like to discuss it," he said, following his first impulse—which was that he didn't quite believe she'd finished the paper. But his second thought was of her diaries, of what he'd read about her genius. Why didn't he believe her? Had it been so long since he'd shared his work with anyone who had the potential to grasp it that he didn't believe it was possible? Or was it that he needed firsthand proof of her intelligence and sanity?

She sighed out a short puff of anger, but he cut in before she could say anything. "I might reconsider talking about the theory," he said, "if you satisfy my curiosity about something first."

"Okay, anything. What will satisfy you?"

Charlie narrowed his eyes at her as the possibilities ran through his mind—possibilities that had nothing to do with math or physics—and he saw her notice, saw her expression change to the one he'd seen in the lab when he'd almost kissed her, saw her swallow hard, and then she averted her eyes to the window again. He took his time to regain his own composure and force his mind back to the theory while he walked the length of the dining table and passed behind her, then sat down to his breakfast—blocking her view of the city. Now she had to look at him, which she did.

He took a bite of his eggs and a sip of his coffee. "Let's talk about my paper, since you're interested in that," he said. "You understood the entire derivation?"

"Not entirely, no. I don't know complex analysis very well so I didn't follow everything."

He laughed again. "That's fine. No one I know of can follow it without more details. I invented a new technique. I meant to write it up as a separate paper, but I never did."

A light of understanding came to her eyes. "Is that what happened? That professor—your advisor—tried to steal it, to take credit for it, but couldn't really understand it? Is that why you quit?"

In light of what he knew about Alex now he shouldn't have been surprised that she'd guessed the near-truth about his past, but he was impressed nonetheless—and so it seemed only fair to give her the whole truth. "In a way, yes. The order of things was a little different. He wanted me to publish the theory early, with manufactured data. There was a grant application due and he needed the publication. He thought it would be fine to lie and collect the actual data to prove the theory after the fact. I refused. Then I left and he tried to publish it without me, but he couldn't reproduce the derivation correctly."

She furrowed her brow, nodding, and he expected her to ask more questions about those events, but what she said was: "Will you show me the technique? Or just give me a few hints maybe, on how it works?"

"Alright," he said, pushing his plate aside and pulling a pen from his pocket. He flattened his napkin out on the table and wrote out a set of equations on it, then the diagrams to model them, and started to explain, jotting down each step as he worked. She got the gist of it with only a few broad strokes. He hadn't even gotten to a second napkin when she cut in to ask a question four steps ahead of what he was explaining—a question that showed Charlie exactly how quick her mind was and how extensive her education. A question that convinced him she was everything she'd seemed to be in those diaries.

"Where did you learn such advanced math and physics?" he asked when he'd finished explaining the technique. "You couldn't have gone to school much as a kid, with your heart condition and all—and you certainly didn't go to college."

She'd been leaning forward to see the equations on the napkin, but at his words she straightened and shifted her eyes to her plate. Then she speared a chunk of melon with her fork, transferred it to her mouth, and chewed slowly, as if it were something unsavory. Charlie waited patiently.

Eventually, she swallowed and said, "I read a lot."

"Books? That's it?"

"That's it."

"Did you work with anyone while reading those books? Someone must've at least, say, checked your work when you were learning calculus? A friend? Your father?"

She nodded. "Yes. My father."

"Psychiatrists aren't usually the type to know quite this much advanced math," Charlie said.

She shrugged, her shoulders lifting and dropping in a small undulation of her body. "People aren't always what they seem."

"Well, that's certainly true," he said, trying to see a reaction, but all he got were those clear, icy eyes. He lost himself to them for a few seconds, then averted his own away and pulled his plate forward to eat a bite of the now-cold eggs. "Is that what you wanted to ask me—about the technique?"

She looked up with a deep breath, as if bracing herself. "No. Your theory…it points the way to physically influencing acoustic waves using electromagnetic waves, and I was thinking—"

"I didn't mention any of the practical applications in that paper," he said.

"But it's obvious—" This time she stopped herself.

Charlie raised an eyebrow. His paper had laid the mathematical and theoretical foundations for the things she was talking about, but it would take an unusual mind to see the implications of that work outside the field. She was trying to hide her intelligence—it was so clear now, in light of the diaries. But why? "In fact, it isn't obvious at all," he said. "But it is true."

They studied each other in silence, he smiling faintly, she stone-faced.

Then she smiled and lifted an eyebrow at him, the way he often did. "I had an idea for Bernak Hall," she said, "but before I tell you maybe you could come with me this morning to hear something?"

Charlie sipped his coffee, taking his time and letting her wait. "Where?" he asked.

"To a church—"

He burst out laughing—a hearty, almost dismissive laugh. "You're going to church services?"

"No, not services. A performance—at what used to be a church."

"Another one of your special acoustic venues?"

She nodded. "It'll only be an hour."

He was about to say yes but stopped and busied himself with his breakfast again, buttering his toast, cutting his fruit, salting the remainder of his eggs. He glanced at her once and noticed that her hands—ungloved—were gripping the edge of the table. How old had she been when she started wearing gloves all the time? When and where had she cut her hand? Why did she keep everything a secret?

He tried to convince himself that the reason he wanted to go with her was to get the answers to these questions, but really, he wasn't even sure what he'd do with that information anymore. He was sure that what he should do was get back to the work of saving EmerSound, to that pile of papers waiting for him on his desk.

Out loud he asked, "When do we leave?"

CHAPTER XXXVI

At ten minutes to noon, Charlie's chauffeured black car stopped in front of an old church in the center of the city. Unlike Martin Hall, this building was well-adorned with gargoyles, crosses, and intricate patterns of stonework. A short stairway led up to a set of aged wooden doors framed by elaborate stained glass.

Charlie stopped to examine a sign at the entrance advertising today's performance—a quartet playing a series of pieces by old masters of the Baroque period. It was fitting that they were in a church—music was Alex's religion, after all. He held the heavy door open for her and then followed her into the church, which was smaller than Martin Hall and only half-full, with most of the audience seated in the center and front pews.

"The best place to listen is up there," Alex said, pointing to a narrow balcony with a high stone wall at the back of the church.

Charlie followed her up the steep stairs to that spot, then stood looking up, noting the angle of the ceiling—she was probably right; the sound would travel well up here. "How do you find these places?" he asked.

"I've been looking at music venues in the city for years," Alex said, slipping the large flat buttons of her wool coat through their buttonholes one at a time. "Bernak Hall works sometimes, for a large symphony orchestra with a hundred musicians, lots of brass instruments, and big percussion—and if you're sitting in certain rows of the front sections. But a quartet like this would get totally lost in there. This church is one of the best places in the city for a small chamber group. It has just the right size and reverberation."

Charlie was coatless and helped her out of hers, then draped it next to him on the balcony wall. She still wore the navy sweater, and he saw that her pants, too, accentuated her form, falling neatly from her thin waist over high heels. These clothes—surely ones that Grace had picked out—made Alex look delicate and slightly fragile, still pale, but not unhealthy the way she had seemed at the coffee stand. The fragility contrasted with her straight posture and gave Charlie the sudden, distinct impression of a peculiar courage, or of a clean strength. Had the clothes of her old life been calculated to make her look ill? Why?

The quartet began to tune their instruments and she leaned forward, resting her arms on top of the stone wall of the balcony to watch the musicians. "Listen for the cello, especially," she said. "It has a huge sound in here."

He could already hear the richness of the hall in the harmonics of each note, rising clear and distinct, as the musicians bowed their instruments. "What are you hoping to accomplish here, exactly?" he asked.

Alex looked over her shoulder at him. "I want you to hear the acoustics here. Experience it yourself."

"But you said you think I already understand it. What more do you think this'll do? Don't you think that if—how did you put it?—if I'm 'trying to kill the part of me' that wants more out of my life…don't you think I'd resent you for dragging that part out? How do you think you can get anything from me in that case?"

She smiled at him, a knowing smile, as if underscoring his words, and he stopped to really consider what he'd said. What had he revealed?

She said mildly, "You remember what I said. Verbatim."

He barked a laugh in surrender. "Alright," he said and leaned forward like she was doing. "I'll listen."

The concert lasted an hour. The music was beautiful and the hall was everything Alex had said it would be. But Charlie was riveted by her. By the curve of her neck as she angled forward with her arms on the stone wall, by the way her breathing seemed to match the rhythm of the music, by the way she leaned her head back and closed her eyes at the climax of one piece.

Then the audience was clapping and putting on their coats and leaving the church.

Alex, however, remained at the balcony, looking ahead, and some instinct made Charlie wait silently beside her. After a while she said, "Do you ever wonder why people go to church? I mean the physical place, and why it's always been the place that makes people feel sublime?"

"Are you religious?"

"No, not at all. But I wonder about people who are… I think a lot of what they feel in these places has to do with the music and the acoustics. There was a time when a composer wrote music, he thought of how it would sound in these churches because that's where his music was performed and heard—the venue is an instrument, too. Whether the churches were designed that way on purpose or not, they're perfect acoustically for that music. And the reverence, that thing people feel in a place like this, it's not God—it's the music."

"The composer as God?" Charlie asked.

She looked at him and smiled. "The music as sublime. It's the perfection of the music, the way it swirls all around you and cuts straight through you—into you. When it's done right...it reaches the real you, something beyond the person you're pretending to be...to the person you really are. Or maybe the person you want to be. The person you ought to be."

He watched the musicians down on stage packing their instruments into their cases, and he heard the faint chatter of their conversation, a buzzing hum that lost coherence as it traveled up to them.

"But it's not just the composer or the musicians or the music that do it to you," Alex continued. "It's you—your own emotions, your response to the music. And my kind of music, when it's done properly, can transport you to this other deeper place. That's why it's so powerful. It's the combination of the music and your real self. It takes courage to let yourself feel that."

He thought that she wasn't talking to him, not really, and he was getting a glimpse at her thought process, her inner state—almost like the continuation of her diaries, except this wasn't the sick little girl. This was the musical genius, the one who could understand the deep structure of fugues as a child and complicated mathematical derivations as an adult—the one who fascinated him.

He said, "So you think if you perform your concerto in the right place and in the right way, you can somehow create this experience for people?"

"Yes. Exactly."

Charlie laughed without amusement. "Let me give you a tip, and save you years of torture: People don't want it. They want things that they know and expect—things that are safe. They don't want the challenge of your music. They don't want someone to come along and wring that kind of emotion out of them. They don't want to feel at all, in fact. Not like that."

There was a sort of question or an understanding in her eyes, or something that was a combination of those things. "That doesn't matter," she said. "I can't control other people. Why worry about them? Besides, the only way to find the people who do want my music is to put it out there."

He looked over the balcony again at the nearly empty hall. She was wrong, he was sure of it, but something about this idea—that it didn't matter whether people understood or not—was seductive. She was an idealist.

And she was doomed.

"I used to think like that," he said. "Before I did put my best out into the world."

"Your theory?"

He nodded. He felt a vibration and thought it was his emotions finally cracking out of him, but it was only the phone in his pocket, alerting him to a call. He ignored it.

Alex's voice gentled. "I don't think you've given it up so completely only because there's no one to understand it. Maybe that was the reason at first. But now...maybe you don't think you deserve to be happy that way. Or like you don't deserve to spend your time doing things you love because somehow you've soiled your soul."

Charlie glanced at her sharply, suddenly feeling exposed, as if he'd lost a mask he hadn't known he'd been wearing and feeling like he needed to catch his breath. She met his eyes with something like challenge—no, more like intensity—and he thought her breath was coming faster, too, because he'd become aware of the rise and fall of her chest.

She smiled then and said quietly, "Anyway, I understand your theory. Just like you understand my concerto."

This is why I like her so much. She understands and isn't afraid to say what she thinks. The words were a revelation and a kick in the stomach. It was almost physically painful—because he knew he was going to destroy her. Because it was the only way to save EmerSound.

Was it the only way to save EmerSound?

"Excuse me up there! We need to lock up." A man's voice floated up to them and Charlie blinked. He'd almost forgotten where they were. Alex, too, looked startled.

"We should go," he said, glad for the reprieve—he didn't know what to say, or what to think about her revelation or his own reaction. Then he held her coat for her, careful not to touch her as she slipped into it, and they left the church in silence.

Once outside on the deserted sidewalk, when he was about to gesture for his car to pull up from where it was parked down the street, Alex put her hand on his arm—his bicep—to stop him, and he turned to her. A faint wind blew wisps of golden hair that had escaped her ponytail, framing her face like rays of light. Her eyes were earnest now. "I had this idea… Maybe we can hire someone to help with the acoustics in Bernak. Fix what we can."

His phone vibrated again, and again he ignored it. "What exactly do you think can be done to the hall?"

"What if we could use your theory and build a device to manipulate the sound precisely?" Alex asked. "Like electromagnetic waves that can target particular frequencies in particular sections of the hall."

"Acoustitech," he murmured, amazed that she'd made this connection, thinking of this project in the lab.

"What?" she asked.

"I've built a device like the one you're talking about."

"Really?" The word came out on a gasp.

But Charlie didn't enjoy her shock this time. He smiled bitterly. "I've never been able to make it work."

A spear of disappointment cut through her expression, but she said, "Maybe you could just think about the specific problems at Bernak? Take a look at it, at least. You might be able to make it work. Any little bit would help."

"Maybe," he said. "But I'm very busy with EmerSound's problems. It's unlikely I'll have much time for it."

The third time his phone vibrated, Charlie knew he had to answer—three in such a short time meant trouble. The screen flashed with the number of one of EmerSound's conference rooms, and Charlie held up a finger to Alex and said, "One second," before reluctantly answering the call.

"Charlie, you're on speakerphone," Jennifer said. "I'm here with Richard. Michael Chap just served us—he's suing."

"And Keller's already pulled sponsorship," Richard added, voice cracking with panic.

And so he should be panicked, Charlie thought mildly; Keller was their biggest advertiser. "Suing us for what?" he asked.

"Wrongful termination," Jennifer said. "He's claiming Alex discriminated against him for his artistic opinions."

"That's ridiculous," Charlie said. "That can't seriously hold up in court."

"It doesn't matter. He's filed and posted about it online already. Discrimination suits are very bad for company reputations no matter how they turn out. It'll be a while before it's reviewed, and even if the case is thrown out, the bad publicity during the wait will kill us. We should offer to settle right away and hire him back. That will shut him up. Minimize the damage"

Charlie looked at Alex, standing a few feet away, figure delicate, head held high, lost in some world of her own—a world he would've liked to be part of. The idea of forcing Chap on her to save EmerSound made him feel physically nauseous.

"Charlie, are you still there?" Jennifer's voice prodded.

"Yes."

"We're going to run out of cash at the end of this week. We have no choice."

"There is always a choice," Charlie said, thinking of his London properties—the assets he'd set aside for an emergency. Well, if nothing else, this situation qualified as an emergency—because somehow, saving EmerSound without resorting to his old sacrificial tactics seemed crucial, as if something much bigger than just the company or Alex's music were at stake. "I can put together a loan to carry us through until this blows over," Charlie said. After all, they still had Brandy.

Richard's voice saying "Thank God" overlaid Jennifer's saying, "Good. I'll release a statement that we're hiring Chap back by the end of day."

"No," Charlie said, his voice stern. "We are not giving any more money or airtime to that insect of a man."

He hung up the phone and turned to Alex. "Come on, let's go. I need to find a way to protect EmerSound from Michael Chap."

CHAPTER XXXVII

That night Charlie jerked out of a nightmare in which he'd been burning EmerSound to the ground—he'd literally lit a match to his desk, walked out of his office and down the stairs, then stood outside watching the building go up in flames. What made his heart beat in a hard staccato, though, wasn't that he'd done it, but that he'd liked it.

He sat up in bed, blinking hard to force himself back to the reality of his bedroom. The clock read 2:00 a.m., and he was wide awake, but he couldn't shake the dream: The idea of annihilating EmerSound, not taking it public or selling it whole, but ripping it apart piece by piece, remained alluring. He wanted to do it.

Frustrated, he got up, dressed, and headed to the library in search of a drink. He went to his desk, intending to turn on the lamp, but stopped mid-reach, arm extended, eyes falling to the stack of papers just visible in the dim glow from the skylight—the stack with all the work he still needed to do in the attempt to keep EmerSound going: the real estate sales to negotiate, the sponsors to schmooze, the people to appease. The heap looked precarious, as if one push would send the whole thing toppling to the ground, and he was tempted to give it the push it needed, but that was the dream talking again. Instead, he switched on the lamp and straightened the pile.

There was a document envelope on top, which had not been there earlier, with a note from Murdoch scribbled on it, informing Charlie that Glen Clarence's latest investigative report was inside, and that he'd found Simone at the penthouse earlier claiming she'd been waiting for Charlie when no one besides the housekeeper had been home—and maybe Charlie wanted to call her? *No, thank you.* Charlie made a note to ensure the staff knew not to let Simone in again. She could be directed to see him at EmerSound's offices.

Then he pulled out Clarence's report, which was a few informal emails that Murdoch had printed out. The investigator had managed to get Donnelly—the neighbor's son who'd spoken to the journalist about Alex—to accept cash for what he knew. The only new information, though, was something about a cousin, a girl, who came over sometimes and was Alex's only friend as a child. Charlie made another note to Murdoch to contact Clarence—the less direct interaction Charlie had with the slimy investigator the better—and ask him to find out who the cousin was and try to locate her.

He wasn't sure why he wanted to find this friend—it wasn't the fabled Katia, he was sure. There was no reason to make up stories about a cousin visiting. But perhaps this was someone who Alex would like to see again. He wanted to help her, he realized, and maybe he could help her even more by helping make her music perfect. The thought felt like salvation—the salvation he'd been thinking of the night he'd watched Brandy perform. Maybe then he wouldn't feel he needed to burn the company to the ground.

The thought brought back images from the dream, and to distract himself from it and give his mind a different fire to ruminate on, he knelt on one knee by the fireplace in the sitting area and rearranged the logs. Then he pressed the ignition button under the mantel to set the fire roaring to life.

He allowed himself the rest of letting everything wait, and sat in an armchair to watch the logs burn, enjoying the way the fire seduced him, the way it monopolized his senses with its radiating heat, its intermittent pops and crackles, its flickering light, and its smoky aroma. Even the room seemed imbued with a different personality, as if lighting the fire had sparked another consciousness to life.

Could he simulate that in a different room and without the fire? Could he fool the senses by presenting them with the sensations of the fire without the thing itself? How dependent was it on the size of the room, the intensity of each sensation, and their relationships with each other? He might start by trying to recreate the feeling of being close to the fire when in fact you were seated farther away from it.

The problem wasn't unlike Alex's concerto in Bernak Hall. What would he do there? How could he make a large room seem small acoustically? She was right that Acoustitech could work for the particular problems at Bernak, especially if he had a model for what he wanted to achieve. He'd never tried it for something specific like that. He needed data, though, and a better look at Alex's preferred locale—Martin Hall—and he needed to map Bernak acoustically to find its problem zones. He'd need to set up the lab to work with its distinct issues, but that could be done easily.

Then he was walking out of the library and down the corridor, EmerSound and its problems forgotten, the fire still roaring. At the door to the lab he paused, realizing what he was doing; he hadn't been inside—really inside to work—for so long that it no longer felt natural to enter the code and walk in for that purpose. The place was alien to him.

The old thoughts reared again: He really shouldn't get drawn back into this work; he should focus on EmerSound because it was safe; he should force himself to go to bed because he had early morning meetings scheduled.

His hand hovered over the keypad momentarily. He thought of the *Red Concerto* and icy blue eyes and salvation, and he promised himself that he'd just spend a little time in the lab, only enough to help Alex and not so much that he'd get obsessed with the work again—then he lowered his hand and entered the code. He smiled at the click of the door unlocking, like the greeting of an old friend. He'd do just a little work—just a few hours—he told himself again, then he pushed the door open and crossed the threshold.

PART THREE
Adagio

CHAPTER XXXVIII

A heavy snow had fallen overnight and the city glistened with it. Alex stopped on the sidewalk, tilting her head back to look up at the trees, whose branches, bare of leaves, were outlined with thick white lines of snow and sparkled in the sun.

The deep crimson voice of Alex's new bodyguard, Tim, cut into her thoughts: "Ms. Weiss, we should go inside. The protesters have seen us." He was a large man, taller than Charlie by a few inches and heavier by a hundred pounds, and Alex liked his professional manner and felt well-protected by him. She nodded and followed him as he pushed past the twenty or thirty people waiting to protest her arrival at rehearsal—as they had done since Michael Chap had filed suit against her and EmerSound a few weeks ago. They'd even trudged through the snow to do it.

Alex would've liked to walk to rehearsal today, to enjoy the way the sound of the city changed, hushed by the snow and muted to softer pastels, but the increased paparazzi, the picketers, and a couple of death threats meant she now needed the protection of the car and the bodyguard. But at least they'd stopped recording for the show in the mornings, because David had decided the footage only highlighted the protesters and gave them unnecessary press.

She'd really become a princess now—practically living in a palace, driven around in cars, having all her material needs catered to—but, also like a princess, she was locked away in a tower, and whether for protection or for imprisonment, it had the same effect. Alex was surrounded by people all the time—the show's crew, the chauffeur, the bodyguard—but she was utterly isolated. And so she kept thinking of escape. Maybe being a princess, rescued or not, was never a happy ending. Maybe a princess was not the thing to aspire to, even as pretense.

But all she had to do was walk into rehearsal to forget all about it. Today, her orchestra was waiting on stage, already arranged into the unconventional seating arrangement she'd figured out a week ago. By moving the violinists forward, the cellists to stage left, and the basses to the back and center, the sound of the concerto in the hall was vastly improved. It wasn't perfect—not even close—but it was something, and a few drops of water in the desert were so valuable, giving a bit of sustenance and a lot of hope.

She walked onto the stage and put her violin case down by the conductor's podium. "Okay, everyone," she announced. "Let's do a few run-throughs of the whole concerto, then after our break I'll join you as soloist."

There was chatter, and a couple of the orchestra members clapped. Aside from Charlie, several of the musicians had encouraged her to do the solo, and though she worried about establishing herself definitively as a master violinist in a public performance, the only other choice was Chap. Surprisingly, Charlie hadn't forced her to hire him back. Charlie, whom she hadn't seen since the day she'd taken him to the concert, and about whose decisions she was nervous. The longer there was no sight or sound of him, the more worried she got. Well, there had been some sound—the unmistakable racket of construction emanating from his portion of the penthouse last week—but was he working in the lab or destroying it? Anything was possible.

With her orchestra now ready and watching, Alex lifted her baton to start them playing, and soon forgot about protesters and princesses and laboratories. Until they took their break.

Willem ran up to her podium, posture tense and expression stormy. "I need to talk to you," he said.

"What is it?"

He looked away, first glancing at the few musicians still sitting in their chairs and then to the back of the room where the camera crew and David were also taking a break, then squared his shoulders and met her eyes to whisper, "Michael Chap released a video, and it's mostly about you, accusing you of being"—he made air quotes with his fingers—"'unhinged and dangerous.' And he says Charlie is sleeping with Brandy Starr…like he does with all his divas. It's gone viral."

Alex couldn't think. Couldn't react. Everything around her seemed to fade away. She just stared at Willem, trying to process the words: *unhinged and dangerous.* What could Michael possibly mean? What could he know? Her vision faltered, going black for a moment.

"Alex," Willem said. "Hey, Alex, are you okay? Alex?"

She blinked, realizing she was leaning hard against the podium to stay standing. She pushed away slowly. "Yeah, I'm just… I haven't eaten enough today, that's all."

He narrowed his eyes but continued. "Ellise just told me that she heard David is waiting for Michael Chap—he's coming here to confront you, apparently, and they're setting up for that. They want to get it all on camera. And even more paparazzi are starting to show up outside. You should get out of here."

"Can I see the video?" she asked, still processing that first part—the part about her.

Willem pursed his lips, but nodded and tapped on his phone, then handed it to her and started talking again, saying something about ignoring the tabloids and lies in the media. She concentrated on watching Michael's video, her chest hurting when he said: "I would wager she has psychological issues. Someone should really check into that. She's unhinged and I really think she could be dangerous."

"Is it...is it his affairs?" Willem asked. "I'm sorry, I just sprang it on you. I thought that you and Charlie...well, I guess I shouldn't have assumed. Listen, it might not be true, right?"

Alex kept staring down at the phone, though the screen had gone dark and there was nothing to watch anymore. She should reassure Willem, she thought, but what would she say? *No, I'm not worried about the affairs; I'm worried someone is going to dig up my past?* Better he think her distraught over extramarital affairs. Though she probably would be upset if she let herself think about it. She knew Charlie had been with Simone, and so the part about the other girls might be true, too.

"But look," Willem said, "Charlie released a statement even before the video went viral that he supported your choice to fire Michael. It's dated for Monday but didn't really go viral until Chap's video. Charlie says some really nice things about you and your talent."

She focused on Willem's words. Even in the midst of all of this chaos and the knowledge that she'd have to run away, Charlie's support made her…happy.

"Come on." Willem took her arm to try to guide her away from the stage. "Let's go to one of the dressing rooms. You can lie low for a while until you're settled."

As she looked at Willem, a spike of affection burned through her, leaving behind only ashes, because here was another friend she'd have to leave behind without explanation, without further contact, without hope. She couldn't bring herself to think about what else she'd have to leave behind.

She tried to smile and failed. "Could you tell Tim"—she pointed at her bodyguard, standing in the back near the doors—"that I'm going to room three, please? I'll meet you there."

"Oh, sure." Willem glanced at the man, then back at her. "And don't worry, this thing's going to blow over like all the rest of it."

"Yeah," she said, though she didn't think it would blow over, and she couldn't take the chance. People were already digging—how long before they followed up on Michael Chap's assertions?

CHAPTER XXXIX

C harlie's promised few hours in the lab to perfect Acoustitech had morphed into weeks, which had then spilled over to work outside the lab: the installation of dozens of specialized microphones and recording equipment at Bernak and Martin Halls to gather data, the finding and contracting of a fabrication lab for Acoustitech panels, and the construction of a special sound room in his own lab—all of which had required various donations and bribes, especially with the expedited timeline required to meet the *Mrs. Music* finale deadline.

With all of that, Charlie hadn't been able to spare any time for EmerSound itself. But he'd been working almost the way he used to work in the early days of his lab—or maybe even before that, in his days at graduate school—and even though he hadn't been able to sleep much, he was invigorated. So he gave Murdoch the task of managing the EmerSound workload, while promising himself that once the finale for *Mrs. Music* was over and the *Red Concerto* had been recorded, he would concentrate on the company again.

At last, everything was ready, and as the day approached early evening, the engineers and installers arrived at Bernak Hall to install the Acoustitech panels, with Charlie to oversee the process.

He arranged them into three hubs of work, one at each wall of the hall, with several men on ladders bolting the flat gray rectangles of Acoustitech to the predetermined spots, as others stood below and chatted in animated tones. Charlie stood on the stage, hands clasped behind his back, watching and thinking of Alex. He hadn't thought of her in the weeks he'd been busy with Acoustitech—not directly anyway—but he knew she'd been there all along, as if an echo from her performance had been bouncing through his subconscious the whole time, driving him to do the work.

He was excited to tell her about this new work, he thought in wonder. She'd understand both the work and his obsession with it—after all, she'd been the one who asked whether his obsession with this work wasn't actually a love of it. Was she right? Was his calling it obsession and therefore treating it as something to be stamped out just a way to make himself believe he didn't love these things, so he wouldn't have to suffer their loss?

"Charlie!" Murdoch called from below the stage. A younger man stood with him, and after a moment Charlie recognized him as Willem, Lawrence's cellist friend.

Charlie jumped down from the edge of the stage and joined them. "Something wrong?" he asked.

"Michael Chap—" Murdoch began, but Willem cut him off.

"How the hell can you not know what's wrong?"

Charlie didn't answer, merely looking to Murdoch for an explanation.

"Michael Chap posted a video, he says you've slept with all the divas. It's harsh about you and Alex."

The supposed affair with Brandy was part of the show. But the rest? The only diva he'd ever been with was Simone. "*All* the divas?" Charlie asked.

Murdoch nodded. "It's gone viral and people are upset. I tried to reach you earlier."

"I turned off my phone so I could concentrate on the panels," Charlie said absently. He tried to get himself back to the context of EmerSound, to create a sense of urgency and get his mind churning on this problem, but none of it would come.

"You are such a bastard," Willem said quietly, as if to himself, but not so quietly that Charlie couldn't hear him.

"Excuse me?" Charlie said.

"I said you're a bastard."

Charlie smiled at him, truly amused. "Yes—but I'm sure that's not new. What's set you off?"

Willem glared at him. "That you've done all this to Alex. How could you?"

Charlie frowned at him. "You mean the alleged affairs?"

"What the hell else? I mean, she didn't say anything. And I always thought this thing between you two was, you know, fake. But she seemed like she cared a lot. She was really rattled. And you don't even seem to care."

Charlie turned and paced away from the two men. *Alex had believed it.* She'd believed he'd had all those affairs—was still having them. And she was upset by it.

Murdoch cleared his throat. "We can't find Alex."

"What do you mean you can't find Alex?" Charlie said,

whirling back to face them.

Willem answered. "After we watched the video this afternoon, she said she'd be in one of the dressing rooms, but then she left without telling anyone, and Murdoch says she hasn't been home, and she hasn't answered any of my calls or texts. It's unusual—she always answers."

"What about her bodyguard? Have you talked to him?" Charlie asked Murdoch.

Murdoch shook his head and sighed. "He says she slipped him earlier, left Bernak without telling him, and he went out to find her, but he's got nothing. He has no idea where to look for her and no clues."

"I think she ran away," Willem said.

Charlie stilled. Alex—run away? No, she couldn't possibly leave her concerto behind because of one video with unsubstantiated rumors about *him*. She'd have to love him—she'd have to love him more than she loved her music to do that. Then, Charlie narrowed his eyes at Willem. He'd made his pronouncement with more confidence than would a mere coworker. Who was this kid to think he had to come to Alex's rescue, to think he knew her so well. "Are you sleeping with Alex?"

"What? No! But *I* care about her. *I* want to help her." Willem said, punctuating each "I" with a slap to his chest.

Charlie stepped back before he gave in to the urge to grab Willem by the collar and punch him. He had no right to do it. Part of his anger, he knew, stemmed from the knowledge that this kid had every right to defend Alex, and even sleep with her.

The other part of the anger was reminiscent of what he'd felt his last day in graduate school when he'd sat in mute silence as his advisor—a man he'd respected, maybe even venerated—demanded that Charlie fabricate data for publication, and then threatened to expel him if he refused. But Charlie could not compromise his scientific integrity and knew he had to quit, devastated to realize someone had the power to take something he loved away from him. That was the day he'd decided that instead of fighting for the thing he loved, he'd shun it—had redefined love as destructive obsession and fought to destroy it, so he would never again be that vulnerable. That was the day he'd begun giving up on his theory.

He thought of the year leading up to that day—the year he'd spent working on the theory, when every minute of every day seemed to be a sunlit paradise. Why had he thought he would be better off denying himself that light? Why had he let all that passion for his work atrophy instead of working to make it stronger?

Could he now revive it? Train it again? Make it strong and bright? Could you restart a sun that had gone out?

He could only find out by acting. His strategy of denying himself and of quitting had led to destruction and misery. What if this time, instead of shying away from the anger and the pain, he acknowledged what they were trying to tell him—that he cared about Alex and her music? What if he used them as fuel for his motivation rather than as kindling for burning his values?

"Come with me, both of you," Charlie said to Murdoch and Willem as he walked toward the dressing rooms.

"What are you doing?" Willem asked, running to catch up.

"We're going to find Alex. And then I'm going to fix this."

CHAPTER XL

Alex waited for the bank manager to leave the room before lifting the lid of her safe deposit box. She was a little numb, going through the motions of taking the envelope out and glancing inside at what, in the past, she'd thought of as her keys to freedom in case of danger: the navy blue square of passport, the shiny driver's license, the thin rectangular social security card—a new identity to ensure her safety. But all she saw today was the looming prison sentence of silence, her concerto left behind, never to be recorded, and the new identity only felt like a great burden. She'd made this plan long ago—made it with a cool, clear mind, knowing she'd need to leave the city at any hint of danger. But she hadn't known she'd feel so reluctant to escape.

She stuffed the envelope and wads of her remaining cash—not too much since she'd given most of it as payment to the orchestra for the Martin Hall rehearsals—into her backpack and walked out of the bank briskly, keeping her head down and clenching the straps of her bag to pull it taut against her back.

Outside, she stood for a moment, shivering, looking up at the gray sky. The temperature had risen just enough during the day to melt the evidence of last night's snow storm but it might rain, and she wondered if she should stop for an umbrella. No, someone might be able to identify her later. She should make her way uptown as far as she could on foot while it was dry, and then take a train out of the city. But she pulled her coat tight and turned toward downtown. She needed one last look at the city, and then she'd follow through with the plan.

She walked for hours then, keeping a rapid pace, taking turns at random anytime she reached a red light, until she realized that she hadn't noticed the city around her at all. *It's not the city you're reluctant to leave.* She slowed her steps and looked around. She'd made it to the narrow curving streets of downtown. During the day, this neighborhood bustled, open-fronted shops spilling their wares out onto the sidewalk in a colorful cornucopia of hats and purses. But it was late now, and the streets were empty and forsaken, as if the darkness had washed away the city's vitality, leaving behind only discarded cigarette butts, food wrappers, and the occasional bent straw lying in the gutter, used and forgotten. Alex couldn't shake the feeling that leaving the city and abandoning her concerto would have that same effect on her life, reducing it to a dark, dirty thing. She walked faster, telling herself that keeping a rapid pace would ward off the cold, while knowing she was trying to escape something that was increasingly inescapable—because it was inside her.

Her phone buzzed and she jerked a little in surprise. During her walk to the bank earlier, she'd silenced Willem's number—he'd called seven times and sent twelve text messages—because she didn't know what to say to him, how to explain. She'd decided to send him a letter when she was far away and settled, to say goodbye. But she hadn't gotten rid of the phone, unable to commit to an act that would finalize her decision to leave. Then she'd forgotten about the phone altogether; no one else had called or texted—until now.

The text message was from Charlie: *Please come home.*

It's not my home, she wanted to write back in protest, but the idea was so seductive she almost turned to walk in that direction. She wanted Charlie's home to be her home. She wanted to go *home* to him. How did this situation—a temporary pretense at playing house with this man—become something she wanted so badly? *I can't have any of it. This isn't my fairytale.*

The phone buzzed again, but this time he was calling. Alex stopped and gazed around her. A dozen feet ahead, several groups of raucous people sat at sidewalk tables under heaters at a pizza place. They were noisy—noisy enough to shield her conversation. She picked a spot near them, in the shadow of a burnt-out street lamp, and leaned against a wall to answer the phone.

"Alex." Charlie sounded cool and composed like he always did. "Are you okay?"

"Why wouldn't I be?" Alex asked, trying for flippant but not sure if she'd succeeded.

"Willem said you were upset, that you'd disappeared. And you never came home."

Alex closed her eyes, guilt and longing and sadness slamming into her. She answered in a low monotone, unable to scrounge up anything more upbeat. "I was avoiding the media."

"Look," Charlie said, "I know it's a lot…but I've been dealing with this kind of thing for years—the rumors, the cameras, the constant annoyance of looking out to see who's following you and who's spying—"

A burst of laughter rose from one of the pizza restaurant tables and Alex watched the group while she listened to Charlie. Just four young people, men and women enjoying the evening, easy and relaxed. Had Alex's life ever been that simple?

"And I have the experience to help you." Charlie's voice was tinged with earnestness. "Let me protect you from the paparazzi."

If only he could protect her from the real threat. "I don't need help," she lied.

"If this is about what Michael Chap said—that I'm sleeping with Brandy—it's all lies. You have to know that. The only one of the divas I've ever been with was Simone and that's over. It's been over for a while."

He wasn't with Simone anymore. The Brandy rumors were for the show. Alex felt a jolt of happiness—like she'd felt when Willem told her about Charlie's press release supporting her. But she shook her head. Why was she letting herself hope? And hope for what, exactly? That she could have Charlie? Make this pretend life real? It was impossible. Even if Charlie wanted it, she couldn't do it to him. She had made a choice a long time ago, knowing she'd never be able to have something like this.

Had she made the wrong decision?

Charlie misread her silence. "If you don't believe me I can   "

"No. It's not that," Alex cut him off. "I mean, I believe you. I just…I don't…care." She ground out the second lie and got only silence in return.

A driver down the street leaned on his car horn for a long few seconds and Alex flinched.

Charlie said, "I might be able to help with Bernak—with the acoustics, I mean. Just give me a chance. I'll show you tomorrow."

It was a terrible idea, but like the night she'd read through Charlie's original contract, knowing she would do anything for the concerto, she knew she had to stay, because the promise of better acoustics was not something she could ignore. "Okay," she told Charlie. "I'll stay."

♪ ♫

Alex didn't see Charlie that night when she got home or in the morning before she left for rehearsal. It didn't matter, though, because she'd clamped down all her thoughts about him and Michael Chap's video—all she could do was wait and see what happened. Tim the bodyguard stoically drove her to Bernak, and they stayed in the car for a moment to gauge the protesters. But the gathering outside the hall today was barely a group, just a few people who didn't even have pickets to denounce the show and were milling around aimlessly. And then inside the hall, where people were normally calm, a small commotion had ensued; the show's crew was huddled in a corner, with David gesticulating wildly at them, while the musicians were crowded together off-stage, chatting heatedly.

Alex forced herself to keep walking—maybe this wasn't about her—and she was nearly to the stage when Willem came rushing toward her from offstage somewhere and hugged her. "I'm so glad you didn't leave," he said.

"Why would I leave?" she asked automatically. Then added carefully, "What's everyone talking about? Is it another video?"

He seemed confused and looked at the hubbub as if he hadn't noticed it before. Then he shook his head. "I'll tell you about that later. But look, he's here. And he's done it." Willem was pointing to a spot along the left wall about a quarter of the way down the hall, where Charlie, in jeans and a navy sweater, stood at the top of a ladder, screwing something into a gray panel on the wall.

"Come on," Willem said, and she followed him down an aisle toward Charlie as he stepped down the ladder. He reached the ground and pivoted, then smiled when he saw her and walked to meet them.

"Is that…Acoustitech?" Alex asked, her voice faint.

Charlie laughed and he looked happier than she'd ever seen him. "I like seeing you shocked like that," he said.

Willem laughed, too. Alex just shook her head.

"It's all set up. Should we give it a try?" Charlie asked.

"You built it?" Alex asked. "And it's working?"

"More or less. I've adjusted the settings to the hall's specific problems—the glaring ones that I could hear and measure. Now I need you to tell me what else you hear and help me tune it to your orchestra."

"Um…yeah, okay."

"I'll go get the orchestra ready," Willem said and jogged off before Alex could answer him. She was still dumbfounded.

Charlie walked away in the opposite direction, toward the back of the hall. "Let me show you something," he said.

Alex followed. She liked Charlie this way, so light and happy, but it made her a little sad, too, thinking of how he'd be affected if she were exposed. Maybe his mood didn't have so much to do with her, and he'd be okay. "What happened to you?" she asked as she fell into step beside him.

"What do you mean?"

"I thought you said you didn't have time to do this."

"Well, I made time," he said, then stopped to point again. "See this back right section? This is where the sound doesn't travel evenly. The balcony right above it does this weird thing where certain frequencies get reflected and other ones get absorbed, and that makes the sound uneven in the rows just in front of it."

"Yes! Back behind Section F, right? The midrange is almost completely muted."

"Exactly. See, Acoustitech can compensate for—"

"Guys!" David shambled toward them, almost breathless. "Good that you're both here. Listen, the reaction to the Michael episode is better than we'd hoped for. A lot of the key players have already turned on him."

"Okay," Charlie said. "Now, as I was saying—"

"But we need a little more to seal the deal," David said. "We need some PDA."

Alex stiffened. The last time David had brought up this idea, Charlie had balked.

But this time he looked around the hall and asked, "Which camera?"

David pointed to one on Alex's right, and before she could take in what was happening, Charlie stepped to her, snaked one arm around her back, and kissed her.

The kiss was not a perfunctory smack of lips for show, not the act of an unwilling man, not clumsy or even hurried. It was a lingering, patient journey, like the deep tones of a cello when the bow is pulled slowly, seductively over the strings. It enveloped her—*he* enveloped her, a hand cradling the back of her neck, an arm wrapping almost completely around her, and she'd never thought anything could match the way music made her feel, but here it was. She didn't move at first, shocked by this contact—this thing she'd wanted, imagined, but hadn't dared hope for—then, her shock wearing off in the wake of desire, she kissed him back, her hands gripping his arms. He deepened the kiss in reaction, but only for a few seconds. Then he pulled back. She let her eyes meet his, looking for answers. Was it an act, did he mean it, what was going on? But she could read nothing there. He let her go and stepped away.

"Did you get that?" David yelled and someone must have answered, because he continued with, "Okay, guys, that's good for now," then wandered off.

Charlie smiled, then turned to walk up the stairs. "Come on, I want to show you this."

Alex watched him go, still in a sort of shock, trying to process the kiss. And then what had David been saying about Michael Chap? People had turned on him? She had to ask Charlie about it all. Well maybe she wouldn't ask about the kiss. She shook herself a little and called after him. "Wait." She hurried to catch up. "What did David mean about Michael?"

Charlie stopped a few stairs above her and turned to look down at her. "Don't you watch the show?"

"The show?"

"The show—*your* show."

Alex shook her head and Charlie laughed. "No, of course you don't. We put together a *Mrs. Music* episode that's sort of a biopic of Michael. David interviewed some of his old music teachers and classmates—anyone who could attest to his less-than-stellar musicianship. That, together with some of the more revealing footage of him playing, and you expressing distaste for it, made a good case for him being fired."

"David came up with this idea?"

His gaze shifted to hers, and in a careful voice he said, "No. I did."

"Oh." She wanted to know the why and the how of all these things Charlie was doing, but his proximity, now that she knew what his arms, his body, his lips felt like, distracted her, and she couldn't string together the words to ask the questions.

Charlie cleared his throat. "Ready to get back to Acoustitech?"

She nodded—it was all she could do—and then he was going on to tell her about the data he'd gathered, explaining how Acoustitech would work in each area of the hall and the different ways it could alter sound waves. He explained at length the physics behind his invention and how he'd applied his wave theory, and how many panels he'd built. She listened, followed, and managed to focus, but all along the echo of the kiss chased her, resonating in the back of her mind and through her body.

Then, finally, he was done explaining and said, "We still have a lot of work to do, though, if we want to have it done by the finale. Let's give it a try and figure out the adjustments I still need to make."

Alex nodded again, accepting it, accepting everything, letting herself pretend she could have this. But a nagging frustration remained and began to morph, slowly turning into rage, because she knew it was too dangerous for her to stay, and she really couldn't have this at all.

CHAPTER XLI

Alex was enamored—by Acoustitech, by Charlie, and by the promise of the *Red Concerto* as it breathed to life in rehearsals. She, Charlie, and the orchestra had worked on Bernak Hall's acoustics for the last week, and now Alex sat in the middle of the first row, waiting for Charlie to finish a few final touches on the Acoustitech software. The orchestra waited, too, on stage, their conversations a low rumble in the hall. The show's crew and cameras had left hours ago, but the orchestra had stayed for this last bit of work—they would play the first movement, conducted by Willem, so that Alex could hear the concerto in the newly tuned hall.

There was a tap on her shoulder, and Tim, who was sitting behind her, held up his cell phone. "Your father is calling. I guess there's something wrong with your phone? Murdoch gave him my number."

Her father. There was nothing wrong with her phone; she'd been ignoring his calls for the past week. But she'd read his texts urging her to "take action before it's too late." So she knew what he was calling about—he'd seen Michael's video or heard about his allegations, and "take action" was code for "get the hell out." But so far nothing dangerous had come out of the missing diaries or Michael's video, and she might be able to get away with having her concerto recorded if she was very careful. She flinched—getting away with something implied that you had acted wrongly. Had she? Had agreeing to marry Charlie really been so wrong?

She thanked Tim and took the phone, but she stayed in her seat. She wouldn't talk for very long. "Hi, Dad."

"What exactly are you doing?" Dennis Weiss asked in that dangerously calm voice.

"I'm at rehearsal and I really don't have time to talk," she said, infusing her own voice with sweetness for the benefit of anyone who might overhear.

"Have you seen any of the things they're saying about you online? A lot of people are calling you unhinged. It's only a matter of time—"

"Yes, of course, Dad, but by that time, I'll have finished what I need to do here."

"And then what?"

"Then I'll take action." She said it knowing he'd think she meant to leave. But she wasn't sure anymore. Would she be better off hiding again? Taking on a new name and a new personality so that people wouldn't notice her? Did she want to go back to that life? She did not. But neither could she see a way to keep this life. She was an imposter here, an interloper, and unless she figured something else out, she would have to leave when the show and Charlie's need of her were over. Maybe she could still be this person without Charlie and his show. But she was so tired of pretending.

"It's ready!" Charlie's voice projected through the hall from somewhere in the back.

Willem came to the edge of the stage to look down at Alex. "Ready?" he asked her.

"I have to go," she said into the phone. "Let's talk again later." She hung up without waiting for an answer, handed the phone back to Tim, and gave Willem a thumbs-up.

Then she sat back to listen to the *Red Concerto*. When the music began, she closed her eyes and watched the swirl of colors, luxuriating in the richness of the music unfolding into the room. It was bizarre and heady to hear her own composition like this—performed properly and sounding perfect—and she wanted the music to go on forever, to be her reality, and her current circumstances and likely dire future to be the effervescent dream.

But like any dream, the music eventually came to an end.

She opened her eyes and across from her, leaning against the stage, was Charlie. She didn't know how long he'd been standing there but looked as if it had been some time—his pose casual, arms crossed, and shoulders slouching slightly. He watched her, eyes intense, and she knew that her music no longer threatened something fundamental inside him, and that she'd finally reached him.

And he'd done this: made her music a reality, given her an orchestra, and made the hall perfect. It was better than Martin Hall had ever been. It was almost better than when he'd kissed her.

She smiled. "I think we got it."

His eyes didn't leave hers, but he turned his face just slightly to call over his shoulder, "We got it. Thanks, everyone."

Chairs squeaked and the voices of the musicians rose, filling the silence as they packed up to leave.

"I'll get the car," Tim said, and Alex got up from her seat but then wasn't sure what to do. She didn't want to follow Tim, didn't want to leave just yet—not when Charlie was looking at her like that. But there was no reason to stay. So she stood there, fidgeting, one finger running over the scarred wrist of her other hand.

"So you're happy with the hall, then?" Charlie asked. "Everything is perfect?"

"Mostly."

"Mostly?" His eyebrows rose, but he gave her his half smile. "What's not perfect?"

"The tones are a little off when I'm up there playing the solo, but I think that's just my violin. It doesn't have the resonance of a really great instrument."

He laughed, and it was a deep, rich blue. Even the sound of their voices was different with the Acoustitech up and running.

"You're willing to accept something not-quite-perfect? That goes against your principles, doesn't it?" he asked.

"No," she said, now laughing, too. "It'd be unreasonable for me to want something that's beyond my means and that's not so important to the performance. I doubt too many people are going to notice that the tone of my violin is a little less full than it could be. The other things…I insisted on those because they were important and within my reach."

"Who might notice about your violin?"

"Musicians. Lawrence, maybe."

"Lawrence certainly knows instruments," Charlie said, his expression thoughtful. "Hang on a second." He straightened and moved away from the stage, taking out his phone and tapping on it for a few minutes. She watched him; he wore jeans and a sweater, just like the day he'd kissed her, or any of the other hundreds of times she'd see him, but he didn't remind her of the Beethoven sonata or the tortured angel anymore. He was just himself now. And he was perfect.

Willem and a few others called to Alex and waved as they left down a side aisle. She waved back, feeling awkward standing there, waiting for Charlie. She was used to him having to stop what he was doing to take care of some emergency at EmerSound—he'd done it dozens of times in the last week while they'd worked on tuning the hall—but today, it felt different. Maybe because today, she didn't have the excuse of the work anymore and had to admit she was waiting for him just to be near him.

Finally done, Charlie put his phone in the back pocket of his jeans and turned to her, his eyes dropping to her hands, where she was rubbing at her wrist again. She stopped and pulled out her gloves from a side pocket and fumbled a little while slipping them on. Charlie took a step closer, watching her, and his eyes were so dark—almost black—that for a moment it gave him that aura of the fallen angel again, but she thought maybe the chains were gone now.

"Why is your piece called the *Red Concerto*?" he asked.

The question threw her a little, coming out of nowhere, but maybe he wanted to stay a little longer, too. And she could tell him, couldn't she? There was no danger in that part of it. "I associate music with color. I can see colors and patterns. And that's the color I see with this concerto. Well, the last movement is more blue, but the rest is predominantly red."

One set of overhead lights went off with a click, leaving them in partial darkness—Bernak was closing for the day. But Charlie didn't move, as if he hadn't noticed. "Why did the last movement turn out to be a different color?" he asked.

"Because your voice is blue."

"My voice?" he asked, a little gruffly.

"I...I wrote that part for you."

His eyes left hers, but only to drop lower, to her lips. She wondered if he would kiss her again. Were they alone yet? She hoped so, but had no idea. She couldn't concentrate on anything beyond Charlie's presence—with his body so close—and her own pounding heart.

He didn't kiss her. But he didn't move away, either. He stood watching her with those fathomless eyes until Tim came back to announce that their car was ready to take them home.

CHAPTER XLII

Alex and Charlie came up together in the penthouse elevator. He'd gotten a phone call in the car—not the one he'd wanted—and hadn't been able to talk to her anymore on the way home. But the last movement of the *Red Concerto, his* movement, echoed in his mind, and he wanted to kiss her—had want to for days—and wished David and his cameras were here so he'd have the excuse, again. *If you need an excuse, you shouldn't be doing it.*

"So what's next for you?" he asked, as they stepped into the bright light of the foyer. "Now that the show is almost over, I mean."

She turned to him and jammed her hands into her pockets, the motion pushing her shoulders up a little, making her look very young—in the sense of being innocent and a little lost, rather than in age. "I'll keep composing," she said.

He sensed it wasn't a complete answer, but her expression had shuttered. He would've called it regret, if that made any sense, but surely, she wasn't sorry the show was ending. He wasn't sorry. Was he?

"What about you?" she asked. "Will you keep working on Acoustitech and your theory?"

"I don't know. I hadn't planned on it originally, but now..." He didn't know what was next any more than she did. It was strange how lost they both were suddenly. How had the final episode of a TV show—one of *his* TV shows—become a defining moment in their lives?

His phone buzzed, and he moved away from Alex to glance at it, hoping this was the message he'd been waiting for. It was, and better than he'd expected. "I have a sort of surprise for you in the library," he told Alex. "Can you meet me there in ten minutes?"

"Okay," she said, eyes widening.

They parted to take separate hallways, she down the east one to her room, and Charlie down the central one, but Murdoch, in coat and tie, headed him off just before he opened the door to the library. He was holding a stack of papers and a pen.

"I have a few items we need to discuss, if you have a minute?" Murdoch said.

Charlie nodded, but a knot of discomfort hit him. *I like Murdoch—why would I dread seeing him?*

"You need to review the plan for Brandy Starr's tour so we can finalize everything," Murdoch said. "And you need to decide if she should do Europe this year or next."

Right. It wasn't Murdoch he dreaded seeing, but EmerSound he didn't want to think about. He'd had to deal with the finances these past few days—that couldn't be helped—but he'd avoided the other parts of running the company. The contrast between his work on Acoustitech and coddling EmerSound's so-called talent or managing Richard was too much. He put his hand on the doorknob and told Murdoch, truthfully, "I trust you to make the plans for the tour. And next year for Europe is fine." He didn't really think about it, but it didn't matter.

"Yes." Murdoch's eyebrows lifted very slightly as he scribbled on his papers—the man must be surprised indeed if he let that much show on his face. "Also, Clarence wants to know if he should call with his report."

"God no. He can email me like last time."

Murdoch scribbled some more. "One last thing. I found Simone here again when no one but the staff was around. They claim they don't know how she got in and couldn't make her leave. Should I have them contact security next time?"

"Security for Simone?" Charlie laughed. "Come on, Murdoch, she's harmless. She's just having a hard time with our separation. Keep throwing her out politely until she gets the message."

"She was ranting about Alex and antipsychotic pills. I'm not sure throwing her out works. Maybe if you talk to her she'll get it out of her system."

Charlie considered this. It did seem like Simone was grasping at outrageous lies to get his attention. "Maybe. Okay, I'll talk to her next time she comes looking."

"Good." Murdoch ran a finger down the top sheet of his stack, then nodded. "Alright, that's it for now."

"We should have more hallway meetings," Charlie said wryly. "They're so efficient."

Murdoch shook his head, but he smiled a little. "Go see Lawrence. He's waiting."

Charlie had texted Lawrence to request violins for Alex only an hour ago, just after she'd told him she wanted a better instrument, and he hadn't expected anything so soon. But he waited until he and his friend were both seated on the library couch, drinks in hand—whiskey for Lawrence and water for himself—before asking, "Where did you get the violins so quickly?"

"I brought two of mine," Lawrence said.

Charlie eyed the violin cases on the desk. Lawrence never sold instruments from his collection. "I told you I didn't want a borrowed one. I want to buy a violin for Alex, no strings attached."

"Surely, you want a violin with strings?" Lawrence quipped.

Charlie chuckled.

"Well, you did also say that you wanted a superlative instrument," Lawrence said more seriously. "Perhaps this time I will sell one of mine—if it's the right fit."

"What made you change your mind?"

Lawrence looked at him, a directed stare, but Charlie wasn't sure what he was trying to say with that look, or what he was trying to see.

"I think," Lawrence said, "it would do both of you quite a bit of good. And to be honest I couldn't think of an instrument that would fit her better than a particular one of mine." He pointed to the violins. "The other one is merely for comparison."

The intercom chimed, then Murdoch's voice announced, "Ms. Weiss asked me to tell you she'll join you in the library shortly."

Charlie deposited his glass of water on a side table and stood up in a rush of energy. He was at a loss for what to do, though, which was an odd new feeling, but he needed to do something, so he paced in front of the couch. When Alex came into the library, she stood for a moment, framed in the doorway, looking at Charlie. They smiled at each other.

"Hello," Lawrence said, standing up. She let him take her hand and kiss it lightly.

Charlie checked a flash of irritation, not at Lawrence himself but because his friend could make the gesture so freely. "Lawrence has brought a couple of violins for you to try, Alex," Charlie said. "I thought you might like something special for the finale."

"A new violin?" she said.

"Well, new to you." Lawrence opened the cases on the desk. "Come have a look."

The lure of the violins caught her easily and she didn't hesitate to pull off her gloves—the same delicate white silk ones from earlier—and drop them on the desk. When Lawrence offered her the first violin, she took it and held it up balanced across her hands, tilting her head slightly to peer in through one of its *f*-shaped holes. The smile on her face froze, and her eyes went back and forth between Charlie and Lawrence.

"This is a Stradivarius," she said. "From your collection?"

Lawrence nodded, smiling.

Charlie laughed, suddenly enjoying himself very much. So this was what it was like to get something he wanted and to feel good about getting it. "Is that okay?" he asked.

She gave him the slightest look of exasperation, then accepted a bow from Lawrence and drew it across the strings, her eyes closed, and tuned the strings carefully. Next, she played a simple scale, and already it was musical, stretched and soft, swelling up then down, like a blanket undulating gently as it fell. For just an instant, she opened her eyes and looked straight at Charlie, and something in her expression made him take a step back.

She started to play again, this time the solo from the first movement of the *Red Concerto*. He spun away to pace the perimeter of the library, hands clasped behind his back. This was the piece he'd interrupted the night she'd moved in, when he'd been so angry about it, when he'd vowed never to listen to her play again. What he'd pretended he hadn't heard and hadn't witnessed had been there all along, every time he looked at her, thought of her, and in every contradictory action he took to destroy her and hated himself for.

But tonight, he felt no anger or denial, only a peculiar kind of relief, as if the music formed a safety net for the tsunami of emotions it elicited. So when those emotions roiled to the forefront, instead of feeling suffocated by them, he was invigorated, cleansed, free. He stopped near the wall of shelves, away from Alex and Lawrence, to marvel at the experience.

He'd seen a documentary once where a cardiac surgeon had cracked a man's chest open, reached in, and grabbed the heart to pump it, so the organ had no choice but to beat. That's what it was like to sit in a room wet with the sound of Alex's music. His emotions were wrung from him, as if squeezed out by her hand, to run through his arteries and veins, to give him life.

Alex finished the piece and held the violin out to Lawrence. "It's lovely, but a little bright," she said. "I like a warmer sound."

"Yes, I can see why you might," Lawrence said, putting the instrument back into its case. Then, as he pulled out the second violin, he continued, "Your style is quite unique—I've only seen one other person bow in that manner. With whom did you study?"

Charlie held his breath, daring to hope she'd answer the question, but she said, "Why is that the first thing everybody asks? Like they're looking for a puppet master."

Lawrence seemed stricken by her statement, and she must've seen it, too, because she added in a soft tone: "I just haven't really studied with anyone famous, that's all."

"The other person I knew who bowed like you wasn't famous," Lawrence said slowly. "She was called Natasha Volkov. Do you know her?"

Alex stood stock-still, and it was peculiar, as if she weren't real but made of something hard, like stone or granite. But then she shrugged. "No. I don't know her."

Her reaction was too strange, Charlie decided—and wondered dimly what Glen Clarence had found out about Natasha Volkov.

"It was only a thought," Lawrence said as he handed her the second violin. "This one's a Guarneri, a *del Gesu,* and has a mellower sound."

She took the violin almost reverently and repeated the same sequence, tuning it, trying a scale and then the solo again. Charlie could hear the differences in the instruments. The second was lower and darker, but he thought that he wouldn't be able to choose between them—they were both exquisite.

But what made them different exactly? Could he recreate those kinds of minute differences in sound quality with software? He'd read that digital instruments were not very good at recreating a true-to-life sound. Those small details could be the key to the whole thing. If he could tweak the high end just right… He got lost in the topic for a while, making mental notes for a new project, and when he turned his attention back to the room, Alex was placing the Guarneri back in its case, saying, "Thank you for letting me borrow this. I'll be really careful with it."

Lawrence belted out a laugh. "I think Charlie means to buy it for you. It's hard to part with, but I think I've been persuaded."

"But this must be worth—"

"No, no, you must take the instrument and go," Lawrence said. "It would be improper for you to know the cost of a present."

Alex finally looked at Charlie—she'd been ignoring him in such an exaggerated way since that glance over the first scale that he'd become convinced it was a mask for its opposite—that she was actually hyperaware of his presence. Now she'd been distracted from her efforts at avoidance by a total bewilderment.

Charlie wanted to grin or to laugh. But he affected his most casual, almost bored voice in saying, "It's true, I'm buying it for you. Go ahead and take it." Then, when she just kept staring at him, he did laugh. "You'd better start practicing. You'll need to get used to that violin if you're going to play it in concert in a couple days."

She nodded, still looking dazed, but picked up the case and whispered a "thank you" on her way out, neglecting to take her gloves.

When the door closed behind her, Charlie crossed to the desk and laid his hand on the gloves. "That violin belongs with her," he said, stroking two fingers along the soft silk.

Lawrence sat down again and slung an arm over the back of the couch. "Yes, it does… You know, old man, I didn't believe a word of that love nonsense they had in the papers, but I guess even they get it right on occasion."

Charlie shook his head and his hand fisted, crushing the gloves. He wanted to deny it—once upon a time, he would've denied it by calling it obsession. Now he knew it for what it was, but love or not, nothing could come of it, and there was no point in talking about it.

And then it struck him: He'd told himself he couldn't have Alex because he'd destroy her, but that wasn't necessarily true anymore, was it? He wasn't the agent of her destruction anymore.

"Why buy her a violin like that one?" Lawrence pressed.

"I wanted to make sure she'll be okay when she moves on." This was true, if not the whole truth. "Besides, she plays too well to be on a lesser instrument. And I can afford it."

"Oh, there was a time when you could've bought my whole collection and not even noticed the cost. But not now. I know you've liquidated your real estate assets for EmerSound."

"I'm not exactly poor. Besides, EmerSound"—he couldn't bring himself to say Brandy Starr—"is going to make me a lot of money very soon."

"Do you have any idea what that particular Guarneri is worth?"

Charlie threw the gloves back down on the desk and headed toward the bar to pour himself a drink. "I'll pay whatever it takes," he said. But he didn't pour the drink, because it occurred to him that he didn't need to numb himself. He wanted to experience this. It felt right…it felt good.

PART FOUR
Presto

CHAPTER XLIII

Alex couldn't sleep that night, and she lay in bed, staring out into the darkness. The day had been intense. She wanted to convince herself that her restlessness was a product of the *Red Concerto* coming to life finally, or of the new violin Charlie had gifted her—a superbly-crafted instrument she'd played for hours already—but she knew it was more than that. She'd seen that look in Charlie's eyes, at Bernak and then in the library, and she kept coming back to it.

She'd finally broken his habitual stoicism, that veneer for some powerful passion, which he controlled with an iron fist. She'd known it was there, but he'd never let her see it before, not in the week they'd worked together on Acoustitech, not even when he'd kissed her. But she'd seen it in his eyes today, and it was the promise of a maelstrom to come. She'd known in that moment that she was in love with Charlie Emerson.

She got up and started to pace, wishing that she had picked a bigger room, or one with more windows, or at least windows she could open. She tried to open one anyway, pulling down on the lever and pushing hard, but it would not budge. She banged on the glass with her fists, wanting to break it, break every damn thing in the stuffy room. Why had she allowed herself to fall for Charlie? How could she go back to any semblance of her old life after that? Of any life without him? How could she tamp down everything she was again? She thumped the window harder, until her hands hurt and the anger subsided. Then she leaned her forehead against the window, letting her arms drop, and focused on the cool flat glass against her face. The night was cold, and she wore only a threadbare T-shirt that hung mid-thigh, but she waited until she was shivering before turning away from the window.

She saw, first, the wedge of light from the hallway on the ground inside her room; second, that the door was open; and third, Charlie Emerson standing on the threshold, looking the way she felt: restless and hyperaware. He wore only pajama bottoms, and she clenched her hands at the sight of him half naked.

She wanted to be able to look away, or to tell him to go away, but she couldn't—wasn't this the maelstrom she'd been waiting for tonight?—and he entered, shutting the door behind him, gently. There was no breach in his control as he moved toward her, just a slow, lupine approach, but his hair was tousled like he'd run his fingers through it repeatedly. Alex wondered how it would feel to run her fingers through his hair.

He moved close enough that his face slid from the shadows into the light streaming in through the window. He had a fierce expression, the one he'd had in the lab when he'd almost kissed her. She moved back a step and her hip hit the ledge of the window. She pushed herself against it. He smiled; it wasn't a kind smile or an amused smile—it was primal and hungry, and she gripped the ledge behind her to keep her hands steady.

She saw the images of her concerto again, as she had all those weeks ago when she'd written the fourth movement. Here it was at last—her music in motion. She smiled at him and saw its reflection in the fire that ignited in his eyes.

"Why are you awake?" he asked, his voice a rasp just above a whisper.

"I was waiting for you."

"Turn around."

He'll find out, a little voice screamed in her head, but she ignored it and turned, raising her arms and stretching them to press her palms flat against the cold glass above her. The action put her closer to him, almost touching, but not quite. He lowered his head slightly and let her wait like that, and she felt his breath on her hair. It was uneven. She closed her eyes and whispered his name.

He moved his body against hers, the cotton of his pants rough on the back of her thighs, and his chest hot against her back, then tortured her with languid movements, his hands coming up to caress her through her shirt, starting from her hips and rising up her sides, over her arms. When he reached her hands, he laid his palms over hers and leaned into her. "I've wanted to do this for weeks." His voice was gruff and she shivered with the pleasure of it.

"Do it then," she told him.

He slid his hands down her body again and then under her shirt, hesitating when he found she was naked underneath. That break told her how much in control he still was. This wasn't the eruption, not yet. His coming here was calculated, considered. *He's going to find out.*

Then he moved, one hand up to her breasts, the other down, and her thoughts scattered. She was an instrument in his hands—like a cello, she thought, the way he held her, the way he moved his hands against her—and she lost herself in the music of it.

When she couldn't stand it any longer, when she had to touch him, she leaned into him, dropping her head back on his chest and bringing a hand to grip the back of his neck. The moment she touched him, he spun her, violently pushing her against the wall next to the window, his mouth on hers, his body crushing her to the wall. He grasped the bottom of her shirt and pulled it off, leaning back to look at her, and she gasped. His eyes bore into her, hungry and a little wild. This was Charlie's soul completely naked, all the things he held in such strict control—the fierce passion and the drive and the genius, all etched in the planes of his face and the intensity of his eyes. She reached out to undress him.

She clung to him when he lifted her up and pushed into her, setting a slow rhythm, and she had the fleeting thought that he was the embodiment not just of one movement of the *Red Concerto* but of all her music and of all her aspirations, and some distant part of herself screamed disaster. But she ignored it because she might never get the chance to experience something like this again. His tempo increased and she let the beat sweep her away. She held off as long as she could, making the crescendo last, and only when she felt him surrendering, did she let go.

CHAPTER XLIV

It was morning, and Charlie was in the kitchen in pajama pants, arranging cups of coffee on a tray to take back to Alex's room. He smiled, humming the theme to the *Red Concerto*, allowing himself the rare exercise of imagining future possibilities for himself—and Alex. Together they'd remake EmerSound and reinvent the future of music and acoustics. He would establish a research department in his company and develop Acoustitech for all the applications he'd once dreamt of. He had so many ideas that every once in a while he had to stop and jot them down on a napkin from a stack on the counter, lest he forget. He'd filled six napkins by the time the coffee was ready.

Alex was still asleep when he came into her room, lying on her stomach, her head turned away from the window. She looked like a painting from some old master—her arms raised and tucked beneath her pillow, the covers pushed down, exposing her to the waist, the bare skin of her back and the curve of her breast smooth and enticing. He tensed with an acute desire for her. Then, inexplicably, he also felt a pang of unease, though he couldn't locate its source.

He shrugged, then set the tray down on the nightstand and sat on the bed next to her, watching the way her hair fanned out on the pillow and the slightly flushed skin of her cheek. She stirred and turned over on her back, then smiled at him, groggy and vulnerable.

I'm vulnerable, too, he thought, wondering if this was the origin of his unease, but he found that it didn't bother him anymore. Instead, the vulnerability seemed necessary—as if that was what had made last night different from his nights with other women. Different and better. He twirled a strand of her hair around his right index finger. "You're beautiful," he said.

Her features flickered, her smile dropping and then reforming, but sadder somehow. He ran his finger along her neck and down her chest between her bare breasts, a light brush against her skin, and a shiver ran through her body. He smiled, admiring her shape and her taut, perfect skin.

Then he froze. That was it—her *perfect* skin. Where were her scars?

He pulled his hand away, wanting to question her, to convince himself what he was thinking was ridiculous, but confronting her seemed like the wrong tact. So he only said, "I brought coffee."

She pushed herself up to sitting, and still half asleep hadn't seemed to register the change in him, though she did pull the sheet up to cover her breasts.

He reached out his hand and gently grasped her wrist—the one with the scar he'd discovered on the day he'd married her—and ran the index finger of his other hand over the raised scar, where the skin wasn't perfect. "Tell me again how this happened."

She swallowed. "My hand got caught in a car door. I wasn't paying attention. It's really not all that important."

He let her wrist go and picked up a mug of coffee from the nightstand, offering it to her, then waited a moment for her to take a sip. "You said you don't like to talk about it," he said. "But that doesn't seem so dramatic that it would traumatize you."

She paused with the mug to her lips and her gaze moved to his, but her expression remained impassive. She drank from the mug again before answering. "It was a bad enough injury that I couldn't play the violin for weeks afterward. That part was very traumatic for me."

"Hmm." Charlie took his own coffee and stood to drink it, looking down at her. He tried to consider his next move, but all he could do was watch his own disappointment—a visceral feeling slowly growing into something that was almost a physical pain.

"Ms. Weiss, David and Grace are here." Murdoch's voice came from the hallway, accompanied by a knock on the door.

Alex shoved her mug onto the nightstand and scooted off the bed, dropping the sheet as she ran to the closet. "I'm supposed to have a photoshoot this morning," she said, "and I'm late."

He saw again the perfectly smooth skin of her chest and thought of the scar on her wrist—a pronounced scar from a major injury that hadn't shown up in any of Clarence's reports. The same reports that had documented instead at least one heart transplant, maybe two—surgeries that required an incision large enough to allow for the cracking of ribs and the removal of her heart. And yet Alex bore no scars on her chest.

He wanted to laugh at himself—was it just five minutes ago that he'd thought he was happy because he could be vulnerable?

It seemed he'd merely reverted to being blind about something—someone—he was obsessed with. He thought of Simone's accusation about the antipsychotic medication, the diaries documenting Alex's alter ego, her constant pretense at being someone she was not.

He wanted to follow her into the closet, to shake her, to yell at her, to demand answers. But he didn't do any of that, calming himself, reminding himself he didn't have enough information yet, not enough data to accuse her, and he shouldn't throw her off balance before her big performance tomorrow night, at least not without proof. And because he was sure she'd lie to him even if he did confront her.

He didn't wait for her to come out of the closet before heading to his desk in the library, where he kept all of Glen Clarence's reports. He found the latest report in his email; this was the one Murdoch had told him about yesterday—just yesterday when Charlie had been so captivated by Alex and her music.

He had a strange sense of foreboding, as if some knowledge were waiting for him inside that message he didn't want to see, something that threatened him and the delicate strings that balanced his new serenity. But a serenity based in blindness was only a mirage, and the longer he was blind, the more devastating the consequences would be when that mirage dissipated.

So he straightened his back and opened the mail. The report was about Natasha Volkov—the woman who played violin with the same strange technique as Alex. Clarence wrote that the woman had died of a drug overdose while still a student at the City Academy of Music, and no one remembered her giving violin lessons. She had been described as a troubled young woman by people who knew her, an immigrant from Eastern Europe, with no real friends and no family, except a daughter, maybe eight years old, who had disappeared into the foster system.

This last fact about the daughter sparked an idea, and Charlie called Clarence immediately for more information, but the man didn't answer. Charlie left a message asking for a call as soon as possible.

Then he turned to his computer to do his own research, typing in various combinations of names—Alex Weiss, Katia, Natasha Volkov, Dennis Weiss, the Greene Institute, *Mrs. Music*— and terms like violin, hospital, and heart surgery, most of which returned either too many results or nothing but pages with long lists of names for members of different organizations.

Finally, the combination of Katia, hospital, violin, and *Mrs. Music* took him to an obscure fan site for the show, though not one of the dozens EmerSound had set up. Charlie assumed "Katia"—the only term not associated publicly with Alex—would be the name of a fan who'd posted a comment, but he scrolled down anyway, because he was out of ideas and still waiting for Clarence. It was not a "Katia" but a person calling himself Joe-the-Fan, who had posted:

She looks like this girl Katia that was at a mental hospital where I used to be a janitor like ten years ago. At first, I thought it was the same chick 'cuz she used to walk around with a violin case but then I remembered that chick was on the crazy ward and then died or something.

It seemed like too much of a coincidence—a Katia at a psychiatric hospital, who may have played the violin, and who looked enough like Alex that someone had remembered it? Was this the Katia from Alex's diaries—and if so, what did that mean?

Charlie had found no answers by the time Glen Clarence called back a while later.

"What was Natasha Volkov's daughter's name?" he asked the investigator, with little preamble.

Clarence stuttered for a bit, then said, "I think it was Katia…. No, wait, Katia was the cousin—you know, the one that Donnelly guy told me about…let me check…. Huh, that's weird. They have the same name. What are the chances of two Katias in one investigation?"

Not two Katias, Charlie thought, three. Katia the daughter, Katia the cousin, and Katia from the diary. But Charlie couldn't see the link exactly—and there was only one person who could be involved in Alex's deception. A person who could both prescribe antipsychotic pills and falsify medical records, thereby turning insanity into heart failure.

CHAPTER XLV

C harlie rode his motorcycle without thinking, without control, without anything but the single-minded devotion to find the truth—a truth he was beginning to see but couldn't quite believe.

He'd tried to reach Dennis Weiss the previous day, but the man had not accepted his phone calls. Then, after eluding Alex that evening with excuses of work—through Murdoch because Charlie couldn't bring himself to see her in person—he'd remembered Clarence telling him that Weiss's usual Saturday morning activity was visiting his wife's grave at a cemetery not too far from his house upstate, which Charlie realized, as he rode, was also near the Greene Institute.

It had snowed again the night before, leaving the roads slippery and rough, and Charlie almost crashed twice on the way: once, when he took a turn too fast and the bike slipped—bringing him so close to the pavement that he tore the leg of his leather pants—and then again when he almost missed a red light and hit the brake hard enough to nearly flip the bike front to back. By the time he arrived, his pants were caked in snow and mud.

The cemetery was a small field covered entirely in a white blanket of snow, bright in the winter sun and marred only by grave markers protruding at uneven intervals, the old and the new, gray stone and shiny marble. He recognized Weiss from a picture in Alex's file. The man was there at a gravesite, standing alone in the cold silence of the day, head down.

Charlie walked up behind him, expecting to find a tombstone with his wife's name, but the marker only bore a single capital letter X. It was ominous, and again Charlie had the urge to turn away, to let it all go and pretend he'd never met Alex. But his night with her wasn't something he could just push away, and he'd been a scientist, once upon a time—maybe he would be again—and knew that ignoring facts didn't change them.

"Who's buried in that plot, Dr. Weiss? What have you done?" Charlie asked.

Weiss spun around, the shock on his face turning to anger when he saw Charlie, recognition in his eyes. Charlie held his gaze with a ruthless one of his own—he'd have his answers, whether the doctor volunteered them or not.

They stared at each other until Weiss at last said, "How dare you harass me at a cemetery? I don't care who you are; you have no right."

"Your daughter is my wife, and the future of my company. My whole life is tied up with hers now. It's absolutely my right to come see you, to ask why you've been lying about her health and why you've been pretending she has heart troubles. Whatever reason you have for hiding her mental illness, it hasn't helped her. It's doomed her."

Weiss didn't immediately respond; he kept staring at Charlie's face, trying to decipher something. Then with a flat, monotonous voice that revealed nothing, he asked, "Why are you assuming I lied about her heart condition?"

"She has no scars from her supposed heart surgeries."

Weiss closed his eyes and shook his head. "I did warn her about you." He said it rhetorically, almost under his breath, but it was as good as a confirmation of Charlie's accusations.

"Tell me what happened," Charlie said, controlling his voice, trying not to show his impatience, his need to punch someone in the face. "Tell me or I'll have to resort to something drastic."

Weiss's shoulders dropped and resignation replaced anger on his face. "My daughter, Alexandra, is buried in this plot."

"Your daughter?"

"Yes, Mr. Emerson. You see, I did have a daughter—a biological daughter, Alexandra Weiss. She was never well—her heart disorder was much more severe than her mother's had been. She succumbed to it when she was just eighteen, like her mother had twelve years prior. The girl you know as Alexandra Weiss was my patient at the institute. I've helped her stay hidden these past years by giving her the identity of my dead daughter."

Charlie moved his head slightly downward in a motion that started as a gesture for Dr. Weiss to continue but was forgotten in the commotion of a mind trying to make sense of the insensible.

"Fifteen years ago," Weiss continued, "your Alex—known as Katia then—came to us for certain behavioral problems. That's what they called it, you see, her gifts. She didn't fit...and she was parentless, homeless. Her caseworker was a woman I knew, and she came to me and asked if the institute could take Katia. She was too vulnerable for the foster system, a prime target for abuse...We'd just opened the children's program—really, it was my colleague, Dr. Shaylan, who was running it—and we didn't have any girls, so we took her.

"Katia was eleven years old. We were supposed to socialize her, teach her to be normal. That's what the program was for. At first, we saw nothing special, just a maladjusted, rather average little girl. Not really unwell enough for the program, but we decided to keep her for a couple of years since we had the space and the money.

"But what we saw…it was only what Katia wanted us to see. Even at that age she had a unique understanding of the world—something that few people gain even in adulthood. She manipulated almost every psychological test we performed so we'd think she was unexceptional. But there was one test she couldn't fake—when I finally realized I should test her.

"Katia is a synesthete. She can *see* sounds, music mostly, as displays of colors and patterns. Sometimes she tastes them. It's a kind of higher-level association of the senses, something between perception and conscious thought. In those early years of her life when the ability first presented itself…it confused her, I think. Especially if the music wasn't logical or harmonious. And I think her mother was afraid for her and did a lot to convince Katia to hide it.

"It was a while before I realized what was going on. Then I began my tests and saw her tendency to retreat, sometimes violently, whenever presented with certain kinds of music. Some of the modern classical composers were the worst. It was intriguing to me on a professional level, to see this little girl draw back in physical revulsion when presented with a certain genre of music and then sit in enraptured awe in response to others. She said the best music produced the most beautiful sights. Imagine being able to visualize your emotions…. I think that's what it's like for her."

Weiss fell silent. He was no longer looking at Charlie, but out onto the cemetery, his eyes unfocused as if he were seeing the little girl as she was all those years ago. He continued to stare off as he went on, his shoulders hunched in his brown coat, his breath coming out in misty bursts.

"Then she started to ask questions about the music she liked—and the questions she asked! I like to think of myself as a somewhat accomplished pianist, but she was already so far ahead of me in terms of her depth of understanding. She was talking about the mathematical theories behind fugues. That's when I really started to see the extent of it—her intelligence, her musical gifts." He turned away with a jerky motion and began to pace back and forth in front of the grave, crunching in the snow, substituting the movement for the emotion he wouldn't show on his face.

"Please go on," Charlie prompted, his tone almost gentle.

"Yes, yes. Where was I? Yes…she was faking. She'd faked every test so we wouldn't know. And you know what that little girl—that little twelve-year-old girl—said to me? She said, 'Average girls are expected and accepted—they're left alone to live how they want.' I'll never forget it. I asked her how she wanted to live, and she said she wanted to be left alone to play the violin.

"Well, you've heard it—she was a virtuoso already, back then. She said her mother had taught her, and I looked into it. It was true. Her mother had been a rising star at the City Academy of Music but dropped out with mental health issues. Started dancing in unsavory places and eventually died of a drug overdose. No record of the father at all."

"Natasha Volkov," Charlie murmured.

Weiss continued: "And here was Katia, with only that old violin left from her mother, and apparently she was sneaking books and videos and recordings from the hospital library to continue to learn. Practicing in empty corridors around the hospital all night. One of the nurses and a few of the orderlies knew about it, I think. They and some of the other patients had helped her. She's always been resourceful."

He stopped his pacing to look at Charlie, underscoring the next part of his story, as if deliberately emphasizing his role. "I was already beginning to have affection for her as if she were my own daughter, and now I knew how vulnerable she really was, and if I'd let her go back into the system, they'd destroy her. So I helped her fake her way through my tests. We made her look just unwell enough mentally to keep her in the hospital. And I helped her with her education—music, too. It was what she wanted. It was what I wanted.

"I took her home sometimes to be with Alexandra and to have violin lessons. She needed the instruction and they both needed a friend. They were good for each other. Katia gave Alexandra the will to live. If I'd been able to, I would've adopted her...but this was the best way... I thought so at the time anyway." The last sentence was said in a low voice that was almost a whisper. Weiss's shoulders sagged more and his head lowered.

"But what happened? Why is she pretending to be Alex now?" Charlie asked.

Weiss lifted his head, and his sad smile was a century old. "The plan was, once she was old enough, I'd say she was well and she could leave on her own. That was the plan...but I failed her.

My daughter—my biological daughter—her heart malady took a turn for the worse when she was sixteen and Katia was fifteen. There was a transplant, but it didn't take. I was distracted, took a lot of time off...and Dr. Shaylan took over Katia's care. Somehow, he'd found out about her violin playing, too, and her synesthesia, and he was fascinated by her case, wanted to study her. He wanted to help her, too, but we had differing ideas on how to do that. I'd managed to keep her as my personal patient, but when I started my absences, Shaylan worked his way in. I think it was bad... Will you think me a terrible person if I tell you I've never had the courage to look into the files? To see what exactly he did to her... to drive her to that..."

"Drive her to what?" Charlie asked, forcing the words out, because he knew already—didn't he?—thinking of the murder Clarence kept talking about, the patient who'd killed one of the doctors.

Weiss's voice was weak when he began speaking again, but it was devoid of emotion. "He planned to give her electroconvulsive therapy that night. The nurses told me. To *cure* her synesthesia. But unbeknownst to me, Shaylan was using unsafe protocols, and Katia knew. She knew what it could do to her. She'd seen it in other patients... One of them eventually ended up killing himself. So she fought back. Shaylan died. That's all I know." There was a note of something secret, something hidden in the last phrase, but Charlie let it go, because Weiss was going on.

"I don't know how she escaped, but she did so that night, in the commotion of Shaylan's death, and she came to the back door at my house just before sunrise. She'd run three miles through the woods with an injured hand.... She was covered in Shaylan's blood, her own blood...and her eyes were shining, but she was clearheaded.

"They'd made a plan, you see. Alexandra had already told me weeks before that Katia could take her identity if...when... and now Alexandra was dying. She was already in a coma...not yet dead. But she was at home, you see, because I'd wanted to take care of her in her final days.

"The authorities tracked Katia to my house, but they had it all wrong." He laughed bitterly. "They thought she was coming for me, too, that I was in danger. They staked out the house and searched everywhere for Katia. But the whole time she was in my basement. Hiding. She stayed with us until my Alexandra was gone, and we buried her together, here. If you pay people enough, they'll let you bury a body without too much paperwork." He pointed to the headstone and smiled sadly.

"Then I gave Katia everything I had of Alexandra's. Her driver's license, her birth certificate, all of it. Clothes even. And cash. As much as I could get without raising suspicion.

"Like I said, Katia was resourceful. She said she knew people who could...who could fix it so she could become Alexandra. I just had to keep Alexandra's death out of public record and make it seem as if I'd taken her to the clinic in Switzerland again—Katia gave me the name of someone to help me. They'd worked it all out. And Alexandra had me convinced this is what she wanted."

Weiss laughed again, but this time it was a sad, resigned laugh. "It was all so easy for me. To give her this last thing and pretend to myself that I was helping Katia and carrying out Alexandra's last wish. Did I help? Or did I doom her? I wonder if I should've...let them take her. I don't know..."

Charlie was missing something. This didn't sound right. "Why did Alex—Katia—have to escape? Surely it was self-defense if this other doctor was using unsafe techniques?"

Weiss slipped his hands into the pockets of his overcoat and averted his eyes toward the ground. "Dr. Shaylan had long been documenting Katia as violent...which I only found out when the police showed up at my door after she'd...after he was dead."

"So you could've just contradicted him—"

"It's not that simple!"

"Why the hell not?"

Weiss flinched and took a step back at Charlie's tone—and perhaps his expression, too. He said, "Katia does need to take medication to help her with a condition related to her synesthesia. Too much loud noise...agitates her. I didn't think I'd be able to protect her in court. They told me there was a lot of evidence of the violence. I'd never seen it, but that didn't mean it didn't happen. And, after all, it was clear Katia and Alexandra had been planning something. Perhaps she'd planned to hurt him. And like I said, I wasn't in the right state of mind."

"I don't care for your excuses, Dr. Weiss. Tell me the facts. What did this Dr. Shaylan write about her? What were the circumstances? Why would you let someone who might be violent out into the world?"

"I...I don't know, damn it! I did what I could, don't you see? I can't go back and change it. I couldn't bear to look at the files. And then they disappeared. She made them disappear."

"So you just let it go? You let *her* go so she could trap someone else?" Charlie fisted his hands, fighting to keep control.

Weiss shook his head and whispered, "I owed her. I was the one who put her in that position. What else could I have done?"

"You could've…" *What could he have done?* Charlie wondered as he looked at the beaten man in front of him, the man who'd been so weak with his own emotions, so afraid of feeling bad that he'd helped an unstable girl possibly get away with murder. And look at him now—defeated, guilt-ridden, all but destroyed, and for what? Love. Love had weakened him.

Charlie felt a surge of disgust, of sorrow, and of hopelessness for the man, and that pity kept him from berating Weiss anymore. He couldn't see the point in it. And perhaps the man had spent the last decade paying for it in his own way.

"I was so tired of the suffering. I had this responsibility to protect and defend her, and I was failing." Weiss's neck was bent, his head hanging as if the burden of it was too much and he was about to break under its load. "I wanted to be done with it. I thought it was done when she got away."

Charlie stilled. These were his own words; hadn't he thought over and over again that he wanted to be done with his theory, with the lab, with Simone, with EmerSound, *with the suffering*? What was the difference between Weiss and himself? There had to be a difference, because Charlie wasn't going to end up like this man.

"Maybe the reason you're not done with it is because you still let Alex—Katia—play you," Charlie said. "You should've turned her in, let her go to jail—cut yourself off from her. That's the only way you could be done with her."

Weiss's head lifted. His eyes and his voice desperate, he said, "I can't just throw away someone I love…. You can't either—you've got to help her. She doesn't have anyone else."

"There's no help for her."

"But you love her. I know you do."

"I don't even know her."

"You know her. You let her have her music. That's the real woman—the musician is who she is. Please help her."

Charlie said nothing and turned to go. As he walked away, he saw, out of the corner of his eye, the old doctor fall to his knees at the grave of Alexandra Weiss.

CHAPTER XLVI

C harlie rode, hard and fast, to the Greene Institute. Weiss had said the files on Katia were missing, and Charlie remembered Glen Clarence telling him many weeks ago that the police files on the murder were missing but the institute might have backup tapes of sessions with the patients. Weiss may not have the courage to face what had happened to Alex—Katia—but Charlie didn't have the luxury of cowardice.

When he got there, though, he stood looking up at the facade of the enormous building, at the countless windows that stared back at him like blank, dead eyes, and at the large double doors, unnerving and beckoning all at once. The wind picked up slightly and blew against his face and hair, whipping his leather coat open.

He still couldn't quite reconcile the Alex he knew with a place like this, or with the story Weiss had told, and when he moved, his steps were forceful and slow, as if he were trudging up a snowy mountain, though the path had been cleared of snow.

In the anteroom just inside the entrance, Charlie relayed his purpose to a guard, then waited, staring down at the rust that streaked across the surface of the guard's desk like dried blood, until a young man in the tan slacks and white shirt of an administrator came striding in.

"I don't know why everyone's interested in this case again all of a sudden," the man said. "I already told the cop I was giving her the only backup copy of the tapes. There are no files. I don't have anything else."

"Everyone?" Charlie asked, aghast that he'd been so blind while others had seen through Alex. Even while living with her and having the diaries, he'd been the last in a line of people who'd figured out who she was.

The administrator nodded. "Yeah, everyone. The private eye who keeps calling to ask questions about the murder. And the cop who took the tapes yesterday. Aren't you a cop?"

Cop. Had Alex had been found out by the police? If so, there was nothing Charlie could do about it anymore. Perhaps he could save the company from the worst of the fallout, but there was nothing he could do for *her.*

So he left, riding home slowly from the Greene Institute. He was tired, and gone was the need to rush—to find out about Alex, to know. He knew now. He knew that Alex—that Katia—had betrayed him. Was she really a murderer? Possibly. Did that change her music? No. Did that change how he felt about her? It should. He kept going around and around, unable to untangle the knot of ambivalence tightening around him.

He returned home thinking he'd have a drink and decide on a course of action after that, but Murdoch came hurrying toward him in the foyer. "Simone is waiting for you in the living room."

"Simone is here?"

Murdoch nodded. "She's up to something." The wariness in his gaze prompted Charlie to head to the living room without more questions.

Simone lounged on the couch, arm thrown across the back, legs crossed casually. She wore the dress that used to be Charlie's favorite—a green flowing thing that wrapped around her like a tunic. She was definitely up to something.

"Close the door and have a seat, darling," she said. "I brought a video for you to watch."

Charlie said nothing—there was nothing to say—and did as she asked. When he was seated next to her, she raised the remote to the video system. The lights flicked off and the theater-sized screen descended from the ceiling, the buzz of its motor filling the room for a few seconds. Then the projector blazed to life, but there was no more sound, only a grainy black-and-white video flickering in the dark silence.

Charlie immediately knew from the low resolution of the images that the video was from a camera meant to project on a much smaller screen, maybe a fifth the size of the one here. But it was clear enough: an interview room of some sort, like the ones in police stations, with a table in the foreground, a chair behind it, and the outline of a door on one of the sterile white walls in the background. There was a glass of water on the table, but otherwise the room was empty.

Then a young girl was ushered in, and at first her face was obscured by a mass of light-colored hair, but once she was seated and facing the camera, Charlie could see that it was Alex. Katia, he corrected. He sat very still, not daring to look away from the screen—if he looked at Simone, he might strangle her with his bare hands.

A sign was briefly brought up in front of the camera: *Katia Volkov: Reaction to Isolation.*

Then it was just Katia, sitting there, her hands clasped together on the table. After a minute or so, she frowned and closed her eyes. After another few minutes, she pushed her chair back and bent over, hands to her head, like she was in severe pain.

Charlie wanted desperately to look away now, unable to witness whatever distress she was feeling, or to believe that she was psychotic somehow. He averted his gaze to the glass of water on the table in the video, thinking *this isn't right*. Something wasn't right. But he forced his eyes back to Katia. *Face it*, he told himself. *You have to face who she is.*

On screen, Katia stood up, crashing her chair to the ground, and then she was pounding on something between her and the camera—a two-way mirror or a window—her lips mouthing something over and over. Eventually, Charlie realized what she was saying: "Let me out. I'll kill you!"

The video paused. "Had enough?" Simone asked.

Charlie blanked out his face and turned in his seat to look at her. The light from the screen gave her face an odd sheen, shadowed on one side and lit on the other.

"She's photogenic, isn't she?" Simone went on. "I told you she was dangerous. And if this gets out…EmerSound is going to be ruined. I mean that doctor's death and this video will put her away for life. They could even charge you as an accessory to murder. You have to get rid of her."

The pieces clicked into place. "It was you yesterday—you pretended to be a police officer to get this from Greene, didn't you?" Charlie said.

Simone gave a self-satisfied smile. "Of course."

An involuntary and momentary relief rushed through him—the administrator had referred to the cop as "she," and if Simone were that "cop" then no real police knew about Alex, and she might yet have a chance. If Charlie gave it to her. "How did you know?"

"Let's just say I pay Clarence better than you do," Simone said, getting to her feet. She glared down at him, hands hanging at her sides, and with the light from the screen behind her now, she looked menacing, almost monstrous. "It was that day you broke up with me, do you remember? Clarence came to visit you. I may not be some kind of genius, but I'm not as dumb as you think. I knew something was up and that Clarence would know. The rest is history."

Charlie kept his tone calm, trying to lean back nonchalantly, as if none of this mattered. As if it hadn't shattered his entire world. "He figured this out?"

"Clarence?" She gave a bark of laughter. "No. It was your own questions about Katia yesterday. He called to tell me about it right after he talked to you. And I remembered the Katia in the diaries. Don't look horrified—of course Clarence gave me the diaries. Did you really think he'd put them back? And I had the advantage of the pills I found in her room. It was easy from there to figure it out and get the tapes from Greene. And after I heard you slept with that girl? I mean, *her* of all people. I had to help you, Charlie, even if I had to do it like this."

"And how did you know I slept with her?" he asked, pressing his hands into the couch, telling himself he couldn't strike Simone.

"God, you're so naïve," Simone said with a groan—of frustration or anger—spreading her arms out wide and throwing her head back. "I have sources everywhere. Your housekeeper is a big fan of mine, you know."

Charlie thought of all the times Simone had been caught here alone, of how he'd assumed she was devastated about him, but she'd just been collecting information, snooping, and stealing things like Alex's pills.

"And now you'll see that I've been controlling things the whole time." Simone's lips curled around her last words with venom.

"And what exactly do you think you're controlling?" he asked.

"The narrative, darling. What else? You think Michael Chap could come up with all that gossip on his own about your affairs? Or that he thought of the lawsuit?"

Charlie had thought the worst way to be hurt was to lose something he loved, so he'd distanced himself from the people who could take those things away, and when his pain hadn't ceased, he'd distanced himself from the things he could love. But he'd been wrong. This—having enabled his own destruction— was worse, and he was starting to see how it had happened. To avoid the things he could value, he'd pushed himself toward the things he could never value, the things he hated—and the only way to do that was to ignore the facts: that his choices for EmerSound were wrong and could only lead to unhappiness, that tainted money could not be redeemed by the promise of future good work, that Simone wasn't interested in loving him and only wanted fame and control.

He gave Simone his half smile—the one that mocked with knowing—and hers faltered a little. "So what's the plan?" he asked.

"Alex will leave—before the finale, so her disappearance can be big news. Then we'll release the story about her slowly, in our own way: She's crazy, a murderer, we didn't know—all of it—and then we'll cash in on the notoriety. Save the company just like that. I've already planned it out with David and Richard. You don't even have to do anything."

"Are you that threatened by her?"

"I'm trying to save you! She's crazy!" Simone threw the remote across the room and the video flickered off, leaving them in darkness but for the dim light coming from the slit at the bottom of the door. "This is the only way to save EmerSound," she added, quietly, with a sudden calm. "And then we can be together again, the way we used to be."

He understood now. She was offering him his old life—by all accounts, a life of comfort and luxuries: a beautiful woman to sleep with whenever he desired without commitment; a company that was easy to run, requiring no real thought from him; a public that would happily empty their pockets into his hands for the most clichéd music. He'd been living it for years. He could live it for many more. But was that grayness living, or was it a slow death by torture?

Ironic that it was Alex who'd fed the tiny pilot light that had grown into the flame of his motivation. Just yesterday he'd thought Acoustitech could be the foundation of a new company—a company that would be the marriage of his science and expertise in business, a company he could be proud of. He might still be able to have that if he let Alex go and handled Simone in the right way. But could he go back to his science, knowing that some part of it was built on Alex's music, buoyed by her tortured past, and at the cost of her freedom? Did he even want to do his science anymore?

"Well, Charlie?" Simone asked, her voice hard.

He looked up at her.

"What's it going to be?"

He shrugged. "You put way too much stock in my spending a night with that girl," he said. "To hell with her."

CHAPTER XLVII

Katia was sixteen years old the day Alexandra told her she was dying. They were sitting next to each other on Alexandra's bed on one of those rare afternoons when Weiss brought Katia home, looking through magazines. Typical teen girl magazines—the kind of thing Katia only enjoyed when she was with Alexandra. As if their special friendship and closeness gave even the most meaningless things significance and imbued them with endless appeal.

Katia was laughing at an article about the special uses of vinegar in beauty routines, when she looked up to see a serious expression on Alexandra's face.

"What's wrong?" Katia asked.

Alexandra sighed. "My heart is failing again. The transplant is not doing well."

Katia's vision went momentarily black, but she breathed her way back to focus. "What does that mean?"

"They won't give me a second transplant—my body can't handle it. I don't think...I don't know how much longer I have. Dad didn't want me to tell you, but I didn't think that was fair."

The two girls stared at each other, and Katia felt a few silent tears make their way down her cheeks.

"It's okay, though," Alexandra said, and the forced cheeriness was a hard thing to bear. "I have a plan. I got my driver's license before the doctors found out that the heart is not doing well. And I thought…well, I thought you could have it."

"What for?"

"You can be me. After—well, just in case that other doctor doesn't leave you alone and you have to get away from him. I know Dad doesn't understand, and he doesn't listen. He may not be able to help you in time. And you said that you couldn't just leave because there's a record of you being at Greene and every-thing—that you needed them to sign off on you being okay. Well, I'm pretty normal. And we look similar enough. You could just become Alexandra Weiss."

Katia shook her head, frowning. "No. No, I can't—"

"Yes, you can. Look, we're both trapped. You by the institute and me by my body. Together we can be free."

Katia had noticed her friend steadily growing paler and weaker for a while, but she hadn't really believed it was dire. Not even as Alexandra unveiled her detailed plans for Katia to take her identity after her death did it seem real. And Katia only assented to the plan because she didn't believe she'd ever do it, because she didn't believe her friend would die.

But one morning a few months later, Katia saw Weiss in the hallway outside his office at Greene, holding a cardboard box. He'd been absent from the institute for several days.

She rushed up to him. "What's going on?"

He looked at her as if he didn't recognize her, or really anybody. "Alexandra had a heart attack a few days ago. They've given her only a few weeks. I'm taking care of her at home until…"

Katia staggered but caught herself against the wall. "Can I see her?"

He shook his head. "I know about her plan. She told me last night. I won't agree to it."

"I don't want it! It's her plan, not mine. Please, just let me see her."

"No. It was a mistake to let you two get so close. I should never have done it. But I won't let you ruin her last few weeks."

He walked away, and Katia stood staring after him. She forgot all about the plans she'd made—to lie low, convince the staff she was better, and try to get out of Greene legitimately when she was eighteen. She needed to see Alexandra before it was too late.

That night she took her usual path to her practice spot in the stairwell, but with jeans and a sweater under her pajamas. She held up her violin case, which was actually empty, and nodded at the guard on duty who knew her and let her practice violin at night.

He waved her through and she hurried to the tenth floor, to the unmonitored fire escape one of the older kids used to smuggle contraband into Greene. The alarm on that door was supposed to sound if opened, but it had rusted through long ago, and for a little money every month, the maintenance staff ignored it.

Katia took a back hallway to the fire escape, and once out on the metal grating, she took off her pajamas, folded them neatly, and placed them next to her violin case by the door. Then she climbed down the ladder and into the back gardens.

The lights were dim outside the building, and she could barely see the path in front of her. She moved slowly, feet squelching on dirt or leaves, and tried to stay in the shadows. But she hadn't been out there alone at night before, so she didn't know about the guard who stood watch on the side of the building and who saw her round the corner long before she saw him.

Shaylan was at Greene within an hour of Katia's capture. He dosed her and had her in the interview room with the blasting music a few minutes after that. It had never been so bad—whatever he'd given her was strong, and she couldn't control the visions and the swirling, or the anger. She held her head in her hands and she screamed, and when that didn't help, she got up and banged on the window. She screamed and yelled until she was hoarse, until they came in with the other needle.

She woke up in a room she hadn't seen before, her arms and legs manacled to a bed, and when she tried to lift her head, she found it, too, strapped down with a band across her forehead. *I know what this is*, she thought. This is what they did to the other kids—the ones who became vegetables. The ones who died. The shocks.

But at least all the drugs they'd given her were out of her system. She felt normal, though her left arm hurt, and she remembered struggling with the needle in her bicep and ripping her skin. She could see in her peripheral vision that someone had bandaged it.

The face of the nurse who'd always helped her, Carry Taylor, appeared above Alex, hands working quickly, unshackling her, saying, "I'm going to lose my job for this, I'm sure, but I can't let them do it to you. I just can't."

When Katia was sitting up and Carry was undoing the final restraint on her ankle, the door opened. It was Shaylan and a burly orderly.

"Nurse Taylor, I've told you to stay out of this," Shaylan said, his voice flat. He gestured to the orderly and the man came forward and took Carry by her arm, pulling her away. Carry looked at Katia with fear in her eyes but said nothing, letting the man drag her from the room. The look said goodbye.

In the split second Shaylan had turned to watch them leave, Katia grabbed at the first sharp thing she could reach—the pair of scissors with the first aid supplies on the table next to her—and shoved it up her sleeve. Then she leaned over and finished undoing the clasp at her ankle.

Shaylan laughed. "I wouldn't bother. Justin will be back in a minute to strap you down again. Just accept the treatment. You'll feel much better afterwards."

"But I'm not sick. This will kill me. The way it did the others."

"Only one of them died, and he killed himself. I was trying to help him. I was just too late."

"No, it was your treatment that made him want to commit suicide. And all the others were worse after your treatments. You broke them. I know, I lived with them, every day."

Shaylan's face grew red and he said angrily, "They were never going to fit in the way they were—and the one who died, well, he was too disruptive, always asking questions and resisting. My treatment worked. It wasn't my fault he was suicidal. And I'll get it right with you."

She got off the bed and stood away from it. "Get what right? There's nothing wrong with me. You know that. Stop lying."

"The world doesn't need someone like you," he yelled, more agitated than she'd expected him to be. "It's your kind that makes all the other kids feel bad about themselves. It isn't fair to them. It'll be much nicer when everyone is normal, equal."

"You want me to be brain damaged," she said, finally understanding. She let the scissors down her arm a little so that her fist was wrapped around them, just below the handle. "You want to take my talent away."

He took in a deep breath, and then his voice returned to its normal, oily tone. "It's because you call it talent that you think you need to keep it. It's an illness. Didn't you see earlier tonight? Music shouldn't do that to you."

"That music would've been too loud for anyone. And you gave me something to make me angry like that. How can you do that to me and call yourself a doctor?"

He walked closer to her, his composure cracking again. "Because what kids like you do to other kids, how inferior you make them feel with your so-called talent, really hurts them. It's the same thing as violence. Other people don't understand that so I just made it into something they would understand. Something they could see: you as violent. Now, just lean back—it'll be over soon and you'll feel so much better. You'll see."

He tried to grab her hands, but she was quicker, pulling her arms away and stepping sideways. He turned to her, moving in again, and this time she tried to push him away but he wouldn't budge. He was too big. He laughed and grabbed at her hands again. She jabbed his forearm with the scissors.

"You bitch!" he yelled, though she hadn't even penetrated his lab coat. Then he had her wrists in his grasp and was pulling her to the bed.

She fought, but he was strong and her bare feet slipped against the cold tiles. He turned, bending over and yanking her right hand—the one with the scissors—back and down into the cuff attached to the bed. He needed both of his hands to close it, and when he let go of her left hand, she grabbed the scissors with it. The metal cuff snapped violently on her right wrist, sending a sharp, rough pain up her arm.

Katia screamed, flailing at the excruciating pain, desperately trying to keep him from hurting her again. He stood, grabbing her by the throat, and the scissors in her flailing hand caught him. They sank in deep. She let go. His grip on her throat loosened and they looked at each other, both shocked. The scissors were in his neck. He reached up and pulled them out. Then he collapsed.

Katia looked down at him, at the blood spreading out in a pool around him. Too much, too quickly.

"No," she whispered, and worked frantically to undo the cuff around her wrist, but the blood from her own wound made everything slippery and it took so long, but then she was finally free to grab a wad of gauze from the table and kneel down next to him and jam the material at his neck, to stop the bleeding, to help, something. But the gauze saturated in seconds, useless, and when she dared to check, Shaylan's eyes were wide open, already blank. He wasn't breathing.

She remained kneeling for a moment more, working through her panic, considering, deciding. No one would believe her. Shaylan had laid the case against her, had been doing so for a long time—he'd even said so himself. They'd think she was violent. That she'd done this unprovoked. She'd be locked up for real.

She thought of Alexandra—of how she was dying but not yet dead. Katia could still go and see her. She could do that much at least.

She got up and ran.

CHAPTER XLVIII

Alex sat at the vanity in her dressing room at Bernak Hall, watching as tiny dust particles floated and sparkled in the last of the day's sunlight—a thin ray shining through a little window at the top of the room.

Only months ago she'd watched Charlie from her coffee stand with nothing but an anonymous appreciation of his beauty, and now he'd become as important as her music. She'd been disappointed not to see him last night, but it was probably better that way because she'd needed the sleep. The previous night, Charlie had fallen asleep beside her after their lovemaking, but she'd stayed awake as long as she could, to savor it all—him and the things that had passed between them—falling asleep finally, grudgingly, in the early hours of the morning.

Plus it was good to have time to think about her next steps. She could stay, she'd decided, if she mustered up the courage to tell Charlie her story—about Alexandra, and her past as Katia, her stay at the Greene Institute, and Shaylan.

For today, it could wait. Today, she imagined herself as those floating specs in the air, suspended and almost weightless, dancing in the light in their easy manner, drifting downward for a while and then suddenly changing direction—like a melody played in a high register, on a violin or a flute, lilting up and down, mimicking the swerving bits of dust in a complicated, unhurried dance.

She let the music flow through her mind and marveled because she didn't feel agitated or restless like she usually did with a new composition, as if her time had expanded and there was no pressure to get it all down right away.

The last two days had lapsed in much the same way. The image of Charlie yesterday when she'd first opened her eyes, the way he'd looked at her, stayed with her as she moved through her days, making her continuously and exquisitely aware of her own body. She took a shower and the water cascaded over her like the caress of warm hands. The smell of a mug of coffee someone handed her during the photoshoot intoxicated her like a glass of wine. Even the lotions and makeup Grace applied to her face felt luxurious in their subtle silkiness. And today when she'd arrived at Bernak Hall, she didn't care at all about the ruckus of the crowds and media with their cameras and questions as she was rushed inside.

This is happiness, she thought, standing up to study her reflection in a full-length mirror. Her hair was piled elaborately on her head, and she wore a black evening gown that was not a dress exactly, but a feminine reference to a tuxedo: wide, flowing trousers with a shiny stripe down each seam, a vest with tight sheer sleeves that made her shoulders look naked, and intermittent diamonds gleaming like shirt buttons on a long strand hanging from a necklace. Despite her usual disinclination for primping and feminine vanity, she found herself enjoying the shimmering gown and dramatic makeup. *Charlie will like it.*

Then he was there, standing in the doorway. She saw him through the mirror—him and Simone. She stood to face them, then frowned, because they weren't dressed for the finale, and because there was something wrong with Charlie.

"What's going on?" Alex asked.

"Don't be obtuse. We know what you've done. It's time to go," Simone said.

"Go?"

"Yes! Get out of our lives, you murdering bitch!" Simone was shaking.

Charlie stood stock-still, face totally blank, lips drawn in a stern line. Alex's eyes moved to the envelope in Charlie's hand.

"That's right. We've got proof," Simone said. "Show it to her, Charlie."

He extended the envelope and Alex tried to see a hint of emotion from him, some recognition in his eyes, but there was nothing, and for a moment she couldn't breathe, as if someone had cut through her windpipe. She forced the air into her lungs and steadied her hands, then took the envelope. There were pictures inside. Stills from a video she'd thought destroyed forever. A rumble of thoughts assailed her: the *Red Concerto*, Charlie, Alexandra, Katia, all she'd risked to reach this point—all of it gone. "Charlie, let me explain—"

Simone laughed. "We're way past that, aren't we? You're caught. I have so much more evidence than this."

Alex met Charlie's eyes but he didn't contradict the statement. She turned her gaze back to Simone. "What will you do with it?"

"We'll start with the police, but the press will get their chance. Unless you leave. Now. Tonight," Simone said.

"You have to go," Charlie said, his voice low and inflectionless.

"Consider yourself lucky," Simone said. "We need to save EmerSound, and for that we can't be directly associated with a psychopath. If you disappear, we can trickle the story out slowly and make it seem not quite as bad."

"Disappear before…the performance?" Alex asked, hoping still that she might have this last thing. This one thing because it would help EmerSound, wouldn't it?

"You think we're going to let you perform?" Simone said and laughed again, this time a bitter, ugly laugh. "Are you that stupid?"

If Charlie weren't here, if it were only Simone threatening her, Alex would fight back, would refuse to leave. But she was looking at him and thinking that this was what he wanted. She'd lied to him and he wanted no explanations. He just wanted her gone. She owed it to him to go, didn't she? He knew what it would do to her not to have her music, and he wanted that as her punishment. And perhaps she deserved it.

She'd kept wondering what she'd done wrong and here was part of it. She could see now that she'd done the very thing she'd accused Charlie of so many weeks ago—she'd put the information she didn't like out of her thoughts and pretended it didn't exist; she'd ignored her worries about the missing diaries, convinced herself that Michael Chap's accusations about her would be treated as baseless gossip, and pretended Charlie hadn't seen any significance in Lawrence's comment on Natasha Volkov. Of course she'd done something wrong. And now she had to pay for it.

She nodded and dropped her head.

"Pack up your things and go," Charlie said. "Simone and I are leaving the city for the night. When the show doesn't go on there's going to be a media fallout. You have an hour, I think."

CHAPTER XLIX

I t took several hours for Charlie and Simone to reach the
house in Connecticut. The snow had made the roads slippery and slow, and the house was secluded enough that
many of the paths hadn't been cleared. Charlie didn't often go
up to the house in winter. He drove the car himself, both to have
a reason to focus on something other than Simone and a reason
to ask her to sit quietly while he concentrated on the difficult
driving conditions. He couldn't stand the idea of listening to
her voice—ironic, since her voice was the thing that had drawn
him to her.

When they arrived at the house, he lit the fireplace and
opened several bottles of wine. Simone drank happily and chatted. He stood by the fireplace, leaning on the mantel, and sipped
his own glass—his first and only.

"Did you mean it? What you said about my having a show of
my own?" Simone asked after her fourth pour of wine.

"I was wrong about Alex, wasn't I? If you're right, then this is
the only course of action for me."

He walked over and topped off her glass with one of the open bottles from the table.

"I'm going to pass out before we get to the main event," she said and giggled.

He turned away from her, thinking, hoping that the night's main event was already taking place—if Murdoch had done as Charlie asked, the *Red Concerto* performance would be happening.

It had been easier than he'd expected to convince Simone they should leave the city right away; all he'd had to do was agree to her plan—Alex disappears and they go back to "the way things used to be." He probably hadn't needed to offer Simone her own show, but he'd done it to ensure she wouldn't suspect his real intentions: to let Alex have her performance and then escape, while he kept the evidence against her from coming out as long as he could, buying himself time to tease out the true extent of her guilt. If her past hit the news, it would be that much harder to find out what had really happened.

He'd brought Simone to this house for the same reason he'd bought it—its distance from the city and its perfect seclusion. Cell reception didn't exist out here, and there was no landline connection to the outside world. There was only a satellite, but the connection was switched off in the winters. They'd have no news, and Simone wouldn't know about the performance until well after it had happened.

He turned back to her now, noticing her silence, and saw that she'd fallen asleep, her hand dangling off the side of the sofa and the wine glass lying sideways on the ground.

He left her there and went out the back door and down the short path to the lake, taking in the serenity of the cloudless evening, the silent snow-covered earth, and the forest of hearty evergreens. The lake hadn't frozen over yet but lay starkly placid, its mirrored surface reflecting the moonlight.

Charlie sat down on a rock jutting out from under a cluster of bare thin tree trunks. He picked up some small stones and rubbed them between thumb and forefinger, feeling the sharp jab of cold against his bare skin. He chose one and hurled it at the lake. It swooshed through the air and hit the water quietly, making only a tiny splash, but the waves from it radiated outward, small at first and then growing larger and larger.

Actions were like that—each individual decision and deed radiated out, eventually touching everything in its vicinity. He'd chosen Alex and pulled her out of her coffee stand and soon she'd be a famous composer and a notorious felon—her music and her past flowing over the world.

Charlie's own world had been drowned. What was left to him now? EmerSound was gone—if not yet in action, in his own soul at least. And he'd never again be the man who'd been willing to get married for a reality show, who'd tried to be something he wasn't, who'd yearned to stop yearning.

He watched the waves. He'd discovered a new way of thinking about how those waves interfered with each other and the range of their effects on everything around them. He'd come up with equations to tie together waves produced by things as disparate as electromagnets and sound.

He stood up.

He was seeing, in his mind, Katia: Katia in that room at the institute. He was seeing her pushed back from the table, not touching it, holding her head in her hands. He was seeing the glass of water on the table, waves roiling on its surface—waves so strong he'd been able to see them in a grainy, low-resolution video. Waves that could only have come from a very strong source of vibration—like a very loud sound.

He could prove she was being tortured.

He ran for the garage and the motorcycle he kept there. Alex would still be in the middle of her concerto and he could get to her before the end, before she disappeared.

Charlie rode, feeling focused and sure, not thinking about his speed or the icy roads. He kept thinking only of the equation he could use to prove that Shaylan was torturing Katia with sound and that her reaction wasn't to isolation but torture—that Shaylan had lied in the files and that she'd killed him in self-defense.

He lost his footing once but managed to stay on the bike. He remembered Murdoch's words: "The way you ride, it's as if you don't care whether you live or die. You have to stop."

Charlie laughed, seeing so much more in that statement now. To be invulnerable he'd have to stop riding. He'd started riding precisely because in order to be invulnerable he had to cut everything else out of his life. This was his only reprieve. The only time he enjoyed himself. Until recently. Until Katia and her music. And the return to his work. He felt like he was living again.

It was the living that had made him vulnerable to the pain, and the sharp stabbing thing he'd felt on discovering Katia's past. They went together, he thought. In order to live you had to be open to the pain, but the pain didn't have to rule your life. In order to live, you had let go of the need to control everything in an attempt to keep from feeling pain. Because hadn't he learned with Simone that you can't control those things anyway? Hadn't he learned that to deal with people, to work with them, to live with them, to care for them, you had to be open to them turning on you, hurting you, betraying you, leaving you? And they didn't all do that—he thought of Lawrence and Murdoch. And now Katia, too. But he had to get to her first.

Charlie had rarely ridden this path on his bike and never in the winter. He wasn't used to the pattern of ice on the road or the way the headlights of the oncoming truck blinded him as he took a narrow turn. He didn't see how close the edge was or how steep the drop—until he was swerving out of the truck's path and riding down the side of the mountain. He strained, trying to keep his front wheel steady and bracing himself against the jarring bumps as he slashed over rocks and sticks in the dirty, snow-covered mountainside. Then he was trying to make the sharp ninety-degree turn that would slow him down and turn him away from a tree. *Don't hit the tree head-on*, he thought, *that could kill you.* And then, somewhere in the back of his mind, another thought raced through: *I want to live. I'm not indifferent to death anymore. And I'm glad.* Then the image of Katia on stage playing her violin flashed through his mind. He smiled.

But the bike continued to slip on the ice-covered ground. There was no way to stop it. Or turn completely away from the tree. He hit it with a deafening crash that ended in a dark silence.

CHAPTER L

Alex was in a daze as she performed the *Red Concerto* that night, but she knew the concerto was going well because the colors were bright and deep and perfect. After the blast of anguish when Charlie had looked at her with those cold eyes and commanded her to leave, there was the confusion of Murdoch coming to tell her that she'd be allowed to perform the concerto, and that she should leave directly afterward and take her Guarneri violin with her. She'd sat there unable to process any of it, until someone—maybe Murdoch again—had come to walk her to the stage.

There was an initial elation when she'd stepped onto the stage, but afterward everything had become veiled—a protection because there were too many emotions and too many disasters to consider.

Then the crowd was on its feet and Alex was walking off the stage and to her dressing room. It was easy because somehow there were very few people in the hallways. Even Murdoch had disappeared.

She found her backpack in a corner of the dressing room. It still held the cash and the envelope with her new identity. She kept those items and her manuscript of the *Red Concerto*, then dumped everything else—including her phone—into a trash can so she could fit her violin case inside. Then she put on a long coat to cover her dress, deciding she had no time to change, and a wool cap to cover her hair, changed from heels to boots, and walked toward the back door of Bernak.

She knew what to expect next—it would be like the day she found out Alexandra was dying. Or the night she'd killed Shaylan. She'd act, she'd move on, she'd feel nothing, and then one day it would hit her like a punch in the gut and she'd have to fight just to catch her breath.

"Hey, Alex, are you going to the hospital?" someone called.

Alex turned, confused, and saw one of the women from the orchestra approaching her. "Why the hospital?"

"Oh my God, didn't you hear?" the woman said. "Charlie got into a huge accident. They're saying he's in a coma and critical."

♪ ♩

Alex wanted to run to the hospital, to call Murdoch, to call Simone, even—anything to find out what had happened to Charlie. But she no longer had that right. And so she had to wait. Surely, the media would report on his condition soon.

Again, she found herself walking the city streets, this time stopping at one all-night diner after another, drinking cup after cup of black coffee, and watching for news about Charlie everywhere: on television sets, in newspapers, in other people's conversations.

She was constantly in fear and on edge and it was no way to live. Yet it was the way she'd lived for over a decade, with only the last few weeks as a reprieve to show her by contrast what she'd done to herself. How she'd conned herself out of happiness by hiding. How faking her identity—whether metaphorical like with Brandy or literal like with Alexandra—had harmed her in a way that Shaylan had never been able to.

Finally, at 10:00 a.m., almost twelve hours after she'd heard of Charlie's accident, while standing in line at a café in midtown, she saw the news ticker running on the bottom of a TV mounted to the wall behind the counter: EmerSound had ceased to exist. It had been completely liquidated, all rights to their music transferred back to the artists. No one knew exactly when it had been arranged, if it had been done before the accident or after—whether it was the execution of a provision from Charlie's will.

With EmerSound gone, part of Charlie was destroyed forever. It was the first inkling of the punch in the gut Alex had been expecting. She actually stood there for a minute, unable to breathe. And she knew she had to see him, today, immediately. Nothing mattered but to see him. She couldn't leave the city forever without one more glance, even if he hated her now. Even if he was unconscious. She had to try, even if he was already dead.

Katia had run to see Alexandra one last time before she died. This time, Alex walked to the hospital to see Charlie. She had a different name and was visiting a different person, and yet it felt the same. A dear friend, someone she loved, dying, and, in fear for her own life, she had to sneak in to get one last look, one last touch. She was back in that drawing again, endlessly walking upstairs, only to be back at the bottom. You could run or walk, or even ride up those stairs, but you'd end up in the same place—exactly where you started.

Halfway through the two-mile distance to the hospital from the café where Alex heard the news, the snow started coming down in wet chunks and turned to sludge on the ground in the not-quite freezing temperatures. She held her coat closed tightly around her and every few minutes adjusted her winter cap, pulling at it, assuring that it was positioned low over her head and that all of her hair was still tucked away beneath it, hating the nervous action but needing it, or else she'd have to stop and scream right there in the middle of Seventh Avenue. She shivered and walked on. She vaguely knew that there were people around her in the street, but she didn't see any of them. They had ceased to matter.

What could matter when she'd never be able to play the *Red Concerto* with an orchestra again, never see Weiss, or Willem, or Lawrence again, if she went to jail forever or lived in fear of it the rest of her life? What did anything matter if Charlie were dead? She felt dimly that this was the last time she'd fight, wondered if trying to take another breath afterward would be worth it. When you got to that point, she knew, it meant you'd gone catastrophically wrong somewhere.

She'd pretended to be someone else, but she sensed that was only a subset of a bigger mistake. She'd kept saying she would do anything for her concerto—and she had. But maybe there were things she shouldn't have done. Maybe she shouldn't have pretended to be all those other girls in the name of being left alone to play violin or compose or record her concerto. Maybe she shouldn't have run from her mistakes—like Shaylan's death—even if it meant she couldn't have her music anymore. Maybe there were things more sacred than her music. Things without which her music was senseless—like her own integrity and the courage to face the consequences of her actions. She'd wanted to give herself to her art, but she'd given herself up for her art. And she wondered: *Who is left to enjoy the success of the* Red Concerto *now that I've destroyed myself?*

Finally, she stood in front of the building where Charlie was dying—had perhaps already died—and took a moment just to breathe. Then she headed to the intensive care unit, where at the far end of the hallway and around the corner was room 43A: Charlie's room.

The media were long gone, having given up on Charlie during the night when the doctors had announced he was in a coma, so there was no one to stop Alex's slow progression down the hall toward that room. Still, she dropped her head low as she passed the nurses' station.

Then, as she turned the corner, she heard a woman yelling, "Let me in! I need to talk to Murdoch. I know he's in there. And I just saw Charlie's lawyer come out. I need to know what this crap is about EmerSound being liquidated. We had a plan. What happened to the plan? And how could he leave me up there in that house? Someone owes me an explanation for what he's done or I'm going to sue them all. I'll make them all pay!"

It was Simone, in last night's dress, black makeup smudged under her eyes, yelling at the man stoically stationed in front of Charlie's room—Tim, Alex's bodyguard. He glanced at Alex and his eyes rounded in surprise.

Simone noticed and turned around. "You," she said. "It's her. It's the murdering bitch!"

Alex thought she should be afraid. But she wasn't afraid. She stood her ground, understanding that she'd come here, without disguise and without pretense, because she wanted to be recognized. She wanted this to be over. Relief washed through her. She'd no longer act the part of someone else.

"I'm calling the police," Simone said, pulling out a phone from her purse.

"You don't have to do that," Alex said. "I'm not going to run away."

"Make sure you ask for Detective Steven Smith."

They all turned toward room 43A, where, leaning casually against the doorjamb, was Charlie. He wore only pajama bottoms, his left arm in a cast up to his shoulder, his left cheekbone bruised, and a bandage covering his forehead under disheveled hair—but he wore his mocking smile, too, and his eyes were bright. He looked the way he had any number of times, watching Alex, always seeing more than she wanted him to see. But he looked more whole somehow. As if despite his injuries, he was...happy.

Alex smiled at him, forgetting the whole of the hospital, Simone and the bodyguard, EmerSound, and the fact that she was probably going to jail. She smiled because Charlie was awake, alive, and his spirit hadn't been broken. She smiled because nothing mattered if Charlie was alive and was looking at her like that.

"Well, Simone, are you going to make the call?" he asked, though he kept his eyes on Alex. "Or should I do it? Jennifer and I have some new evidence for the head detective in the case of Herbert Shaylan's death and it absolves Alex—Katia."

"What new evidence?" Simone asked, her voice low, but angry. "You're just saying that. This woman is crazy and she needs to be locked up."

"She was abused by a corrupt doctor and she was defending herself," Jennifer said, as she came down the hall with a cup of coffee in each hand. "We're gathering proof that he was torturing his patients and using treatments in dangerous doses. He killed a few people."

Jennifer wasn't alone—she was accompanied by Dennis Weiss. Alex blinked.

Weiss quickened his steps toward her, then grabbed her in a powerful hug. "They're going to save you. You're safe, do you hear me? Safe."

Alex hugged him back, muted by the shock of everything that was happening. She was…safe?

A nurse hurtled toward Charlie. "Mr. Emerson, you need to go back to bed. You haven't been cleared to be up by yourself."

And then a commotion exploded: Simone started screaming about betrayal and lies, Weiss let Alex go to yell back at Simone for being obtuse among some harsher names, an orderly came to calm them down, and a second nurse tried to convince Charlie to go back to bed.

Meanwhile, Murdoch and Lawrence sidled their way around Charlie and out of his room. Charlie remained leaning against the door, silent and smiling at Alex, and she remained frozen to her spot, unable to look away from him. People moved around, obscuring their view of each other, but neither one moved, either their bodies or their gazes. *I'm only a few steps from him*, she thought. *I could almost touch him.*

Lawrence put a hand on Alex's shoulder. "Come into Charlie's room. He's been waiting for you."

Alex nodded and let Lawrence slip her backpack from her back and guide her through the chaos to the door, to Charlie. She stopped in the doorway to look up at him.

He turned to faced her. "I've been waiting for you," he said.

"What for?" she asked, smiling.

"To tell you I love you."

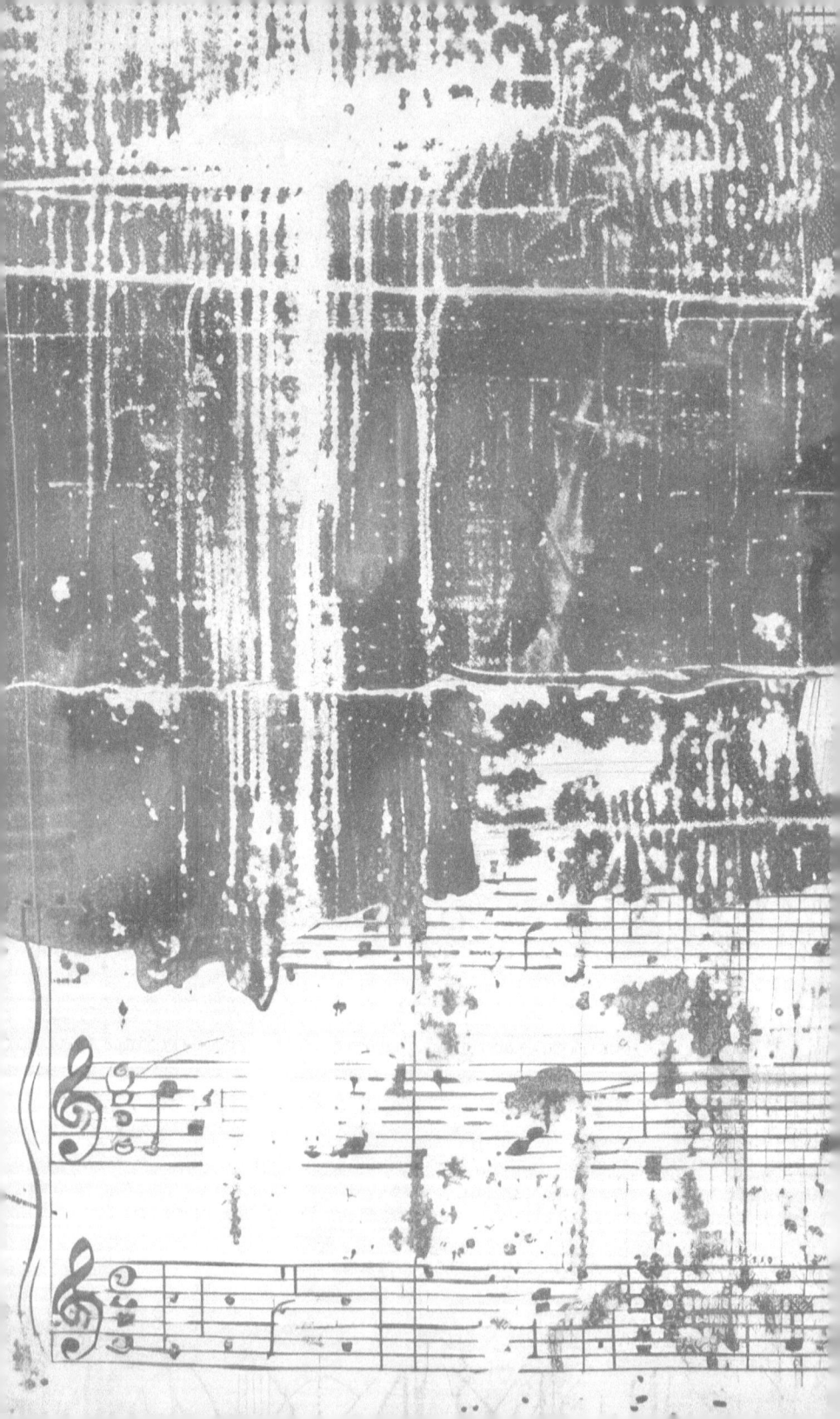

CODA

CHAPTER LI

Katia Alexandra Emerson stood on the threshold—just for
a moment, to watch Charlie hard at work under the lab
bench.

"What are you doing?" she asked. "We have to go in twenty
minutes. I need to do a sound check before the performance."

He poked his head out from under the table. "I promised
Willem I'd bring the new mic to record your symphony, but I
forgot that I soldered it in down here."

He was in a tuxedo, the one he looked so good in, and if she
hadn't been in a full-length evening gown herself, she would've
knelt down next to him. She smiled and waited.

He came out, holding the mic in one hand and wire cutters
in the other. "It's an expensive cord—I was hoping I wouldn't
have to cut it," he said.

"Charlie, EmerTech is worth more than EmerSound ever
was. I think it's okay to cut one wire short."

He looked up from winding the cord around his hand and
smiled at her. His real smile—the one that made an appearance

regularly now. Then he kissed her lightly but held her for a long time.

"Let's go," he said.

THE END

∫ ℓ

ABOUT THE AUTHOR

S. F. HAYES has made a living doing many things: sticking electrodes into insect brains, performing surgery on frogs, consulting on railroads, and teaching aerobics. But she was always one of those kids who was endlessly reading and writing, and finally made it back to those passions (after having two kids). These days she can be found writing in New York City cafes, parks, and subway cars.

S.F. holds a PhD in biology from Caltech and undergraduate degrees in molecular biology and philosophy from UC Berkeley. She lives in the city with her husband, two kids, and two cats, Spark (who hates her) and Pineapple (who does not).